THE VALANCOURT BOOK OF HORROR STORIES

VOLUME FOUR

Also Available

The Valancourt Book of Horror Stories
The Valancourt Book of Horror Stories, vol. 2
The Valancourt Book of Horror Stories, vol. 3

The Valancourt Book of Victorian Christmas Ghost Stories
The Valancourt Book of Victorian Christmas Ghost Stories, vol. 2
The Valancourt Book of Victorian Christmas Ghost Stories, vol. 3

The Valancourt Book of World Horror Stories

THE VALANCOURT BOOK OF
HORROR STORIES

VOLUME FOUR

edited by
JAMES D. JENKINS & RYAN CAGLE

VALANCOURT BOOKS
Richmond, Virginia
2020

The Valancourt Book of Horror Stories, Volume Four
First published October 2020

Translations, editorial material, and compilation copyright © 2020 by Valancourt Books, LLC. All stories copyright © by their respective authors or estates. The Acknowledgments page on p. 10 constitutes an extension of this copyright page.

All rights reserved. In accordance with the U.S. Copyright Act of 1976, the copying, scanning, uploading, and/or electronic sharing of any part of this book without the permission of the publisher constitutes unlawful piracy and theft of the author's intellectual property. If you would like to use material from the book (other than for review purposes), prior written permission must be obtained by contacting the publisher.

Published by Valancourt Books, Richmond, Virginia
http://www.valancourtbooks.com

ISBN 978-1-948405-78-2 (hardcover)
ISBN 978-1-948405-79-9 (trade paperback)

Also available as an electronic book.

Cover by M. S. Corley
Set in Bembo Book MT

Editors' Foreword

MOST HORROR ANTHOLOGIES these days are organized around some kind of gimmick. Sometimes it's a monster (*The Big Book of _____ Stories* [*Vampire/Ghost/Mummy/Werewolf*]), or else a theme (stories in imitation of H.P. Lovecraft, tales written in homage to Stephen King, an entire volume of stories set in haunted houses, or on Halloween, etc.) One problem with these sorts of anthologies is that they can start to pall after a while. When preparing our *Valancourt Book of World Horror Stories*, we came across a 416-page anthology of Romanian zombie stories. It doesn't matter how good the writing is; there are only so many Romanian zombie stories the average person can stand to read back-to-back.

Our *Valancourt Book of Horror Stories* series of anthologies has a gimmick, too, but it's of a very different sort. All of the stories in this book (and in the previous three volumes) are written by authors whose books we have previously published. If we published exclusively new horror fiction, such an idea for an anthology wouldn't be especially noteworthy, nor particularly hard to assemble: we could simply send out a mass e-mail to all our authors, ask them whether they had any stories lying around in a drawer, and then put them together in a book. But instead Valancourt publishes an extremely heterogeneous array of books and authors, spanning from the 1760s to the 2000s, from 18th-century Gothic romances and Victorian-era potboilers to Golden Age mysteries and thrillers, mid-century science fiction, vintage LGBT-interest works, '70s and '80s paperback horror novels, humorous fiction and satire, modern literary classics, translated international works, and much more. A collection of horror stories culled from such diverse writers and such different time periods is bound, if nothing else, to be quite unlike any other horror anthology out there. This curious self-imposed limitation – that the story must be written by a Valancourt author – forces us in some cases to dig deep, and you know what happens when you dig deep: most of the time you don't find anything, but every once in a while you unearth a rare gem. So as we've put these volumes together, we've investigated whether, say, satirical novelist Michael Frayn, 'Angry Young Men' author John Braine, or Booker Prize winner David Storey had ever written a horror story. (They hadn't.) But, to our surprise, Isabel Colegate, an acclaimed author of literary and historical fiction, Christopher Priest, a modern sci-fi great, and Nevil Shute, a bestselling author of adventure novels, all had; and what's more, their stories were terrific – and totally unknown. The resulting volumes have turned out to be weird and wonderful collections where readers can wander the forgotten alleys and byways of English-language horror fiction and might stumble upon an 1801 Gothic poem by Matthew Gregory Lewis alongside a Victorian ghost story by Florence Marryat or a weird 2009 story by Michael Blumlein, a master of contemporary speculative fiction. Although it may sound improbable, the format seems to work, at least if we're to judge from the reviews and reader comments we've seen.

Over the course of the series, one or two readers have been astute enough to discern that we have an ulterior motive in putting out these anthologies. Yes, they make for great seasonal reading in their own right, but they double as an introduction to our large catalogue of some 500 titles. A reader who enjoyed our *Paperbacks from Hell* reprints and purchased this volume to see what new treats *PFH* authors Garrett Boatman and Elizabeth Engstrom had in store for them, but who would normally pass over our reissues of an older work by a writer like Michael Arlen or John Metcalfe, may decide to give the latter a second look after reading their stories here. And those who fancy themselves connoisseurs of literary horror and who would ordinarily turn their noses up at anything so plebeian as to have a 'Paperbacks from Hell' tag on the cover may find themselves reconsidering their preconceived notions about those authors after reading some of their tales included in this book.

The volumes in this series tend to reflect to a certain degree what we're working on at the moment, and this fourth volume is no exception. In 2019 and 2020 we've debuted three new series: *Paperbacks from Hell* (reprints of '70s and '80s horror fiction), *Monster, She Wrote* (neglected works by women horror writers) and *Valancourt International* (translated speculative fiction from around the world), and all three of these are represented in the present book. Elizabeth Engstrom and Lisa Tuttle are featured in both *Paperbacks from Hell* and *Monster, She Wrote*, and both have stories in this book; Engstrom's story is brand new, as is the contribution by her fellow *PFH* author Garrett Boatman. Meanwhile, our first two international authors, Hubert Lampo and Felix Timmermans, both from Belgium, each have a story included here, both of them translated into English for the first time.

Also to be found in this volume are original contributions by Stephen Gregory, Steve Rasnic Tem, and John Peyton Cooke, whose story we think is the most unforgettable in the book – though we'll let you be the ultimate judge of that. And of course, it wouldn't be a *Valancourt Book of Horror Stories* if it didn't include a selection of rare tales from the 19th and 20th centuries, so we're pleased to offer seldom-seen stories by Eliza Lynn Linton, Michael Arlen, John Keir Cross, John Metcalfe, Simon Raven, Robert M. Coates, and Francis King as well.

We took a hiatus from the series in 2019 because we felt there wasn't enough good material out there (one of the pitfalls of publishing mostly dead authors: their stories are a non-renewable resource), but the additions of Engstrom, Tuttle,

Cooke, Boatman, Lampo, and Timmermans to our catalogue made a Volume Four possible, and we venture to think that even if the composition of this volume, with its greater emphasis on new material, makes it a little different from previous books, it should nonetheless appeal to those who have enjoyed the first three entries, as well as those who are new to the series.

As in the other volumes, you'll notice that each story is prefaced with some information about the author and his or her other works, and in some cases with what you might call 'the story behind the story', which often adds an additional layer of interest to the tales. Every one of the books in the Valancourt catalogue has an interesting story behind it, and we hope you'll take some time to poke around on our website and investigate some of the fascinating texts we're rediscovered and republished. Horror fiction may be our emphasis (and yours), but we think if you take a moment to scroll through our offerings of literary fiction, LGBT-interest titles, or 18th- and 19th-century classics, you'll find some unexpected surprises that will catch your interest.

Whether you discover a new favorite author in these pages or encounter a new story by an old favorite, we hope you'll have as much fun reading these stories as we did.

JAMES D. JENKINS & RYAN CAGLE
Valancourt Books
August 2020

CONTENTS

Vivid Dreams	Elizabeth Engstrom	11
Rain and Gaslight	Hubert Lampo	19
The Family at Fenhouse	Eliza Lynn Linton	42
Let's Make a Face	John Peyton Cooke	56
Conversations with the Departed	Steve Rasnic Tem	78
'Happy Birthday, Dear Alex'	John Keir Cross	91
Rain	Garrett Boatman	111
The Coffin Procession	Felix Timmermans	135
Time-Fuse	John Metcalfe	145
A Scent of Mimosa	Francis King	164
Remember Your Grammar	Simon Raven	181
The Other Room	Lisa Tuttle	190
The Fury	Robert M. Coates	203
The Gentleman from America	Michael Arlen	212
The Poet Lewis Bowden Has Died	Stephen Gregory	234

Acknowledgments

'Vivid Dreams' © 2020 by Elizabeth Engstrom. Published by arrangement with the author.

'Rain and Gaslight' © 1945 by Hubert Lampo. Originally published as 'Regen en gaslicht'. Published by arrangement with Meulenhoff Boekerij and the Estate of Hubert Lampo.

'Let's Make a Face' © 2020 by John Peyton Cooke. Published by arrangement with the author.

'Conversations with the Departed' © 2020 by Steve Rasnic Tem. Published by arrangement with the author.

'Happy Birthday, Dear Alex' © 1965 by John Keir Cross. Originally published in *Best Tales of Terror 2*, edited by Edmund Crispin. Reprinted by permission of the Estate of John Keir Cross.

'Rain' © 2020 by Garrett Boatman. Published by arrangement with the author.

'A Scent of Mimosa' © 1975 by Francis King. Originally published in *The Times Anthology of Ghost Stories*. Reprinted by permission of A. M. Heath, Ltd.

'Remember Your Grammar' © 1975 by Simon Raven. Originally serialized on Dec. 25, 1974 and Jan. 1, 1975 in *The Listener*. Reprinted by permission of Curtis Brown Ltd.

'The Other Room' © 1982 by Lisa Tuttle. Originally published in *Whispers*, vol. 5 (Aug. 1982). Reprinted by arrangement with the author.

'The Fury' © 1936 by Robert M. Coates. Originally published in *The New Yorker* on Aug. 15, 1936. Reprinted by permission of the Estate of Robert M. Coates.

'The Gentleman from America' © 1924 by Michael Arlen. Originally published in *The Tatler* (Christmas 1924 issue). Reprinted by permission of David Higham Associates.

'The Poet Lewis Bowden Has Died' © 2020 by Stephen Gregory. Published by arrangement with the author.

Elizabeth Engstrom

Vivid Dreams

Literary fortune is a strange and fickle thing. In the 1970s and 1980s, hundreds of authors made their debuts during the horror publishing boom, and some of them, like Stephen King and Dean Koontz, went on to be household names, their works continuously in print, while others arguably just as deserving, such as Michael McDowell, had their works fall out of print and into neglect. One such author who hasn't gotten her full due in recent years is ELIZABETH ENGSTROM, *who burst on the scene with* When Darkness Loves Us (1985), *which sported a laudatory foreword by sci-fi great Theodore Sturgeon, and which earned good reviews and a cult following. A follow-up, the inventive vampire novel* Black Ambrosia, *appeared in 1988. And though Engstrom never really went away – she's continued publishing and has numerous books to her credit – her early works went out of print and were long scarce and expensive on the secondhand market. We included two of Engstrom's books in our* Paperbacks from Hell *series, and she also has one in our* Monster, She Wrote *collection. We're delighted to be helping readers discover (or rediscover) her books, and the response has been phenomenal, with many hailing Engstrom's work as a revelation. The following tale was written specially for this volume and will no doubt be welcomed by the author's many fans, new and old.*

'THESE SLEEP AIDS HAVE SOME SIDE EFFECTS,' the doctor said as he wrote on a little white pad. 'Take one only when you absolutely need it.'

'What kind of side effects?' Constance nervously twisted the white sheet in her arthritic hands, ignoring the pain.

'The most common complaint is strange, very vivid dreams.'

'Oh, I don't mind that.'

'It's a narcotic, so I'll leave this at the nurses' station.' The doctor ripped the prescription from the pad and stood up. 'If this doesn't do the trick for you, let the nurses know.'

'Thank you,' Constance said. She didn't like pills and didn't want to take a sleeping pill, but the pain in her legs was so severe these days that nothing they gave her settled it down. She hadn't slept a night through for months. The idea of falling softly to sleep and waking refreshed to a new day of pain in her crippled legs was so attractive that she wanted one of the magic pills immediately. She didn't want to have to wait for the prescription to be filled, but she knew that patience was a virtue.

'I don't like him,' Nina said from her bed on the other side of the room. 'He's my doctor too, but he's not long on bedside manner.'

'I don't have to love him,' Constance said. 'If he can find me a solid night's sleep, I'll be forever in his debt.'

Nina snorted.

Soon, the nurse came in with Constance's dose of pain meds, which lightened her mood and made living in this wretched nursing home more tolerable, but did virtually nothing for her twisted, aching legs.

Her day went by as all days before, and she assumed, all days until her death, with a sponge bath, bed linen change, the burly attendant putting her on the commode and helping to clean herself afterward, a game or two of cribbage with Nina while they were both up in their chairs.

Then lunch, a nap, and an hour of some stupid romance book on tape that the church ladies brought in, then television until the nurse turned all the lights out and Constance was left to suppress her moans of pain all night long until daylight softened the windowsills, and the routine started all over again.

But not tonight. Tonight, after dinner, the nurse brought a new yellow pill, the one that the doctor had prescribed, and

Constance eagerly gobbled it down, then lay back and waited for those mysterious, vivid dreams that would take her out of pain and into the sheer joy of slumber.

When she opened her eyes, she was on a hill, overlooking the sleeping city. The small, misshapen moon shone high above. Constance took a step, and then another. She could walk! Her legs were as long and strong and straight as when she had been a teenager, running on the track for her old high school team. The night was balmy and her favorite little yellow cotton sundress felt perfect.

She tested her feet and legs out, running around in a circle, and then as her confidence built, she ran down the street. The only sounds she could hear were her old, favorite tennis shoes slapping moist pavement, and her breath as it came effortlessly in and out of her lungs.

What a glorious feeling, to run again, to run as fast as she could, until she could barely catch her breath. Then she slowed and stopped, hands on her knees, bent over to stave off the stitch in her side. Her hands looked like the hands of a young person, fingers straight, skin clear, not painfully twisted with arthritis, thin-skinned with blue veins popping out of liver-spotted skin.

She was young again!

'Hello.'

Constance straightened up and saw a little girl leaning against the trunk of a big tree. 'Hello.'

'Want to have some fun?'

Fun! Constance wasn't sure she knew what fun was anymore. 'Sure.'

'Let's go!' The little one took off, sprinting down the street, and Constance took off after her, thrilled to be quick, agile, and able to keep up.

They ran for what seemed like miles, Constance luxuriating in the feel of the wind blowing through her long, red hair, perspiration cooling on her skin.

The younger girl stopped in front of a vaguely familiar building, long and low, with many windows. 'Shhh,' she said, then waved Constance to follow.

They walked quickly and quietly through the dewy grass and then behind a series of bushes, to peer into the darkened rooms.

Constance, stunned to paralysis by the image of her young face reflected in the window, couldn't see beyond the glass to look inside until the younger girl punched her on the shoulder. 'See?' she asked.

Constance brought her hands up around her face to shield out the moonlight and she saw two hospital beds in the room. Slowly, she recognized the little figurines on one bedside table, the cheap pictures on the wall, the robe hanging over the foot of the bed.

'Not that one,' the girl said. 'This one, over here.'

Tiny Nina seemed lost in the enormous bed, sleeping soundly with her mouth open. Constance felt a rush of affection for her roommate that she hadn't felt before.

This was all so very weird.

'Let's kill her,' the girl said.

'What?' Constance awoke with a start, and it was morning.

She had slept through the night for the first time in years, and she felt wonderful. Even the pain in her legs wasn't as severe as usual.

Those pills were indeed magical, vivid dreams and all. She could definitely put up with vivid dreams of youth and health and vitality.

That evening, she told Sally, her favorite nurse, that she wanted another of her sleeping pills, as the one the previous night had done her so well. Sally frowned, and read the label, striking terror into Constance's heart. What the hell did they care if she got addicted to some stupid drug? She was old and sick and in pain and would die soon anyway. Sooner than later, if she had anything to say about it. This was no way to live, and

VIVID DREAMS 15

if a good night's sleep with strange, vivid dreams was all she had to live for, they should not deprive her of that.

'Please?' she asked in a tiny voice, inwardly furious that she had to beg for something that should be her right to take.

Sally shook one out of the bottle into her hand and handed her a glass of water.

Constance pulled her covers up and waited eagerly for sleep to take her to the land of health and vigor.

'Hi,' the girl said when Constance arrived back on top of the same hill. 'Ready to go for a run?'

'Yes!' Constance said, and they took off down the hill, flying like the wind.

Soon, she was out of breath and they stood again in front of the familiar building, the nursing home. 'This way,' the girl said, and they walked through the foundation shrubbery on the north side. 'This room.'

They both peered into the room, and Constance saw old Esther McCoy in her bed, a line of spittle attached from her lower lip to the pillow. Old Esther spent her days in her wheelchair, bent over so her head rested on her knees, moaning.

'Let's kill her,' the girl said, and Constance believed that there could be no greater act of mercy.

'Okay,' she said, and then in the strange way of dreams, they were in the old woman's room.

'Put a pillow over her face,' the girl said, and Constance did as she was told.

The old woman put up no fight at all. It was as if she were on the brink of death anyway — as she surely had been for months.

'Good.' The girl nodded her approval as Constance put the pillow back where it belonged, and just like that, Constance awoke to Sunday morning, and time to get ready for a wheelchair ride to the little chapel.

The first thing the minister said was that prayers needed to be said for Sister Esther McCoy, who had passed in the night.

Constance felt the flush of shame, and she dared not look

around, lest everyone in the chapel see the guilt on her face. She heard nothing else for the entire sermon.

Just a dream, correct? It was all just a dream. Strange, vivid dreams, the doctor had said. Surely this was all just a huge coincidence.

Still, that night, she asked Sally for another sleeping pill.

'Those are addictive, honey,' Sally said.

'So what?' Constance snapped. 'You deny an old woman a good night's sleep because of some stupid fear that I might get addicted to it? *You* try being stuck here in this bed with these legs and see how well *you* sleep the night through.'

Hurt, Sally left the room and silently brought her back a pill and a glass of water.

The little girl was at the same place, and without asking, Constance knew where they were headed when they began to run. The night air filled her lungs with freshness and joy, and when they arrived back at the nursing home, she felt none of the remorse at the passing of old lady McCoy that she had in the chapel that morning.

'Not me again,' Constance said. 'It's your turn.'

'Okay,' the girl said, and then they were in the room of Mr Miner, the old railroad engineer. Blind, deaf and of no use to himself or anyone else, the girl picked up the pillow and held it down over his face.

As with Mrs McCoy, he put up no struggle whatsoever, and soon the deed was done.

And it was morning.

'Did you hear?' Nina asked. 'Philip Miner passed in the night.'

'It's about time,' Constance said.

'I agree.'

After two nights of good, sound sleep, Constance felt good enough to be helped into a wheelchair go to the smelly cafeteria for lunch, the first time she had made an appearance there in years. Kate, the aide with all the tattoos, wheeled her in and found her a place to sit at a table with other ladies who were younger, or at least more ambulatory. Everyone seemed glad to have Constance join them, but she was not up for small talk, she was looking around the room to see who might be the next candidate to be put out of his or her misery.

She saw several.

That night, she asked for her pill and countered Sally's hesitation with a stern look. She was going to take no crap about it, and Sally complied. Constance knew a note would be made in her chart, but she didn't give a shit.

She and the little girl ran through the night. Soon they were back at the nursing home, drawn there as if by a magnet. The little girl navigated them back to her own room.

'That one,' she said.

'That's Nina,' Constance said. 'She's still full of life.'

'She's not,' the girl said. 'Let's kill her.'

'You do it,' Constance said. 'If she's your choice, then you have to do it. I can't, because she's my friend.'

'That's the job of a good friend,' the girl said. 'You're her friend, and that's why you have to do it.'

'No.' Constance was adamant. 'You have to do it.'

'I can't. And it must be done. Come on.'

They entered the room through dream magic, and a moment later, Constance stood over her friend's bed. She looked at the girl and saw a greedy eagerness on her face. 'I'll miss her,' Constance said.

'*Do it*,' the girl commanded.

Reluctantly, Constance picked up a pillow and approached her old friend's bedside. Nina slept quietly and peacefully, but as the pillow came down, she opened her eyes and looked Constance in the face.

Did she nod, just before the pillow snuffed out her air?

There was more fight in Nina than in the others, but not all that much.

The girl, standing behind her, laughed and then just as Nina gave up her ghost, the girl sighed. 'Yes,' she said quietly.

In the end, Constance knew that she had done her old friend a favor, just as the girl had suggested.

But when she put the pillow back and turned around, the girl was gone.

She immediately awoke to commotion coming from the other side of her room. Before she could chase away the cobwebs of her dreams, attendants had wheeled Nina's bed from the room with Nina's lifeless body still in it.

Constance felt a pang of loneliness, as her companion of so many years had now gone. No telling what kind of roommate she'd get to replace her. One who played cribbage, she hoped.

The next night, Constance ran like the wind, but her little companion failed to show up and join her. She ran and ran until she thought her heart would burst with the exhilaration of it all, and when she awoke, Nina's family was there to clean out her personal belongings.

'Excuse me,' Constance said, and Nina's eldest daughter, box in hand, turned around. 'Might I have something to remember your mother by? We were such good friends.'

The daughter looked down at the open box she carried. 'Here,' she said. 'Here's a picture of Mom when she was younger.' She picked out a small framed photograph and handed it to Constance.

The photograph was of the young girl in Constance's dreams. Somehow, Constance was not at all surprised, only that in her final moments, Nina had been so treacherous as to manipulate Constance to do her bidding, and then left without offering Constance an escape route.

'But who's to take care of me?' she asked no one in particular.

'The nursing home,' Nina's daughter said as she walked out. 'That's why you're here.'

'No! That's not what I mean!' Constance shouted. 'I mean who will take *care* of me?'

But by that time, they had all gone and she was left alone with her pain.

Hubert Lampo

Rain and Gaslight

The term 'magical realism' is typically associated with Latin American literature, but the Dutch-speaking Flanders region of Belgium had its own magical realism movement in the mid-20th century, the foremost practitioner of which was HUBERT LAMPO (1920-2006). *Many of Lampo's works reflect his fascination with the strange and fantastic, as well as his interest in such topics as Atlantis, Stonehenge, and the Holy Grail; his works also include a novel about the medieval Satanist and serial killer Gilles de Rais and a Dutch translation of Jean Ray's horror classic* Malpertuis. *But by far his most famous work is* The Coming of Joachim Stiller (1960), *which went through forty-four Dutch printings, was translated into fifteen languages (including English, in a 2019 Valancourt release), and adapted for a 1976 film. In this novel, a mild-mannered journalist has his life suddenly upended by the occurrence of a series of bizarre and inexplicable phenomena relating to a mysterious individual calling himself 'Joachim Stiller'. Like* Joachim Stiller, *'Rain and Gaslight' is a tale that deals with the uncanny and inexplicable. It first appeared in 1945 and is translated into English for the first time here.*

IT WAS ONLY WHEN the door of the little pub had closed behind me and I was met with the smell of tobacco smoke that I felt how soaking wet I was. My overcoat weighed like lead and the water dripped off my hat's beaten-down brim. On that November afternoon I had gone to inspect our storage facilities in one of the farthest outlying corners of the harbor. When I arrived I committed the stupid mistake of sending the company car away. It had cost me over an hour's walk in the rain. The damp cold had penetrated all the way to the marrow of my spine. Instead of having a clandestine drink at the bar and immediately phoning for a taxi, as I had at first intended, I took a seat by the old-fashioned stove and asked for a cup of coffee.

In the small barroom – card-playing ship captains with blue caps, a melancholy stray dog at my feet, and the gorilla-like figures of a team of forgotten sports heroes on the wall beside a miniature ship in a whisky bottle – the soft, warm atmosphere of a lost afternoon reigned in the twilight, where the clinking of glasses being rinsed, the purring of the fire, the dull rustle of the rain on the windowpanes, the occasional flaring-up of a squabble between the card players, or the wailing of a ship's siren on the Schelde formed an unbreakable whole with the silence. At the moment I began to sip my steaming coffee, the clock on the wall struck four. I clearly remember the preceding groan of the machinery and how I counted each stroke. Behind the wet windowpanes the harbor streetlamps shivered.

It was now almost completely dark, and the innkeeper lit the lamp. I blinked a little at the light and looked away. It is owing to this that I suddenly caught sight of Clemens Devriendt. Although he sat in the corner by the window, wholly in the shadows, I recognized him at once as he sat staring at an empty beer glass with philosophical restraint. It struck me how changed he was since I had last run across him a couple of years earlier near the Stock Exchange. I have seldom seen anyone grow so old and broken-down in such a short time. Did I express my surprise through any sudden gesture? Did he feel my glance resting on him, or was it only coincidence that he looked at the clock? In any case, he raised his eyes unexpectedly and we looked dazedly at one another. After a short hesitation – what drama played out meanwhile in his innermost self? – he rose wearily and came over to me.

'You don't recognize me anymore, do you?' he asked.

There was a connection between the hoarseness of his voice

and the blurryness in his eyes. I did my best to laugh unconstrainedly, but he didn't give me time to answer. 'And even if you did recognize me,' he cut me off, with a sudden pained twitch at his thin mouth, 'then you would rather pretend you hadn't, right?'

'I don't understand what you mean,' I said calmly, then motioned to the landlord, who was dozing behind the bar, and ordered two Bols. When I looked the other man in the face once more, the bitterness on his lips had given way to a helpless embarrassment that made his eyes human again. As soon as he sensed I had caught him in a weakening of his standoffish attitude, he tried to look right through me. The hoarse sound of his words, however, betrayed his emotional state.

'Don't mind me. I've been really nervous lately . . . Life isn't always what we'd like it to be, Bert.'

'Don't you worry, old boy,' I interrupted him obligingly, 'all of us have a rotten day now and then. With weather like this, black thoughts are only natural. Cheers.'

'Yes,' he said with a groan, 'that rain, which never stops, just like on that awful day . . .'

His hands lay helplessly on the tabletop, alone and abandoned. When I saw those hands, I understood that it was a defeated man who sat before me. Even without his threadbare jacket and disheveled necktie I would have noticed it.

'Just like that night,' he echoed himself with obstinate resignation, and I wondered whether those words were still addressed to me.

For a moment total silence reigned and I heard the wall clock tick. Until the door opened and an attractive young woman came in, accompanied by the wind's increasing tumult, and took a seat by the window, unnoticed by my poor friend, who sat with his back to her. My glance met hers briefly – she had remarkably large grey eyes – and I thought I saw her hesitate, or perhaps even start in fright, although in a self-controlled manner.

'Just like that night,' he repeated stubbornly, 'exactly one year ago today,' – as if he wanted to torment himself, and by now I was certain that he was speaking exclusively to himself. Yet at the same time I felt convinced that he sought to free himself from an almost unbearable burden. His mumbling to himself was worse than any outburst of despair. I laid my hand on his forearm. 'Speak,' I urged with the greatest possible assertiveness, 'speak. If I can help you...'

'Yes,' he hesitated, 'yes... For a year now I have dragged it along with me, like a vicious black dog that follows me everywhere, and until now I haven't spoken of it to anyone. But I want to tell it to you. No, no one can help me. But it'll destroy me if I keep it quiet any longer. Maybe you will understand me, maybe you will laugh at me. All the same...'

While he lit the cigarette I had given him, I noticed that his fingers trembled like those of a seasoned drunkard.

* * *

It happened on a rainy day just like today, one of those endlessly depressing rainy days with contrary wind gusts, low-drifting clouds, and an early falling dusk. You know, the kind of day where in the evening the gaslight in godforsaken streets drips out of the streetlamps onto glimmering cobblestones, while behind certain windows, one or two stories up, you nonetheless suspect a domestic warmth that you yourself will never know, and you suddenly realize you have never really been happy and that there's no chance left you ever will be. That's the kind of day it was, just like I'm telling you.

Was it because of the rain that I had been walking around since early that morning in a depressed mood? Was I worried again – despite the faint hope the doctor had given me some time before – about the condition of my wife, who had been diagnosed a couple of months earlier with an incurable heart defect? In any case, that afternoon I was summoned to the boss's office. No sooner had the office boy come to inform me than I knew what to expect. The crisis in the insurance company was starting to spread at that time like an oil spill. The boss sat like a pasha behind his fake Renaissance desk, his fat face gleaming. First he stared at me rudely for a moment, like an astonished frog, as if he didn't know why I had come.

'You sent for me?' I said peevishly.

I looked him straight in his gelatinous eyes. He shifted back and forth in his overly deep chair. The rain whipped against the windowpanes, the heating pipes hissed, and it was unbearably hot in there.

'Look,' he began, 'you yourself know what a hard time we're having right now keeping our heads above water in our line of work, and that's why ... Anyway, I regret to inform you of an order from the management board that ...'

'That you're firing me?' I asked tranquilly, surprised at my own calmness, even though his slimy voice was making me furious and the blood had drained out of my face.

'You mustn't take it like that. It's only that we wanted to advise you that you should look for ...'

'Another job?'

'Precisely,' he answered with relief, satisfied with his own diplomatic handling of the situation. 'An employee like you will surely soon ...'

He smiled stupidly, finished the sentence with a gesture of his hand, and his eyes swam like frog spawn behind his glasses. I was happy with my self-control. From the outset I had despised him too deeply to hide it, so that it would have been obvious even at a glance – if he had not been immunized by his insensitivity, I mean.

But when I went out into the street with my lunch bag under my arm, shivering in the cold – the rain streaked along my hot forehead and my ears were burning – I felt a boundless self-pity rise up in me, something that until then I had never experienced. Defeated, I looked ahead to my return home.

I knew what a deep impression such things made on Louise. Hadn't the doctor made clear to me that she must be spared from any strong emotion whatsoever? It rained on and on. It could not have been otherwise: it had to rain, that day. The rain made me calmer, and after a while the miserable feeling gave way to a flat tranquillity, oily like the stillness of water on a stormy evening.

The full weight of it hit me: here I was, in the middle of a period of economic crisis, with no job and three months' salary in my pocket. And, uninterrupted, that rain and the reflection of the miserable gaslight on the cobblestones. My shoes were waterlogged and I had the feeling that I would walk in wet shoes until the end of my days. A profound dread prevented me from going home. I was not thinking only of my wife's illness. There was above all the slow acid that for some time had been eating away at our relationship. If there was ever a man who married a woman for love, I was that man, I swear it. But as I walked in my misery through the wet streets, anxiously wondering how I could share the bad news with her in the gentlest way, I realized for the first time that what little remained of the happiness I had originally known and dreamed of with Louise was doomed. Maybe it seems ridiculous to you that I let myself be influenced so deeply by my despondency ... But I was a man of forty who suddenly felt his youth crumbling away. Closing my eyes, I imagined how it would be when I came home. I saw Clemens stumble up the stairs and open the door hesitantly, felt the weary gaze of my wife weigh upon me. She would be sitting in the kitchen mending clothes or with her hands in her lap staring in front of her, even though she knew I hated her hanging around there in the evenings. She would not ask me why I was coming home so late, but would meekly and silently place my dinner plate in front of me and remain silent, not sullen but with exaggerated resignation; in bed, after the conventional nightly kiss, she would turn her back to me and pay no heed to the hand that I would lay on her breast out of habit. I wouldn't have the nerve to speak, conscious of how irrevocably too late it was for us to find one another again and that, yet again, Louise was slipping like sand through my fingers. Really I had always known it, and I had not been blind in my love. During the fifteen years of my marriage I had waited in vain for an absolute rapprochement. It had never come. What was to blame for our gradually having lost one another? The narrow circumstances in which we lived? Our completely opposite natures? The heart trouble that influenced her physical and moral condition more deeply than we had yet suspected? The certainty that her condition would never allow us to have a child? God, I don't know ... Maybe it lay much deeper ... How little we really know ourselves ... The light from the streetlamps was indescribably depressing. Don't think I'm being dramatic if I keep talking about rain and gaslight. Despite the incomprehensible aspects of my adventure, it remains first and foremost the story of a man in the rain, who stares mindlessly at streetlamps, at the yellow reflection on the cobblestones, the blind wall with its mange of saltpeter stains, the wooden fence with its posters half torn off, the lit panes behind which an inaccessible life unfolds, the display window of an old-fashioned grocery store somewhere in the impoverished neighborhood of Sint-Andries with its narrow, deep streets. I began to walk more slowly and stopped, gripped by an inexplicable emotion, to look at the landscape through the condensation on the shop window, just like when I was a young boy holding onto mother's hand, a landscape of jars, boxes of oatmeal, and on top a bunch of half-ripe bananas, cleaning cloths, sponges, pieces of blood sausage and a flytrap on the now-unused gas nozzle.

Something tender slid over the pain, something out of my childhood years, something very early and melancholy, perhaps the memory of a happiness that one has blindly passed by. I saw myself again as a boy, safe in mother's presence, walking past the display windows on St. Nicholas' Eve, or around

Christmastime under the fragrant pines on the Groenplaats. Maybe there was also something of the spring mornings at school, when outside the windows the clouds sailed by and the laburnum bloomed in the neighboring gardens. Around that time Louise had come, girlish and translucent like the spring itself, but unusually introverted and with something of a guilty look about her, just as she has always remained since: a closed book. The Louise of that time – the scent of the lindens and lilacs carried on the approaching twilight, as I sat by the open window at exam time, bent over my Homer and filled with thoughts of her – was dead. Or better: my illusions were dead, like chrysanthemums at the end of November. I loved her so inexpressibly much, my friend, and that evening, when I stared aimlessly through the window of a shabby little store as memories full of melancholy tenderness weighed upon me, I loved her still. But all the same I knew it was all finished and that there was no starting over. And suddenly the misery of the situation shot through me once more as I realized with resentment that my inborn, albeit laboriously concealed, sensitivity must triumph over my laboriously acquired stoicism.

'I am a coward,' I thought, as my eyes filled with tears. 'Otherwise I would take the tram immediately, keep my dismissal quiet from Louise and tomorrow go out and look for another job... Aren't I a man, after all?'

Then I thought of you. I don't know when I had heard it, but in any case it suddenly occurred to me that you had a good thing going at the Transatlantic Commercial Company. The thought that all I had to do was to call you up in order to find someone who could maybe help me, or arrange an introduction, filled me with hope. I found a little café with a telephone number on the window, something like this pub. It was in a little square where I had never been before and where, despite the rain, children in the porch of an old church were whining a counting rhyme that I remembered vaguely from my youth. There was a crumpled directory by the telephone in the little passage behind the barroom. It smelled of roasted herring and I noticed suddenly that I was hungry. Forgive me for not sparing you such details. Just like the rain, the streetlamps, the poor people's shop, the weathered wall with its pockmarked spots and right in front of me the Coca-Cola girl on the wall, they all belong here in this story. I found your number right away. But when the bell at the other end of the world stopped ringing, I heard the voice of your wife.

'I don't know for sure when he will be home,' she said to me. 'But I can give you a couple of numbers where, with a little luck, you might reach him . . .'

I made a note of the numbers on the thumbed edge of the telephone book. At first I felt disillusioned at being fobbed off without any success. You were expected any moment, or you had just gone out the door. I've never been lucky in those things. But afterwards I caught myself taking an unwholesome pleasure in creating a little game. Every time I dialed a number it seemed as though infinity began at the tips of my fingers, and in my imagination I saw the city lying beneath the rain like an endless desert of roofs, boulevards, streets, squares and alleys, while it seemed to me that I had a boundless power that allowed me to penetrate to wherever I wanted. I thought of the dollhouse my sister had when I was a little boy, a complete house in miniature, where you could just look inside because there was no outside wall. There was moreover something in it of the feeling that would come over me around dusk, when I and my fellow scamps would ring doorbells in a posh street and then peep round the corner to see if the maid would come and open the door. I don't know whether for my pals it meant anything other than wanton troublemaking, but in any case it gave me the satisfaction of an ecstatic longing for adventure. As the rotary dial turned, softly ticking as it dialed the sixth or seventh number, it suddenly seemed to me that I had put in the wrong final digit: an eight instead of a seven. Not entirely convinced of my mistake, I waited for someone to answer.

The bell rang vainly in the distance nine or ten times and I was just about to hang up when someone picked up on the other end of the line. There was something in that distant female voice, although distorted by the telephone equipment and wires, something bewilderingly charming and something intimate moreover, like the memory of something one has never experienced. Yes, that is the right expression: the memory of something you know you've never experienced, yet which fills you with a familiarity never before offered by reality. 'I can't tell you, darling, how happy I am to hear your voice. I've been waiting an eternity for you already. Why did it have to take so long?' Before I had the chance to get a word in, or to apologize for my mistake, I heard the soft murmur in the device that told me the connection had been broken, as if there was no more to be said and the unknown woman knew that our conversation was merely an accident, an expression of impatience that would now quickly be silenced. I stood staring at the phone in a daze. At that moment I began to feel like a stage player who is simultaneously an actor and the spectator of his own character – something like the emotion that must come over a sensitive film actor at the premiere of his own work. The raindrops drummed obstinately on the panes of the glass roof and the water groaned in a drain pipe.

I have never figured out what impelled me to act. Without thinking about it, I dialed the number of the information service. The drawling and businesslike voice of the telephone operator annoyed me, all the more since a vague feeling of guilt was coming over me.

'Please ... Could you give me the address for 3-9-6-5-9-8? ... What was that? You aren't allowed to give it out? It's a matter of the utmost importance ... Yes, miss, you can rest easy. You are very kind ...' Finally I got what I had asked for: the name of a street, which I placed vaguely in a part of the town unknown to me, and a house number. Although outwardly calm, I felt myself overcome by a sort of trance that manifested itself in an accelerated heartbeat and stifled breathing. I telephoned resolutely for a taxi. Then I went to the barroom, where a grey cosiness reigned around the fire, drank two glasses of rum one after the other and waited until the car pulled up. Behind the windows the rain spun long threads in the light under a statue of the Virgin Mary.

After the door had closed behind me and the car had set off again with the sticky noise of the rubber tires, I realized where I was. It was in the vicinity of the city limits, in an abandoned street, on one side of which was a long whitewashed wall, behind which I descried a manor house and garden. On the other side of the street rose the side wall of a high, red stone building that I took for a brewery because a bitter odor of malt seemed to float over the whole neighborhood. In addition there was an old-fashioned inn with lowered though brightly lit shutters and three leafless linden trees in front of the door. I stood up to my ankles in mud before a wrought-iron gate. I did not see a bell, and the gate itself was closed. But a small barred door, set apart in the heavy fence of the right-hand wing, stood open a crack. Without stopping to consider, I walked along the gravel path under the dripping trees into the garden. It was a manor house in late Flemish renaissance style, the kind you find many of on the outskirts of the city: a weathered brick building, covered by a protruding slate roof and with a forged iron lamp over the steps in front of the entry door. An unusual clarity took hold of me at the sight of the light behind the upper windows. And although I had not the faintest suspicion of what I was doing there, the feeling came over me that I had always been waiting for that moment, that every thought, every word, and every action in my life had been the preparation for the miracle that began when I tugged the finely curled bellpull and heard a soft clanging within. Again there was the intimate familiarity with things that I seemed to have experienced long before I was born. The peephole in the door was opened and I heard a female voice ask, 'Who's there?' It is strange that I did not feel shy about answering but simply said, 'It is I.' Even stranger is that this proved to be sufficient for the door to be opened and for the maid to admit me as a matter of course. Now I was fully playing the role that I had always felt called to and whose words and gestures had waited within me, God knows how long, previously hidden under the cloudy sediment of joy and sorrow. The pleasant warmth inside the house swept across my face. Meanwhile my glance wandered through the vestibule. This curiosity alone contrasted with the natural and slightly melancholy-tinted acquiescence that made me accept everything passively, as if it could not be otherwise. There hung a heavy copper lantern with green and yellow glass that spread a dampened light, the floor was covered with large black and white tiles, the rain rustled behind high stained glass windows.

'Madam requests you to come upstairs at once,' said the girl, and she preceded me up the monumental staircase.

The unknown woman stood before the mirror of a low dressing table, her face turned away from me. It afforded me the opportunity of quickly taking in the atmosphere of the spacious room. There were an oversized citruswood bed in a harmonic mixture of Louis XV and modern-day styles, with a light-blue canopy of silk voile and a great deal of airy lacework, a screen and a coiffeuse in the same style, very delicate drapes on the high windows, and before the open hearth fire a smooth ultramarine carpet of heavy wool. But above all there was a bright and autumnal perfume, somewhat akin to old English lavender, but less permeating and more intimate, an aroma that since then I have never again encountered. 'It is the fantastic orchids in the dark vase by the floor lamp giving off that smell,' I thought to myself, 'oh, yes, that must be it . . .' but then it occurred to me that orchids give off no fragrance whatsoever.

I waited for the girl to say something that would draw attention to my presence, but she proved to have suddenly disappeared and had closed the door behind her. Then the unknown woman turned her face towards me. I gasped, my heart seemed to come to a standstill in my breast: that woman was *my wife*, I observed in bewilderment.

Miraculously enough my panicked amazement lasted not even a second. I have never been what you would call phlegmatic, but nevertheless I was suddenly completely calm and ready to accept everything, whatever might happen. I was playing my role again while at the same time I stood by as a spectator. My only emotion must have been a somewhat unhealthy, curious jealousy, imparted to me by the character I was playing. I took off my hat and felt that the hairs on my neck were wet too. A log crackled in the fireplace and the pungent, autumnal scent of the burning wood moved me to my innermost core.

'I have waited a long time for you,' said the woman – my wife? – quietly.

I felt my heart pounding calmly but heavily in my chest. The voice contrasted completely with the familiarity in her appearance; indeed something vibrated in that sound that caused a very old memory, rendered formless by the gnawing of time, to ripple deep inside me on the surface of everyday feelings and thoughts, yet the recognition went no further. It could have been the memory of a dream, not of reality.

I stared into the flames around the wood, whose resin was causing sizzling noises. An unruly lock of wet hair fell across my forehead. As I brushed it away, I finally looked at her calmly, my glance moving up along her body. She was wearing a long white dressing gown of a very thin woolen fabric that allowed the silhouette of her legs to be seen. Never before had she worn her hair combed up in this way, with a full head of broad curls, nor had I ever known that it was so dark, with the purple gleam of beech leaves in the light of the fireplace and the floor lamps. Only her face was inexpressibly familiar to me, although I had the inexplicable impression that I had seen that gentle, introverted expression on some other face than hers — yet wasn't she my wife? Despite the heat I shivered.

'I have waited a long time for you,' she repeated and I asked myself whether she was smiling; you do not notice that the clouds have parted, but suddenly the river's water seems much bluer and deeper and thus you see that the sun is shining again. 'And all this time you have walked through the rain for me while I sat here waiting for you. I have waited years for you, you know. But when the phone call came, I knew immediately that it was you. I knew that it would be on a rainy autumn evening, and so today I was full of hope and certainty...'

For a moment she seemed to listen to the rain, a calm rustling now, which seemed to come from the end of the world. I wondered where I would wind up if I left the manor house now and whether I would once again find the road with its streetlamps, the pockmarked wall, the pub with the three lindens, and the sinister factory on the opposite side.

'It is all so strange,' she continued as if speaking to herself, and she arranged her hair with calm, yet above all mature gestures, 'for years you pass by one another, for years you live like small people without a soul, without a body even, and then suddenly you know it. You know that you must believe, believe profoundly, so that someone will come, you know that you must desire, so that your desires will at last be fulfilled...'

Somewhere far off in the house a clock struck the hour.

'Louise...' I said hesitantly. It was the first word to pass my lips.

'You know my name?' she smiled, surprised. 'Ah yes, why shouldn't you know my name? But forgive me, I am going on and on and you are cold and wet from having come so far through the rain to me. In the dressing cabinet in the room next door you will find dry clothes...'

I was dizzy as I left the room. The feeling that I was no longer myself, that my soul must have sailed into the corporeal shell of a total stranger, now seemed complete. Beyond and stronger than all the strangeness that had so far befallen me, there pervaded also the certainty that I had already experienced all of this before. It was not a vague feeling of shapeless familiarity, such as we often experience, but was instead a mysterious certainty, convincing and overwhelming, although every point of reference was missing. Can things happen to us that lie outside our own lives?

In the boudoir, which brought to mind the paintings of eighteenth-century French masters, I found a luxurious robe and a pair of black leather slippers. I did not recognize myself when I stood before the mirror dressed in those expensive things. The plaid robe concealed my muddy pant legs, whose thighs I knew showed the gleam of age, and the accompanying scarf hid my crumpled collar and poorly fitting tie from view. It had never struck me before how thin I was, yet if previously that thinness reflected nothing more than the poverty of an ill-paid office clerk who lacked fresh air and freedom of movement, now it conferred a certain distinction on me that with a little goodwill could be regarded as a sort of philosophical asceticism.

'Now you are your old self again,' she smiled, when I timidly entered her bedroom once more. 'Ah,' she corrected herself, 'I expressed myself badly; not your old self, I mean, but the man that I have always suspected was in you. Do you know, darling, that you would be an outstanding actor? Or no,' she continued mischievously, 'better yet a film star in the romantic roles that Valentino wasn't suitable for in his time . . .' She laughed brightly and endearingly, but without mockery. She sat up on the low bed, her slender legs folded underneath her body and supporting herself on her hands, which rested behind her with fingers spread. She perceived my shyness and my hesitation. 'Come sit beside me, won't you?'

The wind chased plaintively through the branches outside the window and soon the rain clattered against the panes. The log fully caught fire at last and the flames blazed up high. I looked at her from the side; her eyes gleamed darkly when she lifted them towards me, slowly and poignantly.

'How did you know that you had to come at last? What was the sign that revealed it to you?' she asked as she looked at the ring she wore on the middle finger of her right hand – old gold and emerald, I thought automatically.

'I was trying to phone a friend of mine,' I answered. 'The number is 3-9-6-5-9-7. How it happened I don't know, but I dialed 3-9-6-5-9-8. Then I heard your voice and came here. Why, yes, why?... I don't know.'

'There is no such thing as coincidence, my dear.'

'No,' I answered, 'perhaps you're right. Quite possibly there is no such thing as coincidence.'

She took a comb from her coiffure and began to comb my hair caressingly. My hair was brittle and I trembled as I heard it softly crackle, as if her fingers were extracting electric sparks from it. Finally it became silky smooth, like in the days of my boyhood, and I felt a wild pleasure course through me, which seemed to stretch out beyond the limitations of my body into space as well as time. She had not stopped conversing with herself:

'The poorer we are, the more importance we attach to coincidence. But if we strive towards perfection there comes a day of maturity, when we've outgrown all coincidences. Only then have we reached the absolute.'

'Maturity ... outgrown all coincidences ... the absolute ...' I parroted her mechanically, without understanding what she meant. And slowly the melancholy images from the past rose up again, how we had loved each other when we were still almost children, yet how fate had later made pawns of us and made us harsh toward one another. Although I resisted stubbornly, my curiosity disturbed the elysian calm that had gradually filled me. Why had fate singled out me, Clemens Devriendt, an obscure office clerk, to experience – after that miserable day – such an unexplainable, even crazy adventure? Was this woman really my wife, or was I being led up the garden path by a fantastic resemblance? And if she was my wife, what did her transformation to mistress of this manor house mean? Or had she been leading a double life for years, of which I had never had the slightest inkling? Had she forsaken the mediocrity of sharing my small, grey life and gone her own way, an existence I had never suspected? Who had paid for the house, the clothes, the maid? Was she caught off-guard and trying to hide her anxiety and astonishment by playing this role, a suddenly inimitable actress?

'What are you sitting there thinking about so seriously?' she asked.

I realized vaguely that, despite my silence, she knew more about me than I dared to imagine, and I looked at her helplessly.

'I'm wondering what all this means. I would like to know what...' She laid her hand on my mouth and pulled me closer to her.

'No one will ever be able to answer that question. We've crossed the threshold, and then it's of no use, questioning the meaning of things...'

'If all of this isn't a delusion, you are indeed right,' I agreed musingly, embarrassed at the banality of the words.

'There's no use in questioning,' she continued in a persuasive tone, 'not because it is so complicated, but rather because it is of a simplicity whose essential perfection we have not yet reached, a purity that does not belong to the ordinary world of cause and effect.'

I lit the cigarette that she offered me and blew the smoke out pensively.

'I'm just a man without much imagination. I feel more at home in insurance policies, you see...'

'Why, you men,' she smiled and brushed her cheek against mine, 'you are always trying to understand, like children in a train who absolutely want to know why the moon is riding along. While the only thing you must consider is that both of us, through all of time, were predestined to love each other on this night, through all of time and despite all detours and difficulties...'

Her voice had become touchingly soft. I laid my arm around her waist. She was naked underneath her white gown and not for a moment did I notice the thinness I had always associated with that body. Her eyes and her mouth were close to my eyes and my mouth.

'Through all of time,' she repeated, echoing herself dreamily. 'We were separated from each other like the core of all beginning and end. Tonight we have finally found each other again; that has been the mysterious circle to ourselves...' She laid her hands on my burning forehead. I saw tears in her large, suddenly girlish eyes, as I tossed the cigarette into the fire. Then, moaning, she pressed her body against mine. Beneath my trembling fingers the rediscovered paradise began. It rained against the windowpanes. The rest, as Hamlet said in his time, is silence.

* * *

I don't know what time it was when I finally reached the neighborhood where I live, yet it seemed to me as if I had come from very far and that I had roamed for days, weeks, yes maybe months or years, through an unknown world. I knew that I must be weary, and yet I did not feel my body. It had stopped raining long before, but the wind swept tattered clouds theatrically past an unhealthy-looking moon.

It is a sad suburb where I've lived all these years with Louise. First you walk a long way past the railroad yards of the still little-used Zuidstation. Further on is the gas factory with its reservoirs and when the wind is low, like that night, the disgusting stench of a nearby candle foundry hangs over everything. Then you must walk further, past formerly derelict plots that have since been parceled out to the unemployed to use as vegetable gardens. With the most heterogeneous supplies – oil cans hammered flat, rusty bedsprings, orange crates, corrugated iron plates – each of them has put up a little hut, which in the intermittently penetrating moonlight gives the appearance of an archaic village from a bygone world. When the gas streetlamps finally resume, you've landed in a completely isolated neighborhood, called forth out of the ground by the grace of God knows what land speculators, in a place where there is only room for garbage dumps, a burnt-out little castle, and the canals of dead factories. It was because of the low price that we took up residence here a couple of years after our marriage.

I saw that the light was on upstairs. I inserted the key in the lock mechanically, walked through the hall without turning on the light, and stumbled up the stairs. I was at the point of throwing myself numbly onto the bed when it struck me that it was empty. Reluctantly I went to the kitchen.

The terrifying scene that made me freeze in the doorway was enough to bring me back to reality at last. Between the table and the unlit stove, Louise lay on the floor with her stiff arms spread out, dead. 'Her heart,' I sobbed aloud, 'that bad heart of hers. I should have thought of it . . .'

Then I stood with wide-open eyes staring mindlessly in front of me. At first it seemed as though I had grown completely calm, yet I felt that something deceptive was hiding behind this unnatural self-control; shock had paralyzed my panic, like a frozen waterfall. Then suddenly all the sorrow in the world crashed down upon me. I howled like a raging animal, vainly called out her name and knelt down by the corpse, a broken man.

She lay face down, dressed in a brightly colored, yet worn-out, floral dress from her younger years and her head was full of grotesque, pitiful-looking curlers. Had it been a final attempt to look charming for me when I came home? My glance fell on the calendar: November 24, her birthday – the last thing on my mind! A boundless pity flowed through me and I knew that for years now this pity had been stronger than any romantic love. I stroked her forehead, just as in olden days when on a summer evening after the noisy student assemblies we would sit on a bench by the pond in the park, awaiting the coming of darkness. It was cold like marble in the shade. She must have been dead for hours.

I sobbed noiselessly. All the miseries and all the rigors of the past seemed never to have existed. All that remained for me was that last pathetic gesture of hers, that shabby little dress that I had once loved so much, the lipstick on her parted lips, the poor attempt to do up her hair...

I took her cold hand in mine and suddenly groaned in pain and disbelief: on her middle finger she wore a golden ring with a heavy emerald, which I immediately recognized, but which had never been hers...

'So for a full year an unspeakable feeling of guilt weighed upon me,' Clemens Devriendt concluded his story, and I saw tears run down his grey cheeks. 'Because not only do I bear my sadness, but I'm obsessed above all by the thought that *I'm* the one who killed her. I knew – the surgeon had informed me – that her heart could withstand very little. And the night that I spent with that woman, you see, it was...'

'Come now,' I interrupted him for the first time, 'aren't you just imagining that your wife and that unknown woman...?'

He shrugged his shoulders and extinguished his umpteenth cigarette in the ashtray.

'I don't know,' he sighed, 'I don't know. Sometimes it feels like I'll go completely crazy if I brood over it any longer. But no, physically it wasn't the same woman... The doctor assured me the following morning that it had happened the day before at around nine o'clock. But yet... The whole thing is so insanely dark...'

'Have you never gone back to the manor house?' I inquired.

'That might be the strangest thing of all ... I found the house again in the street with the pub, the blind wall, the brewery, and the wrought-iron gate.'

'And?'

'In the inn with the linden trees I had a drink and questioned the hostess. The little castle, as the old woman called it, had been vacant for years awaiting a buyer. And might I perhaps have taken a fancy to it? she asked me as she called to her husband, who knew more about it. I found the question of how long the house had been unoccupied to be a perfectly acceptable one for a potential buyer. The fellow, with his lazy eyes and his handlebar mustache, seemed to agree with me, especially since I treated him to a drink. He counted on his fingers:

'We had gotten married the week before,' he said, 'and a couple months ago it was exactly thirty-eight years since then. Then the last owner died, a young unmarried woman. She died of a heart defect on a rainy autumn night. I remember it very well because I had a drink with the coachman right where we're standing now, after he'd come back out of breath from notifying the doctor. Yes, on this very same spot. I still see it clearly before me, it was the 25th of November, very early in the morning.'

After I had warmed myself by the fire, I walked to the gate. The brick-red gravel that led to the little flight of stairs was thickly overgrown with grass, moss, and weeds. The house itself was in a state of complete ruin and almost all the windows were broken. I had certainly not known it like this. Then it struck me that Louise too had been thirty-eight and that her birth coincided with the death of the last resident. I went back to the pub and with the last of my money I got myself stinking drunk.'

I asked the innkeeper for two more Bols and paid at once. Clemens Devriendt seemed to see an unspoken cue in this, for we had hardly emptied our glasses when he made a move to stand up.

'I've kept you long enough with this foolish story.' He smiled painfully. 'Besides it's my time. I found a little job as a tallyman, you know, and tonight we unload a ship full of hides from South America. It'll be hard work in this rain, and then that stench...'

'If I can help you in any way, financially or whatever...' I offered.

He answered my proposal with a gesture of refusal. His expression seemed calmer now that he had poured his heart out.

'Thanks, Bert. I manage to earn a living now. But thank you most of all for your patience. I had to talk this over with someone, you see, I just had to.'

As we moved in the direction of the door, a few steps from there, he slipped his arm amiably in mine. The woman who had come in shortly after me, and who during our conversation had sat silently staring at the rain, fixed her gaze on my unsuspecting companion, who up till then hadn't taken any notice of her. Now, though, he looked up quickly, as though struck by the intensity of her grey eyes, and I felt how a shock like an electrical discharge went through his body. For several astonishingly long seconds they stared at one another without speaking. My friend had suddenly gone completely pale. His arm trembled under mine.

'Louise,' he groaned. 'Louise...'

The woman smiled. I expected him to walk over to her. Only a few steps still separated them from each other. Then suddenly he grabbed me roughly by the elbow and feverishly pushed me outside. The damp wind brushed my overheated temples and I saw his eyes gleam excitedly in the light of the café window. The raindrops poured down on us mercilessly.

'Believe me, Bert,' he panted, 'believe me. I am not crazy. But that woman in there, it was her, one of the two of them I mean, or maybe both . . . I'm not crazy, I swear it, although I know that you won't believe me anymore . . .' His voice caught in his throat. 'Farewell . . . You can't help me find the solution either, no one can. Forget what I've told you. Farewell . . .'

Then he disappeared into the darkness, where the streetlamps had barely any hold. I knew that it was useless to walk after him. A week later I read in the newspaper that his body had been found by children playing in the reeds along the water a little way downstream from the town.

Translated from the Dutch by James D. Jenkins

Eliza Lynn Linton

The Family at Fenhouse

ELIZA LYNN LINTON (1822-1898) *is said to have been the first woman to earn a salary as a journalist in Great Britain; she was also the author of over twenty novels. Despite being known as a bold and independent woman, Linton often held rather conservative views, with a reputation as a staunch anti-feminist and opponent of women's suffrage, among other stances. Her novels, like* Realities (1851), *published by Valancourt, focus mostly (as the title suggests) on realistic, contemporary social subjects. The foregoing description might not sound like that of an author given to indulging in flights of fancy or penning tales of terror, but in fact Linton did write a number of fine macabre stories. We previously featured her 'Christmas Eve at Beach House'* (1870) *in* The Valancourt Book of Victorian Christmas Ghost Stories, vol. 2, *and indeed the following tale might have featured in a Christmas collection as well, being published as it was on December 22, 1860, in Charles Dickens's weekly magazine* All the Year Round. *To give some perspective to the literary chronology, it appeared in the same issue as chapters five and six of* Great Expectations, *so that Victorian readers would have turned the page from young Pip's adventures to find this very atmospheric and rather sinister tale of murder and hereditary insanity. It no doubt made for particularly creepy Yuletide fireside reading.*

I WAS TO BE A GOVERNESS; but I could not obtain a situation. My poor mother had been insane for many years before her death; one of my brothers was deaf and dumb, another was deformed, while none of us showed either health or vigour.

In a word, there was no escaping the fact that we had the seeds of some terrible disease sown thickly among us, and that, as a family, we were unhealthy and unsafe. I was the eldest and the strongest, both in mind and body, but that was not saying much. I was always what I am now, tall and gaunt, with the spasmodic affection which you see in my face, as nervous as I am now, and nearly as thin; short-sighted, which made my manners doubly awkward, and they would always have been awkward from my nervousness and ungainly figure; and with an unnaturally acute hearing, often followed by attacks of unconsciousness, which sometimes lasted many hours, and rendered me, for the time, dead to all outward life.

Unpromising as our family condition was, when my father died and left us destitute, it was absolutely necessary that those of us at all capable should get something to do, and that the rest should be cared for by charity. The last we found more easy to be accomplished than the first. Many kind hands were stretched forward to help the helpless of us, but few to strengthen the weak. However, after a time, they were all settled in some way or other, and were at last secured from starvation, while I, who had been considered the most hopeful, was still unprovided for, looking vainly for a situation either as governess or companion. Both were equally difficult to procure. On the one side my manners and appearance were against me, on the other, my family history. As I could not deny my inheritance of disease and insanity, mothers, naturally enough, would not trust me with their children, and I was not sufficiently attractive for a companion. People who can afford companions want something pliant, bright, animated, pleasant. No one would look at my unlovely face, or hear the harsh tones of my voice – I know how harsh they are – and pay me to be an ornament or pleasure to their lives. So, as I tell you, I was refused by every one, until I began to despair of success, and without blaming any, to understand that the world was too hard for me, and that I had no portion in it.

As my last venture, I answered an advertisement in the *Times* for a companion to a lady in delicate health, living in the country. My letter was replied to in a bold manly hand, and a meeting arranged. I was to go down that next day by train to a place about twenty miles from London, and find my way from a certain railway station named, two miles across the country — conveyances not to be had — to a village called Fenhouse-green. A mile farther would bring me to Fenhouse itself, 'the seat of Mr and Mrs Brand.' The note was couched in a curiously sharp, peremptory style, and pompously worded. I remember, too, that it was written on a broad sheet of coarse letter paper, and sealed with what looked at first sight to be a large coat of arms, but which, when examined, proved to be only a make-believe. With my habit of making up histories out of every incident that came before me, I decided that the writer was a military man, wealthy and high born; and that, about to leave on foreign service, he wished to place his young and beautiful wife in careful hands so as to ensure her pleasant companionship during his absence. I made quite a romance out of that peremptory letter with its broad margin and imposing seal.

'They will never take me when they have seen me!' I sighed, as I settled myself in the third-class carriage which I shared with three soldiers' wives and a couple of Irish labourers, and I wished that I could have exchanged my fate and person with the meanest among them. Though they were poor, they were not under a curse, as I was; though man had not uplifted them, Fortune had not crushed them as she had crushed me. I was weeping bitterly behind my veil, overpowered with my own sadness and despair, and almost decided on not going farther to meet only with fresh disappointment, when the train stopped at my station, and I let myself drift down the tide of circumstance, and once more dared my chance.

Asking my way to Fenhouse-green, much to the astonishment, apparently, of the solitary station-master, I struck into a rugged by-road, which he said would take me there. The two miles' walk seemed as if it would never end. The road was lonely, and the country desolate, ugly, and monotonous; nothing but a broad ragged waste, without a tree or an autumn flower to break the dead dreariness of the scene. I did not meet a living creature until I came to an unwholesome-looking collection of cottages, covered with foul eruptions of fungi and mildew starting out like a leprosy upon the walls. Where the village-green should have been, was a swamp, matted with confervæ. It was a place to remember in one's dreams, from the neglect and desolation, the hopeless poverty and feverish squalor of all about.

If this was the village of which the writer had spoken so pompously as his property, and of which I had imagined all that was charming and picturesque, it did not argue much for what had to come; and I began to feel that I had painted too brightly, and, perhaps, had ranked my chance too low. The place frightened me. I went through, glad to escape the stupid wonder of the pallid women and children who came crowding to the doors, as though a stranger were a rare and not too welcome sight among them. Indeed, some seemed to have a kind of warning terror in their looks when they pointed in the direction of the House, as they called it; and one old witch, lifting her stick, cried, 'Surely, surely, not there belike!' in a tone which froze my blood. However, it was too late now to recede; so, full of an indescribable terror, I went on my way, until I arrived at Fenhouse, where my future was to lie.

It was a lonely house, standing back from the road, completely shut in, in front, by a tangled shrubbery, while at the rear stretched a close dark wood with a trailing undergrowth of briars and thorns. The gate hung broken, supported by one hinge only; the garden was a mass of weeds and rubbish; the flower-beds overgrown with grass and nettles; and what had once been rose-trees and flowering shrubs, left to wither and die, stifled by bindweed and coarser growths. The house was of moderate size, two-storied, and roomy, but so neglected and uncared for, that it looked more bleakly desolate than anything I had ever seen before. My dream of the young and beautiful wife had vanished, and I felt as if about to be ushered into the presence of some fantastic horror or deadly crime. The wet leaves plashed beneath my feet, and sent up their clouds of autumn odour – the odour of death: unsightly insects and loathsome reptiles glided before me with a strange familiarity, which rendered them yet more loathly; not a bird twittered through the naked branches of the trees. The whole place had a wild, weird, haunted look; and, shivering with dread at I knew not what, I rang the rusty bell, hanging lonely out of the chipped and broken socket. The peal startled me, and brought out a small terrier, which came running round me, barking furiously and shrilly. The door was opened by a ragged, slip-shod servant-girl, and I was shown into a poorly furnished room, which seemed to be a kind of library; to judge at least by the open bookcase, thinly stocked with shabby books. The room was close and musty; the fire in the grate was heaped up carefully towards the middle, and the sides blocked in by bricks. It was a mean fire: a stingy, shabby fire.

After waiting for some time, a gentleman and lady came in. She was a pale, weak, hopeless-looking woman, very tall, fair, and slender, with a narrow forehead, lustreless light blue eyes with no eyelashes, scanty hair, straw-colored ill-defined eyebrows, and very thin pale lips. She was slightly deformed, and carried her arms thrust far back from the elbow, the hands left to dangle nervelessly from the wrists. She stooped, and was dressed in a limp, faded cotton gown, every way too scanty and too cold for the season. When she came in, her eyes were bent towards the soiled grey carpet, and she never raised them, or made the least kind of salutation, but sat down on a chair near the window, and began to unravel a strip of muslin. The gentleman was short and thick-set, very active and determined looking, with dark hair turning now to grey, a thick but evenly-cut moustache, joining his bushy whiskers, the large, square heavy chin left bare; overhanging eyebrows, with small, restless, passionate eyes beneath; in his whole face and bearing an expression of temper amounting to ferocity.

He spoke to me peremptorily and haughtily; asked me my name, age, family condition, previous history, as if he had been examining me on oath, scarcely waiting for my answers, and all the while fixing me with those small, angry eyes till I felt dazed and restless, as creatures under torture. Then he said, abruptly:

'You have a strange look – a scared look, I may call it. How have you come by it?'

'I am of a nervous temperament, sir,' I answered, pulling at the ends of my gloves.

'Nothing else? Nothing hereditary?'

'Yes, sir,' said I, as steadily as I could; 'there is hereditary misfortune among us.'

'Father or mother?'

'Mother.'

'Ah!' said the man, rubbing his moustache, and looking at me with eyes all aflame; 'so much the nearer and more dangerous.'

'I am not dangerous,' I said, a little too humbly, perhaps; but that man was completely subduing me. 'I am nervous, but I have no worse tendency.'

He laughed.

'Perhaps not,' he said, with a sneer that made my blood curdle; 'no one ever has. Don't you know that all maniacs are philosophers, when they are not kings and queens? Shall I take you on trust, then, according to your own estimate of yourself, or discharge you at once, according to mine?'

'I think I may be trusted, sir,' I answered, looking everywhere but into his face.

'What do you think, Mrs Brand?' he said, turning to the pale woman unravelling her strip of muslin, and who had not, as I thought, looked at me once yet.

'She is ugly,' said she, in a dull, monotonous voice; 'I don't like ugly people.'

Mr Brand laughed again.

'Never mind that, Mrs Brand; goodness don't go by looks, does it Miss – Miss what? Are you a name or a number?'

'Miss Erfurt.'

'Oh, yes! I forgot – Jane Erfurt – I remember now, and a queer name it is, too. Does it, Miss Jane Erfurt?'

'Not always, sir,' I said, moving restlessly.

'Well, Mrs Brand, what do you say?'

'She is ugly, and George will not like her,' said the lady, in the same half-alive manner.

'Who the deuce cares!' shouted Mr Brand, flaming with passion on the instant. 'Let him like it or not, who cares for a stupid fool, or for what he thinks? That, for his liking!' snapping his fingers insolently.

The lady's face grew a shade paler; but beyond a furtive, terrified glance at her husband, she took no notice of his words. He then turned abruptly to me, and told me that I was to hold myself engaged to perform the duties of companion to Mrs Brand, and that I was to enter on those duties early next week.

'But without the lady's consent?' said I, too weak to resist, and too nervous to accept.

She put away her muslin and rose. 'Mr Brand is master here,' she said; 'do what he tells you: it saves trouble.'

The week after I went to Fenhouse, as the companion of Mrs Brand.

The first day's dinner was a strange affair. After we had seated ourselves, to what was a very scanty supply, there lounged in a youth of about seventeen: a heavy, full-blooded, lumpish being, with a face devoid of intelligence, but more animal than imbecile; not specially good tempered, but not vicious, a mere idle, eating and drinking clown, scarcely raised above the level of a dog or a horse, and without even their instinctive emotions. What an unwholesome, unnatural circle we made! I longed for a little healthy life among us, and turned with a feeling of envy and relief to the commonplace servant-maid; who, if not intellectual, was at the least more in accord with pure ordinary life than we.

There was ill-blood between Mr Brand and Master George, as the boy was called; and I soon understood why. His mother's only son by a former marriage, and heir of the neglected lands lying round Fenhouse, he stood in the way of his step-father, whose influence over his wife was supreme, and who, but for the boy, would have absolute possession of everything. He had married for money, and had been balked of half his prize. I used often to wonder that the two were not afraid to trust themselves in the hands of one so passionate and unscrupulous; but, though Mrs Brand was undisguisedly afraid of her husband, and the boy was not too stupid to understand that he was hated, and why, neither seemed to look forward to evil days. I do not think that they had mind enough to look to the future in hope or dread. Mother and son loved each other, with the mute instinctive love of dumb animals – a love in which both would be helpless to save if bad times came. They were not much together, and they seldom spoke when they met; but they sat close to each other, always in the same place and on the same chairs, and Mrs Brand unravelled her eternal slips of muslin, while her son gathered up the threads and thrust them into a canvas bag.

I had been there a fortnight, and I never saw either of them employed in anything else; and I never heard half a dozen words pass between them. It was a silent house at all times; and, more than this, it was a house full of hate. Save this dumb-animal kind of love between the two, not a ray of even kindly feeling existed among any of us. The servant was the mark for every one's ill-temper, while I stood out as a kind of pariah among them all, not even dignified by active dislike. I was shunned, and could not understand why I was there at all. The lady never spoke to me, not even to say good morning;

she gave me no duties, but she forbade me no employment. I was free to do what I liked, provided I did not make my existence too manifest to her, and did not speak to her husband or Master George. If by chance anything like a conversation began – for Mr Brand had his talkative moods in a violent, angry kind of way – she used to order me out of the room, in just the same tone as she used to speak to the dog. If I remonstrated, as I did once, her only answer was, 'You can go if you like; *I* did not hire you.'

One thing especially troubled me. It troubled me because, like all morbidly imaginative people, anything of a mystery terrified me more than an open danger; and this, of which I am going to speak, was a mystery. The boy took no notice of me at the first. He never spoke to me when he came into the room; he passed me in the fields as if he did not see me; indeed he had always that manner to me – he did not see me – I did not exist for him. I was well content that this should be; but, after I had been there a short time, Mr Brand began to make distinct mischief between us. From brutish indifference, Master George passed rapidly to brutish aggression. When he met me in the lanes and fields he made mouths at me, and once he flung stones and mud as I passed him; at table he would kick me silently, and whenever I caught his eye he made hideous grimaces, muttering in his broad, provincial accent, 'Mad dog! mad dog! We hang mad dogs hereaway!' His insolence and brutality increased daily, and Mr Brand encouraged him. This was the mystery. Why should he wish this lad to hate me?

There was a plot underneath it all which I tormented myself to discover. Day and night the thought haunted me, till I felt growing crazed with dread and terror. I could not conceal my abhorrence of the youth – I was too nervous for that – nor hide the fear with which that wicked man inspired me. I was as helpless as the poor pale woman there, and as thoroughly the victim of a stronger fate.

One night Master George had been more than usually

intolerable to me. He had struck me openly before both father and mother, had insulted my misfortunes, and spoken with brutal disrespect of my family. It was a wild winter's night, and the howling wind shook the windows and dashed the trailing ivy-leaves sharply against the panes: a fearful night, making all visions of freedom and escape impossible; a night which necessitated one to be content with one's own fireside, and forbade the idea of wandering farther. Yet it was something worse than death to me to be shut up in that mean room, with its squalid furniture and scanty fire, with such companions, and to feel that I could not escape from them – that they might ill-treat me, mock me, persecute me as they would, and I was bound to bear all without protection or means of escape. The stormy night had excited me, and I felt less than ever able to bear all the insolence and brutality heaped upon me. When Master George struck me again, and called me 'mad dog,' something seemed to take possession of me. My timidity and nervousness vanished, and I felt as if swept away in a very tumult of passion. I do not know now what it was that I said or did, but I remember rising passionately from my place, and pouring out a torrent of bitterness and reproach. I was almost unconscious of what I was doing, for I was literally for the moment insane; but I remember the words, 'You shall die! you shall die!' rising like a scream through the room. I have not the slightest recollection of how I left the parlour, nor how I got to my own chamber, but it was past midnight when I awoke from what must have been a kind of swoon, and found myself lying on the floor.

The wind was still raging, howling through the trees outside, tearing down branches, and scattering the dead leaves like flakes of frozen snow upon the ground. Every door and window shook throughout the old house, and the wild moaning in the chimneys came, startling, like the cries of tortured beings. Confused and giddy, I rose up out of my trance, stiff with cold and scarcely conscious. But as my brain grew clearer it grew also feverish, and I knew there was no rest for me to-night. My hearing began to be distressingly acute, and every painful thought and circumstance of my life rose up before me with the force and vividness of living scenes actually present to my senses. I paced my room for some time in a state of despair, wringing my hands and sobbing violently, but without tears. By degrees a little calmness came to me, and I determined to go down-stairs for a book. I would get some quiet, calm, religious book, which would soothe me like a spiritual opiate, and take me out of the abyss of misery into which I had sunk. What friend, indeed, had I in the world, save the Great Father above us all?

As I opened the door I fancied I heard a stealthy step along the passage. I held my breath to listen, shading the candle with my hand. I was not deceived; there *was* a step passing furtively over the creaking boards in the direction of Master George's room. I shrank back into the doorway. Yet there was nothing to alarm me. A quiet footfall at midnight might be easily accounted for: why should it affect me with mistrust and dread? and why should I feel this overpowering impulse to go towards the sound? I scarcely knew what I expected to find; but something stronger than myself seemed to impel me to the discovery of something horrible; and placing the candle on the floor, I crept noiselessly along the passage, every nerve strung to its utmost tension.

Master George slept in a room at the end of the back-stairs gallery, which ran at right angles to the passage in which my room was situated. My door faced Mr and Mrs Brand's; Master George's faced the kitchen stairs, and was properly the servant's room, but she had been moved to a small closet near to me, Mr Brand not approving of her holding so large a chamber for herself, neither willing to allow the boy anything of a better class. When I stood by my door I could see Mr and Mrs Brand's room; but it was only by going the whole length of the back-stairs gallery that I could get to Master George's.

I could see now, however, that his door was open, for a ray of light fell along the staircase wall, and I could hear his heavy snoring breath. And I heard another sound. I heard a man's step in the room; I heard the boards creak and the bed-clothes softly rustle; I heard an impatient kind of moan, as of someone disturbed in his sleep, and then a heavy blow, a stifled groan, a man's deep-drawn breath, and the quick, sharp drip of something spilt upon the floor. Dumb from terror, I stood in the doorway of the boy's room. Pale, heavy, motionless on the bed lay the youth, his large limbs carelessly flung abroad in the unconsciousness of sleep, and his face as calm and quiet as if still dreaming. The sheets were wet with blood – red – the light of the candle glistening upon a small red stream that flowed over the side of the bed, on the floor beneath. At a little distance stood Mr Brand, wiping a knife on a handkerchief. He turned, and our eyes met. He came up to me with an oath, caught me by the throat, and drew the knife across my hands. I remember no more until I awoke in the broad daylight, and found myself in the midst of a crowd gathered round my bed.

Curious eyes stared at me; harsh voices mocked me; rough hands were laid upon me; and I heard myself branded with the burning name of Murderess. Red tracks made by a woman's naked feet – made by *my* feet – led from the boy's room to mine; each track plainly printed on the bare uncarpeted floor – tracks of a woman's feet, and of none other. There was no explaining away these marks and signs of guilt. Who would believe me, a half-mad lonely stranger with such a family history as mine, and, according to popular belief, at any moment liable to make a murderous attack against anyone offending? Had not this unhappy youth notoriously offended, and had I not, only that very evening, openly defied and threatened him? Escape was impossible. To all the evidence heaped up against me with such art and cunning, I had but an unsupported assertion, which would be set down as maniacal raving, and only deepen the case against me.

All day I lay there; all that weary sobbing winter's day; and when the night came they fastened me with cords, and left me once more alone. I was so well secured – bound hand and foot, and triply bound – that it was not thought needful to watch me; and they were all too much excited and overwrought to wish to remain through the night with a lunatic murderer, as I was called. So they went, and Mr Brand locked the door, saying, as he turned away, 'We must have no more such dangerous fits of madness, Miss Erfurt!' with a sneer on the word.

I was too hopeless and desolate to think of any plan of escape, feasible or not. The reaction had set in, and I was content to lie there in quiet, and to feel that I had done with life forever. It had not offered me so many joys that I should grieve to leave it, and for the shame – who cares for shame in the grave? No; I was content to have done with all that had weighed upon me so long and heavily. I had no one to mourn for me, no one to love me, with a broken heart and a sorrowful faith: I was alone – alone – and might well die out at once, and sleep tranquilly in my murdered grave. And I was not unhappy, thinking all these things. Perhaps my brain was slightly paralyzed, so that I could not suffer. However it might be, it was a merciful moment of calm.

It was nearly three o'clock, when I heard a light hand upon the door. The key was turned softly in the lock, and, pale and terrible, like an avenging ghost, the poor bereaved mother glided into my room. She came up to my bed, and silently unfastened the cords. She said no comforting word, she gave me no kind look, no pitying human touch, but in a strange, weak, wan way, she unbound me limb by limb, until I was free.

'Go,' she then said, below her breath, still not looking at me. 'I do not love you, and *he* did not; but I know that you are innocent, and I do not want your blood on my head. My turn is to come next, but I do not mind, now he has gone. Go at once; that sleep will not last long. I made it come for you.'

Without another word she turned from the room, leaving

the door open. I got up as she bade me. Without energy, without hope, I quietly dressed myself, and left the house, going forth into the darkness and desolation, more because I had been bidden to do so, than to escape a greater peril. I wandered through the by-roads aimlessly, nervelessly; not shaping my course for any goal, but simply going forwards, to wherever chance might lead me. A poor woman gave me some milk, and I slept, I believe, once beneath a haystack. I remember lying down there, and finding myself again after many hours. In time – I cannot tell you how or when, nor how long I had been out in the fields, but it was evening, and the lamps were lighted – I was in London, reading a description of myself posted up against the walls. I saw myself described as a murderess and a maniac, and a reward offered for my apprehension; my dress, my manners, appearance, gait, voice, all were so minutely noted, as to render safety impossible. Seized with terror I fled: I fled like a wild being haunted and pursued, and I have never rested since.

John Peyton Cooke

Let's Make a Face

JOHN PEYTON COOKE got his start towards the end of the paperback horror boom when, at the young age of 22, he published his first novel with Avon Books, The Lake *(1989). With its inclusion of gay themes, the book was ahead of its time and was followed by a novel that was even more daring for its day, the explicitly gay-themed vampire novel* Out for Blood *(1991) (republished by Valancourt in 2019), in which a young gay man with leukemia gets his wish – and eternal life – by becoming one of the undead. His other works include two crime novels,* Torsos *and* The Chimney Sweeper. *Horror fans haven't heard much from Cooke for a while, so we're excited to offer this brand-new story. Brace yourself: you will have a strong reaction to this story. You may love it, you may hate it, but we can solemnly promise you that you will never forget it.*

THE PRODUCERS HAD KEPT HER HERE in this windowless ochre room for the duration of her convalescence. 'How long has it been?' she had typed the other day for Nurse, who was the plainest nurse Helen had ever seen, probably a four or a five, as plain as herself, as dull and unappealing as a dried kelp cake. Nurse smiled down at the question pounded out in black ink on the slightly foxed sheet of paper emerging from the manual typewriter. She said that if Helen didn't know, it was all to the good, as her not knowing would work in her favor and would only increase the drama and sympathy and tension on the night of the final reveal. It might add immensely to her popularity score, whatever her final beauty rating.

They had provided her with this typewriter from the Olden Days as the easiest means for her to communicate with them until the bandages came off. The wrappings encasing both of her hands were drawn so tightly they permitted no free movement of her fingers. She could hardly feel them, balled up and confined as they were. Helen imagined herself something like an ancient Chinese princess; her feet were rigidly bound as well. Nurse had to lace onto each hand a sturdy leather mitten affixed with a short, blunt peg that allowed her to depress the keys on the typewriter one by one by means of the traditional hunt-and-peck method. This meant her communications to Nurse or to the producers remained short and blunt.

'Bed not comfortable,' she typed out slowly, banging the machine character by character.

Nurse smiled down at the statement and advised she would check with the producers. Several hours later, as far as Helen could make out, since she had dozed a bit in between, cheerful plain Nurse returned and said, 'They said it's too late now to change rooms or replace your mattress. We're almost to broadcast.'

'When?' Helen typed out.

'Oh, any day now. Soon as they've stored enough solar.'

Nurse spoke absently, as she was busy hooking up a clear bag filled with some sort of puréed pale green soup mixture to the rusted pole by Helen's bedside and fitting the low-hanging end to the dirty-brown latex snake of her feeding tube. It could be pea or celery or sorrel or broccoli or kale or leek or spinach or lowly kelp, but Helen would never know, as it would go straight down the tube through her nasal passage, down her esophagus and into her stomach, and even if she managed to belch, she would barely be able to taste it.

By the time her dinner was prepared, her wrists were always back in the leather straps that kept them secured to the siderails of her bed, so she couldn't even type out a query to find out what was in the bag. As she wouldn't be released again until Nurse's next visit — if she was even awake when that happened — she would not likely waste the energy to ask what she had been fed several hours previous, so she tended not to know. They always assured her it was packed with superfoods, which was a great treat, as these were usually rationed only for sevens and greater.

The straps, the producers had explained to her, were for her own safety and protection. Early on in the run of the show, apparently, certain disobedient contestants had taken it upon themselves to remove their own bandages prematurely, thus ruining the celebrity surgeons' work or exposing themselves to infection or at the very least ruining the surprise for themselves and for the audience. Not to mention violating the terms of their contract, being liable for a severe penalty, subjecting their extended family to certain deprivations, and ruining their own chances at greater worldwide exposure and popularity.

Helen was *not* disobedient and did *not* want a reputation for being so. As it was, she felt she was being a bit of a bother by even asking these few innocent questions. But the typewriter was a great outlet for her fears and frustrations, minor and petty as they were. She trusted the producers and was grateful for her brief moments with Nurse. Her main concerns were when would this all be over, when would all the bandages come off, when could she finally see her new improved self, and how highly would the audience rate her?

That the producers wouldn't give her a new mattress or a different room she attributed to the obvious fact that she was not the only contestant they were looking after. All along the corridor, one presumed, judging by how many contestants popped up on the show on a weekly basis, were so many other girls just like her. Everyone had had their own procedure and had their own care needs. Poor Nurse was probably stretched thin attending to everyone.

Helen had never in her life had cause to act like a diva,

and she would be mortified if she thought they saw her as an emerging one. If she became a nine or a ten, then of course she could do precisely as she pleased, but until that day she at least had to appear humble. She resolved that on Nurse's next visit – provided of course Helen was awake – she would let her know the bed was all right and she was sorry if she had caused any trouble. No doubt all the other girls were weighing Nurse down with all their hysterical requests of the producers at all hours of the day and night. She didn't want to be one of *those*.

She watched the soup mixture gradually gurgle its way down her gullet until the bag was emptied, aside from some remnant gloppy residue sliding slowly down its translucent insides. In the partial view of herself in the mirror, she saw the discolored latex tube threaded into one side of her fully bandaged head, just off center and below her two dark eye holes, just above her fully sealed chin. Her jaw seemed to be strapped tightly shut, and her tongue must be perpetually numb, because she couldn't feel it. She couldn't even find it. Finally, dinner was at an end, and she would have to wait for Nurse to return, disconnect the bag, check the status of her catheter, and empty her bedpan.

All she could do now was stare at her own partly obscured oval-shaped, mummy-like head reflecting back at her in the mirror, propped up against the pillows. Mummies she also associated with royalty, as she had seen the exhibits in museums of eternally wrapped princesses. If she didn't like looking at herself, she could stare at the blank ochre walls and follow the cracks as if they were a strange wallpaper pattern. Or she could choose to switch her glance to the screen hanging from the ceiling on the other side of the room, projecting its endless stream of nines and tens, glamour, wealth, luxury, travel, adventure, sun, sand, fun, flesh, fitness, sex, and, above all, survival.

There was a call button installed within reach of her strapped right wrist, which she could engage by bumping against it, if she needed anything or was ever in a panic. But she never pressed it. She did not want to be considered difficult, and sooner or later all her needs were attended to. They were pampering her, she had convinced herself, as if they were all drones and she the queen bee. The superfoods in her feeding bag were her own royal jelly, aiding her wondrous transformation.

As long as she could remember, she had been plain, and it didn't help that officially she was considered a five. It was true her mother was a nine, and her father a two, but you would think that would average out to a six, not a five. Her mother had once gently explained to her that it was the policy of the directorate to round down rather than up in equivocal cases, to avoid people asking for more than was their natural-born due.

She had lived her life thus far outwardly as a five, as noted on her public directorate profile, but inside she was convinced she was at least a six. Not only a six, but a six deserving of improvement. Growing up the daughter of a nine, she had never wanted for anything, but as she emerged into adulthood, the awakening was rude.

Her impossibly beautiful and accomplished mother had tried to be reasonably supportive, perhaps out of pity, since Helen was naturally the product of her own mixed marriage. But her mother could not restrain herself from often coming out with negative discouragements for which she would then quickly apologize, telling Helen she was only trying to look after her realistic possibilities for future happiness, and after all, what was so bad about being a five, when at least she wasn't a two like her father? She would have fair opportunities for a job in service to the superior numbers, but she would never be a spokesmodel like her mother or otherwise appear on telly.

She hadn't any right to expect that.

And yet she did. She expected it. She aspired to it.

In her senior year, she applied for a Face Grant but was

rejected, as the raters concluded from her screen test that she was '... *a perfectly adequate five, with no particularly remarkable inherent physical characteristics (other than a history of beauty on the maternal side of the family) that would lead us to believe she could attain any rank greater than a six, for which the directorate concludes that a grant is not cost-effective and is therefore denied.*'

Her mother had professed to share her disappointment, but Helen was sure that she was actually relieved. Mother couldn't bear to face the competition, could she? What if Helen had emerged as a nine herself, or even a ten? While her mother succumbed to ageing and had to live off her faded glories...

Once she turned eighteen, Helen saw her only chance as trying to make it as a contestant on *Let's Make a Face*. It wouldn't be easy; the auditions were likely to be just as harsh as what she had been put through by the grant raters. The auditions themselves would be broadcast, subjecting all the plain girls and the ugly girls to global ridicule and harassment, even if they didn't make it as a contestant. Everyone knew that some of these girls were deliberately tricked by the producers into participating in the auditions, when clearly so many of them weren't up to scratch. Simply because it was entertaining for all the world to laugh at this gaudy parade of self-deluded grotesques, and it boosted the show's ratings and sold more luxury products to the viewers, leading up to the real competition and the finals.

'You don't want to draw attention to yourself!' her mother had warned her. 'You're really not that bad looking. Why not just find a fellow five out there and settle down to the five life? No one will bother you, and you might even find happiness of a sort.'

Of course, mother didn't know what she was talking about. On top of that, this ignorant comment brought back Helen's longstanding resentment over the fact that her mother hadn't married a nine herself but had perversely married a hopeless two (probably to piss off her own parents), in which event

Helen either would have been born a nine herself or would have been entitled to a new face if she needed it, instead of having to grovel for a grant or try her luck on a reality show once she was of age. She conveniently set aside the fact that she would not even be Helen at all if it weren't for her father the two – her mother's common riposte whenever this squabble had bubbled up in the past.

Needless to say, she did not speak to her father these days, partly out of embarrassment, partly owing to the impracticalities of communication and travel. Her mother had thrown him away a long time ago, and he lived in a shack in the lowlands somewhere, monitoring the inexorable rise of the sea, a vocation eminently suitable for a two, but something one didn't want to talk about in polite company.

Ultimately, she owed her success in the audition process to the unbelievable support of her friends at the Five School. As soon as she had announced her intention to apply, all of her schoolmates had come out of the woodwork to support her – even those like Becka and Elsie and Freddie, who had never before given her the time of day despite being fives themselves. She had been deeply touched that everyone else in the school finally saw her potential for improvement and rallied behind her. They came with her to the auditions, cheered her on, took her out afterward for kelp flatbreads and frozen soy creams, and generally gave her such confidence that her auditions went off smoother than she could ever have hoped for. Of course, the criticism was unduly harsh, especially from the celebrity judges, who were all tens and could afford to be haters. And she couldn't bear to watch herself on telly being subjected to their endless spews of bile and ridicule.

It was the amazing viewer support that put her over the top and into the finals, and Helen was sure this would never have come to pass without the active social campaigning of her new school chums. And once she made it to the finals, her future success was assured, because the wizards on *Let's Make a Face* had demonstrated time and again that they could do absolutely anything they put their mind to, with nearly any face or body.

After the night of the finals, she spent many hours reliving the heady experience. When she wasn't contemplating her mummified features in the mirror or watching telly, her eyes would drift along the cracks in the dim ochre walls, and she would think about how that episode had gone. Rather well, she must admit, or she wouldn't be sitting here now, awaiting the cutting of the bandages!

The episode had also been replayed a number of times on the screen in her chamber during these weeks (*how many midnights?*) of her recovery. It was an out-of-body experience to think of yourself on telly, being interrogated by the celebrity judges and coddled by the celebrity host. Every time she watched it, she grew more distant from it, as if she had never really been there. It was almost as if it wasn't Helen at all sitting there on stage, getting critiqued for her imperfections and hearing the expert commentary by the celebrity surgeons: what could be done, what couldn't be done, what was hopeless, and what was salvageable.

And it *wasn't* really her. Not anymore. The pathetic caterpillar was about to break out of its chrysalis and go soaring a glorious butterfly. She thought often about giving herself a new name, once she was a celebrity in her own right. *Anabella? Fiona? Aurora? Hera?* (And perhaps she should keep it to just the one name only, like celebrity judge Veronique.) What kind of a show would she want to host for herself? Perhaps a luxury yachting show taking place in the Med? Ones, twos, and threes were literally slaving away day and night building the new hotels and resorts along the grossly expanded shoreline, replacing the now Atlantean hotels of her parents' generation. Helen fancied herself a future Med travel expert, guiding the young yacht-set generation of nines and tens to new, ultra-modern destinations that reflected none of the charred memories of the Olden Days.

'And now let's meet Helen!' celebrity host Peter Lamb had bleated out on that last night of the finals. 'Come on out of your hole, little lady, you're the next contestant on *Let's Make a Face!*'

Helen came out on stage to a thundering of applause, much of it from her own support contingent from the Five School. Becka, Elsie, Freddie, and even her mother were all in attendance to cheer her on. Her father would never have been permitted to leave his post and travel upland to the studios, and she didn't believe twos were even permitted to get tickets. Anyhow, she was glad he couldn't come.

Peter Lamb addressed the audience: 'Here she is, our Helen! What's to become of her, ladies and gentlemen? Will she be elevated to the status of a nine or a ten? Or will she become the latest popular attraction in Dr. Bob's Freak Show Caravan, making its way soon to a gated highland community near you?'

Helen wore a dowdy dress appropriate for a five, actually much dowdier than anything in her own closet, which she took pride to modify to make herself look at least a six. But the producers were in charge, and the makeup and wardrobe department was tasked with making the girls as hopeless as possible, so that the before-and-after comparisons would be suitably jaw-dropping. The makeup itself accented all of her imperfections, so that in the glare of the studio lights and in the camera close-ups, nothing would be left to the imagination.

'You're quite sure you're a five and not a four?' queried the lead celebrity judge, Nigel Soames, not even looking at her but down at his cards. Handsome Nigel was billed as every woman's dream husband, though he was in reality a bachelor who careered across the globe on his yacht from port to port and woman to woman. Helen had often dreamed of marrying him; despite all the abuse of the auditions, she still held out the hope that he would warm to her.

'Quite sure, sir!' Helen said winningly.

'I can't say it's nice to see you again, Helen, as even for a five you look a perfect horror!' Laughter from the studio audience as Nigel shook his head sadly and then glanced over conspiratorially at the judge next to him, the celebrity supermodel Veronique (just the one name, darlings).

'Hmmmm,' Veronique said, musing aloud with her index finger set aside her plump red lips. She was a ten, there was no gainsaying, everybody knew she was. In classic ten fashion, she had even gotten away with murder, having shot her second husband, a three, six times with a .38. This was many years ago, during the Loose Decade when mixed marriages had been so trendy and available. In fact, it was the not-infrequent incidents like Veronique's that had contributed to the rise of the New Conservatism and led most jurisdictions to enact laws banning such unions. Her trial had been dismissed before it could even start, one presumed because of the dark-channel deals and payoffs so common among the tens. The prevailing story passed down ever since was that Veronique had married a right beast far beneath her station who had used her and disrespected her, and had finally done so once too often, and it was all perfectly understandable that the helpless woman had to resort to use of the revolver to stop this powerful monster from bothering her.

'Hmmmm,' she said. 'Heaven knows, Helen, I'm quite sympathetic to your story. Although you must realize, I aborted my own child from my second husband precisely because I knew she'd never be a ten. I'm not here to second-guess the wisdom of your own birth mother, but really, darling, don't you find it humiliating being paraded around on our dear-lamb-of-a-Peter's stage, in front of a billion-odd people (and I do mean *odd!*) watching in their little hovels, all of them knowing you're nothing but a five from a shotgun nine-and-two?'

'I ... I'm not humiliated,' Helen said, maintaining her smile, though it was indeed how she felt. *Anything for a new face,* she thought. *Anything!* She used the line the producers had coached her to do in such a situation: 'I'm a strong girl, I am!'

Veronique rolled her eyes, her trademark move enlarged in full close-up on all the repeater screens, eliciting an eruption of laughter from the studio audience. She loosed her catchphrase: 'Oh, what a bore!' And threw her cards in the air as she'd done a hundred times.

You wouldn't think by looking at him that the third celebrity judge was a ten. Antony Smith had been one all his life, having been born of a famous ten-and-ten couple, and had never looked any better or worse than he did now, and of course Helen was in no position to judge anyone, much less a legit celeb. She was also fully aware that the directorate had quite different standards for men than for women. Everybody knew that. All the same, he didn't seem even as handsome as her own father, who was, as a two, by definition quite ugly. And yet she would rather gaze at an old capture of her father any day of the week than to have to stare for too long at Antony Smith's face.

'How you holding up, hon?' he said. His role on the show was that of the empathetic counterweight to the awful Nigel and Veronique. And yet when it came down to the hard decisions, Antony Smith could be quite cold, as if it was your own fault he had been forced to judge against you, and how dare you be so faithless as to put him in such a position? Helen had seen it on the show over and over again. Antony Smith could turn like that and become your worst enemy. One had the impression the only calculus that mattered to him was his own viewer ratings.

But all Helen needed to succeed in the finals was two out of three judges' votes, after which all the final decisions were up to the studio audience. The fact she had made it this far meant the judges were still rooting for her, no matter what act they were putting on for the sake of entertainment.

'We all understand how you must feel, hon,' Antony Smith

said. 'It must be rough growing up a plain Jane. I'm encouraged you've got such a ginormous fan club in the audience from your school! What great friends you must have! You really want this, don't you? I'm going to be hard on you, Helen, but that's because I love you. What makes you think you can be a nine, maybe even a ten? Why should we waste the talents of our surgeons to turn this plain duckling into a swan?'

'Go on, Helen, tell Antony how you feel!' Peter Lamb prodded, literally, as he stabbed a finger into her ribcage. 'Go on, girl!'

'Well, you see, Antony,' Helen began, 'I've never felt it was quite fair that I was a five. My mother raised me all by herself, of course, and all her friends were beautiful. She never consorted with anyone below a seven. Not around me, anyway! My father was just some kind of fluke, you know, some silly toy. And beg your pardon, Veronique, but I'm sure you know all about that! Then as I grew older, and I realized what I was, and that I'd never get to live among the beautiful people, I don't know, I just...'

'Did you cry?' Antony said. 'Did you have a little boo-hoo?'

'I cried myself to sleep every night. Knowing I'd never be beautiful. Knowing I'd never be popular.'

The studio audience was prodded by an assistant producer into letting out a collective *awwwww!* of sympathy.

'Especially with the boys,' Helen said. 'Never be popular...' And she felt the tears come spilling out and roll down her cheeks. 'Can you imagine? I mean, I don't disagree with the law, but for me to be forced to marry a five! I don't see myself as a five, and I don't want to marry a five. I feel like I'm a ten trapped in a five body.'

'Indeed, indeed,' said Antony. 'We all feel your pain, hon. If I weren't a ten, I think I'd probably kill myself. Not that I'm proposing you should do any such thing if you don't make it through.'

'Some days, I do feel like that,' Helen said. 'I mean, I respect my school chums, but most of them seem to be totally content to be fives. They aren't equipped with the aesthetic sense that's inherent to a ten. They look at themselves and they think they're just fine. Well, I'm not just fine! I won't accept being a five! I just won't! And I thank God every day for giving me this chance on *Let's Make a Face!*'

'Whatever God you pray to is not going to help you,' Nigel said. 'We're God here, us lot, up on this phony dais. We're the Holy Trinity incarnate up here, me, Vee, and Antony, and don't you forget it.'

'What does that make me?' cried Peter Lamb.

'Head priest,' Nigel said. 'Pope. Whatever. Take your pick.'

Peter laughed chummily. 'Now let's hear from our surgical team. You've looked her over top to bottom. You've made clinical assessments of her muscle tone, bone structure, cellulite deposits, and skin quality. You've read her psychiatric evaluation. What do you think? Can you change this fiver into a tenner? What say you, Doctor Bob?'

'Stand up straight, girl!' ordered the chief surgeon, a tall wiry ten of distinction with a full head of black hair, greying just at the temples. 'Whirl round a bit, there's a good girl!'

Helen did as she was told, feeling her face flush with embarrassment as she did a classic girly twirl in her plain dress.

'Now stop!' Doctor Bob took out a long stick and used it to refer to various parts of Helen's body as he spoke. 'Overall, the skeleton is adequate. Bone scan reveals a classic five, nothing too grotesque, but nothing beautiful, quite a plain old skeleton, all in all. We're all in agreement. Could be pushed either way, though. We could push it if we had to. Not much limiting us there. Leg muscles rather middling, as befits the plodding life of a five. It would take some work to tone them up to a nine or a ten. Not outside the realm of possibility, though. Female parts down below are fully matured, but nothing special. Upper parts would need some serious augmentation to get them into ten territory. I believe that's obvious! Shoulders rather slumped, we'd need to get them straightened out, and we'd need to suck out quite a lot of fat here and there, tummy, buttocks, thighs, the usual problem spots for fives....'

'What about the face, Doctor Bob, the face?' Peter whined. 'I think that's all she really cares about, isn't it? Realistically, Bob-O, what are this girl's chances of being made beautiful?'

Doctor Bob shrugged his shoulders. 'Anybody's guess, really! The facial bone structure is tolerable. Classic five skull, no doubt about it. Awfully plain nose, lips nothing to write home about. Cheekbones rather chipmunkish, if you ask me. But the whole point is to turn this one into something she's not, and frankly we can do whatever we want as long as we get paid. If there's a will, there's a way, as I always say. If the judges and the audience will it, we will build it.'

Doctor Bob's catchphrase. It always made Helen smile!

'Well, that's that, then!' Peter Lamb said. 'First it's up to the judges! Judges? What's it going to be?'

Whenever Helen went over this in her memory, she skipped past the long minutes of suspenseful music, the secret discussions of the judges, their animated facial expressions as they publicly bickered and Veronique rolled her eyes and scattered her cards. The further turn of the screw as Peter Lamb said they had to give him their answer, and what was it going to be? Because of course everything had come out all right in the end, with a unanimous decision. Three green circles, not a single red X. She had cried with delight and given Peter Lamb a hug.

'We knew that all along, didn't we, dearie?' he said to her. 'Now let's turn to the audience, for the all-important decision. What's it going to be, you little devils?'

Peter Lamb drew his arm around Helen's waist and escorted her away from the judges' dais and across the stage to stand in front of the four doors. The beautiful spokesmodel (who was never allowed to speak) was already standing there, ready to gesticulate at the gaily colored doors as they were called.

As they moved to their new mark, Helen scanned the faces in the audience – Becka, Elsie, Freddie, and the rest – until she found her mother staring at her out of dim blue light, giving her courage.

'Let's get this on you so there's no monkey business,' he said, as he put the leather hood over Helen's head and locked its collar in place around her neck with a padlock. It had no holes for eyes or mouth, only two discreet reinforced grommets over her nostrils. Early on in the run of the show, they had used a simple blindfold, but the hood had proven far more dramatic, and invulnerable to cheating.

Helen felt perfectly comfortable in the hood, though the smell of the leather was sickly sweet and made her slightly nauseous. Her heart began racing, as she knew her friends in the audience were about to choose her new look. It was so exciting to be in the actual finals!

'Now she's ready, there's a girl!' Peter Lamb sounded condescending, but she was sure he wasn't, not really. 'As a reminder to our viewers at home and all round the world, we've now fixed it so as Helen can't see anything at all. Nor can she object! That's how we like our girls on *Let's Make a Face*, don't we?'

Thunderous applause and cheering.

'Studio audience, are you ready?'

'Ready!' they shouted.

'Ah, my little lambs!' Peter Lamb said. 'Our esteemed celebrity surgeons have done up some lovely renderings of what they *think* they can do with our poor Helen, and it will be up to the studio audience to make that choice for her!'

Lots of cheering, some jeering. Helen couldn't tell the difference, to be honest.

'Each of the four choices are blown up in all their glory and currently hidden behind our famous doors. Or should I say infamous? Because as always, our surgeons have come up with three looks that *might* make Helen a ten ... plus one that would *definitely* make her a zero! How awful would that be, eh? Though it's such a rare occurrence on this show, it's not something we dare contemplate!'

Helen had no worries about this. The studio audience was packed with so many of her school chums, it was statistically impossible for her to be voted a zero. She had seen it happen before, though, watching on telly from home, and it was always quite a shock, not least of all for the contestant, who knew of course what she was getting herself into and would just have to take her lumps. Some people said this was what everyone watched *Let's Make a Face* for, just as they might watch Formula One for a car crash or Olympic skiing for a disastrous run on the slopes and a poor skier's shattered bones.

'Of course, only the studio audience will be lucky enough to see what's behind our doors. All of you folks at home will just have to suffer in suspense until the big reveal some weeks hence!'

Peter Lamb was really working the crowd up into a lather.

'Now it's time for the beauteous Jackie Mackey to reveal what's behind door number one!'

Approving applause and *oohs* and *ahhs*.

The opening of the other three doors followed, all to the same reaction, as far as Helen could make out. Then came the vote, held over the familiar suspenseful music. It was revealed that the studio audience had chosen door number three, and they all cheered for Helen. Helen was congratulated by Peter Lamb. Someone led her offstage, still locked within the cloying hood, and she was taken backstage and prepped for immediate surgery.

These many weeks since that exciting episode had been trying, and she had gone back repeatedly for several more procedures. She had been re-dressed and re-bandaged several times, but always while she was unconscious, lest she catch any glimpse of her new self.

Nurse had explained that for a five like her, such a radical transformation could not be expected to happen overnight.

Helen understood. She was not daft.

Ultimately, one day, she came back to awareness in the dim ochre chamber, with Nurse standing over her smiling nervously and saying, 'It's time, love. The producers are ready for you.'

Helen expelled a huge sigh of relief. Her heartbeat increased noticeably, thumping against the walls of her chest as she grew more excited. She could hear the rhythm in her ears, as every part of her except her eyes remained encased in wrappings. *Today was the day!*

Nurse brought the old typewriter over to her and rolled a fresh piece of paper on the platen. She fixed the typing mittens on Helen's tightly bound hands and let her type out whatever words she wished.

Slowly, Helen moved her arms up and down, hunting and pecking: 'Don't know what to say! Over the moon! Thank you, Nurse!'

Nurse extracted the feeding tube from Helen's nasal passage and esophagus, did whatever she had to do with the urinary catheter, and put fresh eyedrops in Helen's eyes. Two orderlies, likely twos or threes, came in and helped Nurse detach the bed from the wall and rolled Helen out into the corridor.

In the green room, they removed the bandages from her head, not allowing her any mirror, then locked her back up in the leather hood. Although it was scary and uncomfortable, she reminded herself how lucky she was, when so few of the girls who applied ever made it this far.

She felt a lightening of herself, body and spirit, as they cut off the remaining bandages from every part of her. She felt herself rising up to meet her new destiny. Who would she become from this point forward? *Anabella? Fiona? Aurora? Hera?*

They transferred her to a new clean bed that would be more

appealing for the show than her filthy, lumpy old thing. But they locked her wrists back up to the metal sides, using leather straps as they had done for all these weeks. They used similar straps to secure her ankles to the other end. She thought all this a bit strange, although she had seen it done on some previous episodes.

'This is just to help quell your excitement,' one of the producers said. 'We can't have you hurting yourself now or damaging the final result, can we? Plus it's in your contract.'

Helen mumbled her assent. She discovered that after all those weeks under wraps, she had lost the use of her jaw or mouth muscles, somehow, and was presently unable to speak.

'Ready?' the producer said, but didn't wait for a response. 'I think she's ready. Time is money. Can't keep 'em waiting. Let's go!'

'And now, let's bring out our famous contestant Helen from that memorable episode a few weeks back!' came Peter Lamb's voice over the loudspeaker system. 'Round of applause for Helen!'

Although she was still in the hood, she could tell the difference as she was rolled out from the green room to the soundstage. She could hear the raging applause of the studio audience, feel their eyes upon her, and feel the heat of the lights bearing down. She realized she was entirely naked on the gurney as they wheeled her out, but of course, she had seen that done on a few of the episodes as well, at least when there was more work done than on the face alone. It felt like sunlamps gently bronzing her skin. She imagined she was sunbathing on one of the man-made beaches on the New French Riviera. *Back to the yacht, James!* Oh, how nice it would be to have a servant! A one or a two of one's own. Her own father had started out that way but had been granted his freedom after the divorce.

'Let's all take a good look at Helen, shall we?'

Someone was unlocking the padlock at Helen's neck, and wriggling the hood off her head. It took quite a while for her eyes to adjust to the bright lights, and as she struggled with this, Peter Lamb kept on talking.

'Let's bring out Doctor Bob to tell us what he's done, shall we?'

Great applause and some nervous laughter.

'Not sure even our studio audience can see what's going on here just yet, not until we can get the cameras closer in here. Tell us, please, doctor, what have you done to our poor Helen?'

'Quite simple on the face of it,' Doctor Bob said.

The audience laughed at the pun.

'But an awfully complicated operation in actual fact . . .'

Helen was batting her eyelashes and struggling to get her eyes accustomed to the light, after so many weeks in relative dark. She saw some people wheeling across a three-paneled mirror that they were setting in front of her, while two cameramen also came in closer to direct their lenses on her. One camera was coming in close to her face, the other crouching down between her spread and bound legs.

Helen looked out into the audience, looking for the face of her mother, but found only an empty seat next to Becka, Elsie, and Freddie, where her mother had sat on the previous show. Becka was elbowing Elsie and laughing like a cow. Freddie was hiding his face.

'What the audience voted on, and what we have done here, is what we like to call a total labial transposition. We've taken Helen's *labium superius oris* and her *labium inferium oris* from up here, and switched them with her *labia majora* and *labia minora* from down there.'

'So, sort of a lip switch!' Peter Lamb said in amazement. 'First of its kind?'

'First of its kind. We've been looking to do this a long time but needed a suitable candidate. Helen seemed perfect, so we put this forward as her zero option. The team and I were delighted to be given the opportunity by our lovely studio audience.'

Polite round of applause.

Helen's eyes had adjusted as she was listening to the surgeon's clinical description of what they had done to her. She could not believe the audience had voted her a zero. There must have been a mistake somewhere. There would have to be a do-over...

'But that's not all you've done here, surely, doctor?'

Doctor Bob laughed. 'No, Peter, not at all!'

Helen tried to make a sound. She couldn't figure out how to make her jaw work. The muscles of her throat struggled and strained, but the lower structure of her face remained rigid, unable to move. She looked down at her hands and saw that she had none. She looked down at her feet and found they were gone.

'The transposition is to a large degree superficial. What you see on the outside is precisely the effect we wanted to achieve, with this really quite nice *labia majora* and *labia minora* here, just beneath her nose, of a vertical rather than lateral arrangement, as you can plainly see. With other critical lady parts hidden inside. These sexual organs had to be connected to the former oral canal and the esophagus so that it could be at all useful to those lucky gents who will be buying tickets to the Freak Show.'

'Coming soon to a gated highland town near you!' Peter Lamb crowed.

'And that created the problem of what to do with the upper palate and lower palate, and all the dentition, as that could get in the way and create quite a danger for the user. My colleague, Doctor Steve, came up with an ingenious solution. Why not complete the flip? Replace the jaw structures, tongue, vocal cords, everything we commonly associate with the upstairs, and place it all downstairs?'

'My word, that's clever!' Peter Lamb said.

The three celebrity judges came down off their dais and were crowding around the lower-parts cameraman, leaning in for a closer look and grinning.

'Pure genius,' said Nigel Soames.

'*Total* zero!' said Veronique, rising up to look into Helen's eyes. 'Your mother's proud of you now, I'll bet!'

Antony Smith said, 'But can it *talk?*'

'Some physio is likely required,' Doctor Bob said.

'Maybe we can get her to give us a right old scream!' Peter Lamb said. 'Take a look in that mirror, sweetie! Like what you see?'

Helen didn't need to look in the mirror anymore. The upper cameraman had come in close and she could see her new face enlarged across all the monitors throughout the studio (and being broadcast to all those with the luxury of electricity). She could see the tears on her cheeks, and the alien-like flaps of flesh that should never have been put there.

'She wanted to be beautiful, and she wanted to be popular, ladies and gentlemen! One out of two ain't bad! Now how's about that scream?'

Helen didn't know how she could do it. But she was worried she might be punished if she didn't at least try. She had no status here. Whatever little status she once had was now wiped out with the work of the surgeons' knives. She worked the muscles she could find in her lower belly, searching and straining somehow to use what they had grafted down there.

'Open up, at least!' Peter Lamb said, giving her thigh a slap.

'It's moving,' said Nigel Soames. 'By God, I can see the teeth.'

Helen watched on the monitors as the cameras focused in on the mouth between her legs. The makeup artists had smeared bright red lipstick on her lips. Somehow she managed to part them and expose her teeth. Bearing down, she found the means to extend her tongue, and slowly it emerged from between the widening jaws.

'Go on, then, give us a scream!' Peter Lamb repeated, cackling with laughter. He reached down and started tickling her tongue. 'Look at that thing! Do you feed her through here, then?' He looked up at Doctor Bob.

'No, actually, we couldn't find a way to hook all this back up to the esophagus, and we needed the esophagus to remain where it was, for obvious reasons. She takes her nourishment through a feeding tube, and that's how she'll have to keep on with it from now on, I'm afraid.'

While Doctor Bob was rambling on, and Peter Lamb was listening intently to what was coming out of the surgeon's mouth, Helen was concentrating with full intensity on mastering the muscles between her legs. The host kept playing with her tongue, tickling it, squeezing it, getting an obvious kick out of pulling it.

'We also recommend that end-users stick with the upper and steer clear of the lower,' Doctor Bob said.

'And why's that?' Peter Lamb said, still toying with her tongue.

Helen mustered all her strength and bit clean through Peter Lamb's finger at the second joint. She might be a freak and a zero, but the viewers needed to know she retained her dignity.

As she savored the iron taste of the warm blood on her tongue, she was shocked to discover she could. Doctor Bob and his team had indeed worked wonders.

She resolved right then that her stage name would be Hera.

Steve Rasnic Tem

Conversations with the Departed

An author well known to aficionados of horror and weird fiction, STEVE RASNIC TEM *perhaps needs no introduction. He has published close to 500 short stories, along with numerous novels and collections, over a forty-year career during which he has won the World Fantasy Award, British Fantasy Award and Bram Stoker Award, among other accolades. In 2018, Steve personally chose his best and most representative tales from throughout his career and collected them under the title* Figures Unseen: Selected Stories, *which is available from Valancourt. We were pleased to feature his excellent tale 'The Parts Man' in volume 3 and are delighted to welcome him back for volume 4 with this brand-new story, which makes its first appearance anywhere.*

FIRST THING THAT MORNING John thought he'd call Del to invite him to a movie. Then he remembered what day it was. The chair by the window wore his good suit coat. The shoes by the bed were freshly polished, waiting for him. He wasn't ready for this, not any of it.

He hadn't slept well. Every time he dozed there had been a burst of noise, an overheard bit of whispered discussion, someone's plaintive late-night complaint. Once or twice – he wasn't sure – he got up to peer through the blinds expecting to see some fight or assault, but the street was empty, rendered in intaglio blacks and whites.

He sat on the bed staring at his hands. They were his dad's hands, the skin both crepey and membranous, with dark spots floating just beneath the surface. He wasn't sure when they'd gotten that way; it seemed a few months. He wondered if someday he might see clear through to the carpals, metacarpals, and whatever the finger bones were called.

Low conversation leaked up through the floorboards; soft exchanges seeped out of the walls. John's neighbors – he didn't know any of them – were up early. He'd been in this apartment over forty years and dozens had lived here before him, and before that this entire building had been the grand home of someone with money and status. After years of idle study, he could tell what walls had been added and where walls had been taken away, where some temporary fashion had inspired unfortunate changes in door frames and ceiling heights. But not everything made sense. Sometimes sound travelled curiously and the walls seemed thinner every year, the residents gradually erasing them.

Again, the sounds of those unseen neighbors, as if their lips were but inches away, and yet John couldn't hear everything. He caught a few tantalizing phrases – 'you never' and 'you're crazy,' 'you always,' and 'I want' – and was glad he'd never married, but that lasted only a moment. Because a marriage, he imagined, might have been wonderful, and he'd always regretted his failure of nerve prevented him from finding a partner. At least with a marriage he might have felt he'd accomplished something.

If they were trying to tell him something, he wasn't getting it. Sometimes these marginally audible dialogues came from empty apartments. Del, the only person he told, said these events sounded like 'auditory pareidolia.'

People perceive words in random patterns of sound, within the drone of an air conditioner, or in background traffic. The words they hear reflect their own fear and anxiety.

It could be annoying, how much Del knew. Had known. He often heard Del's voice in his head. Recently it appeared to have encroached upon John's own inner voice, a smarter version, so John's own words didn't stand much of a chance.

This was a dangerous perception. He didn't want to be one of those old men speaking to the sky because there was no one else left to talk to.

The day began chilly and overcast, and John would not have ventured out at all if he had not been obligated. Two hours before the funeral the clouds started to dissipate, unveiling a sky of tarnished aluminum. The sounds of the surrounding traffic were strangely dulled. He was a nervous driver at the best of times, and now expected an accident he'd be unable to prevent.

He usually drove everywhere with Del, who kept him updated with directions and warnings, and a bounty of advice, much of it irrelevant. Following Del's directions had become second nature. He missed having him in the passenger seat.

Turn here.

John did and knew immediately he'd made a mistake. Tall weeds crowded the pavement on both sides of the narrow lane and after the first quarter mile the roadway faded beneath a skin of black mud. No signs of a funeral home or the promised chapel. He stopped the car and got out, stepping onto a raised patch of grass so he wouldn't muddy his polished shoes.

He'd driven into an abandoned development. If there had been warning signs, he hadn't seen them. He couldn't quite fathom how the city tolerated such an ill-kept property. The thick brush indicated no attempts at trimming and trees were still down from the storms several months back. Thousands of dead and broken branches lay denuded and sun-bleached like the bones in a killing field. Standing or half-standing among them were the remnants of various unfinished houses, unbarricaded and open to the elements, their materials leached to a monochromatic gloom.

Several yards to his left fractured timbers protruded from an overgrown basement excavation, fronted by a flight of cracked concrete steps leading to nothing. A similar pattern of aborted construction was repeated at more empty building sites along the vanished lane. John was unsettled by this enduring display of incompletion, projects begun and abruptly abandoned.

The world is always telling you things, but you must be willing to listen.

Again, this was Del's voice, unmistakable and startlingly close. He looked around for a speaker regardless, not ready to admit his old friend had taken over and seized the reins. 'Look what you've gotten me into,' John whispered, and bit his tongue in alarm. He'd always thought losing his mind would be the worst fate possible.

Gazing around at these ruins, tasting his own blood, John put together a notion of his whereabouts. When he was younger there had been several blocks of low-income housing in this vicinity. All of it came down in the nineties with an urban renewal scheme for upscale custom-built homes. He remembered the newspaper coverage of certain improprieties, how the executives went to prison. No doubt they were all out and doing splendidly.

Yet another botched job.

He could see the remains of the original concrete wall at the far limits of the property, layered in coarse graffiti. He imagined these overlapping scribblings recorded crosstalk involving decades of deprivation and suffering, becoming increasingly inarticulate as such conditions persisted over generations. The decaying wall separated the long-vanished neighborhood from the wealthier communities beyond. The poor who once resided here, living or dead, were exiled far from home.

It is too late to help those people.

A few trees were visible above the other side of the wall, backgrounded by a slow-moving milky haze. John was nearsighted, but the vagueness still troubled him. He could see nothing through the mist, and anything he imagined was terrible. He heard a coarse, static-filled howl suggestive of crowd noise, whether panicked or thrilled it was impossible to say. He couldn't tell how far away the voices were. They might have been just over the wall or trapped somehow in the clouds hovering above him. He didn't know much about sports, although he'd sat through many a televised game as Del attempted to explain the intricacies. This sounded like a crowd at such a competition, whether football, baseball, or some sort of gladiatorial combat. Listening carefully, he heard patterns in the noise, and imagined he could hear a few coherent pleadings rising above the din having to do with *despair*, and *sorrow*, and *misery*, perhaps. If the dead had a voice, this is how their combined voices might sound.

Pareidolia, Del said again, and John resented having his perceptions so easily dismissed. He had his own life, his own opinions.

He had turned the car too early. He still wasn't sure why. *Turn here.* Was it a random impulse or had it been advice from Del? Del was perhaps the last friend John would ever have. It was normal to wonder if he would be next. Each slip in competency was a step in that direction. The exit he required was the next one off the main road, or the one after. To his shame he wasn't sure.

Back up into the grass and turn the car around. You don't want to be late for the viewing.

More than a thought but less than a whisper.

You've grown senile. Best drive out of here while you still remember how.

It required a few minutes to get the car pointed back toward the entrance. He heard the slow murmurings continue to build behind him. He hated heavy traffic, but now he was anxious to once again merge with the flow.

The mortuary was down a hill and across the street from the oldest cemetery in the city. John had been there before. He and Del sometimes attended the funerals of old men — some they knew and some they did not. John had never thought to do such a thing until Del invited him one weekend to go to two of these services, and he couldn't have explained why this had become a regular event. But there was a group of them who did the same – old men attending the funerals of other old men, a club which understandably grew smaller as the years passed.

Several nice cars had pulled up to the main entrance. John was embarrassed by the state of his own vehicle so parked a good distance away. The service itself was scheduled for later in the afternoon. He'd been surprised by the invitation to the viewing. He'd never met Del's family. He was the one who found Del in his house, dead between collapsed bookcases, covered in volumes of obscure local history. Apparently, it merited an invitation.

As he walked toward the entrance the crowd noise became evident again, louder and echoing off the asphalt, practically on top of him. He looked up and saw nothing but the lowering clouds.

Stepping into the interior of the chapel he felt a sudden loss of sense. In the dim light all color faded, and his vision was awash with grays. 'You must be John. Where would you like to sit?' The man in the black suit appeared so abruptly John's hands began to shake. He crossed his arms and tucked his fingers inside to make them stop. The sanctuary beyond was empty except for a few older people sitting in the front row a few feet away from the open casket.

'Well, I presume that's the family in the front row. I'm not family, just a friend.'

The man smiled. 'You are welcome to sit anywhere you like.'

John mulled it over anxiously. If he sat too far away, he would stand out. 'The second row then? Behind them?'

'Of course. Before I forget, would you care to sign the remembrance book?'

The leather-bound volume was displayed on a nearby lectern. Each member of the family had signed, and several had added notes, addressed to 'Brother' and 'Del,' with something about missing him, but feeling like a voyeur John didn't want to read too closely. The ink was smudged, and there were several fingerprints on the page, which seemed unfortunate, and debris – what was it? Bending over to look John thought it resembled bits of dead skin.

Of course, everywhere we go, we leave dead skin.

Del's voice was startingly loud. John glanced at the funeral director for any reaction, but the man had retreated to his station by the front door.

After John sat down in the second pew the woman at the end of the front row turned and nodded. He thought she might be one of Del's sisters. She shared Del's high forehead, his particular nose. A small, much older woman sat next to her, Del's mother perhaps, head bowed in reverence or sleep. Her white hair was done up in a tight, perfect bun, and her neck was incredibly thin, as if she were a skull floating above a black Victorian mourning dress. He heard soft, monotonous speech, a chant or prayer. He couldn't tell who was speaking. They all looked still.

He had never cared much for this chapel. It was modern: tall clear windows topped with half-moons of stained glass in earthen colors. Each had a rectangular section at the bottom that could be cranked out for ventilation. Outside, the wind had picked up. Thin trees were swaying, and nearby bushes writhed. An insect hit one of the windows and stayed, followed by another, by several more, dozens. He could faintly hear their congregated mumbling, some sort of insect chorus, and swarms of dark bits gathered along with the racing clouds. It all seemed too indistinct for language, but that didn't discourage John from listening for words.

He made himself look away. Scandinavian-style pews and the highly polished casket were made from a similar yellowish wood. There were smudges along the casket rim near Del's waxen face. More fingerprints? And a bit of lace hung off the open half-lid, or could that have been skin? John tried to make himself stop imagining things – he was too far away to see anything clearly.

The chandelier hanging over the sanctuary was enormous, perhaps the largest John had ever seen. It was a spiky thing with needle-like protrusions several feet long extending from a central globular swirl of gold-colored metal. Tiny lights were embedded at random locations throughout the center and the needles. It was the singular beautiful object in the room, and the one item evoking the spiritual, but he couldn't help picturing its fall at some point during the service, and all the mourners it might impale.

His interest in churches was purely architectural. He had no religious beliefs he was aware of. He did believe in mystery. He wanted to understand just enough about how the universe worked to get through an average day, to run errands, to perhaps have conversations, but he did not think he understood much beyond that. He had no inkling of the big picture, nor did he want one.

That's sleepwalking. You're sleepwalking your way into death.

Again, so loud, and clear, as if he himself had said it. He hoped he hadn't. No one appeared to have noticed.

Apparently, he was the last one here for the viewing. Del's misdirection into the abandoned development had made him late. He had never attended a viewing before – was he just supposed to sit here? In movies the mourners filed by the casket – had they already done that? Perhaps they had and they were waiting for him to do the same. Or maybe it was too late for that and if he went up there now it would be a terrible breach of etiquette.

The sister stood and helped her mother walk to the open half of the casket. Both were unsteady on their feet. The mother reached into the casket with an incredibly long, painfully thin arm, and for a moment John thought he was seeing the impossible, but as she withdrew it, it appeared normal length.

One by one the others visited Del. One of the women sighed. 'Oh, Dalbert.' He had no idea that had been Del's given name. It had been 'Del' on the funeral notice.

John was the last to go up. He stood for a moment over Del's still form, wanting to touch his friend's folded hands, but could not bring himself to do it. Del wore a soft blue sport coat, white shirt, and a red tie. That was Del's first date suit. He dated a great deal, many different women, and John admired that in a man their age, the nerve to put himself out there. He never bragged about it, never suggested he was any sort of ladies' man, and John respected him for it.

But this thing in the casket did not look like Del. He'd never been this clean-shaven, this shiny, his steel-gray hair never this short or so perfectly combed. Never this calm. Never this expressionless. The last time John had seen him, sprawled in his pile of books, Del's mouth had hung open, and he'd been hideous to look at.

John waited, but for the first time that day his old friend Del had nothing to say to him. He turned and looked at the family. Some peculiarity in the lighting made their flesh recede, hollowing eyes and cheeks. The mother appeared to be pulling the corners of her mouth down to make herself frown.

He followed the others out of the chapel. The service was two hours away. He heard the family intended to go for coffee. He wasn't invited, nor would he have come.

'Excuse me?' The sister had waited for him by the door, Del's mother still clinging to her. 'My mother wanted to say hello.'

He offered the woman his hand. 'I'm so sorry, Miz Lawson.' She nodded but didn't take it. Her eyes were milky; she was blind, or nearly so.

'Mother was saying Del talked of you a few times, said you were great friends. We wondered if you might want to share your thoughts, at the service?'

'I – you're so very kind. Maybe. Maybe I could do that.' Of

course, John didn't want to, couldn't imagine sharing anything personal before all those people, but he couldn't say no.

They walked out in front of him. He turned to the undertaker, stationed there in his silky black suit. 'Could I go back inside and sit with him a little while? He was my best friend.'

The man frowned, watching the family as they climbed into their cars. 'I understand. I don't suppose it would hurt anything. Everything's prepared, and I have papers to organize in the office. Take your time.' He shut the door, turned, and left through a side corridor.

John walked back into the darkened sanctuary. At first, he had no idea why the lighting had changed. He could barely see the area where the casket rested. He glanced at the windows, and thought they were shaded. Then he saw the little twitches, the shifts. Insects, birds, squirrels, bats, field mice, a variety of creatures filled the windows, pressed against the glass as if from a great wind or other force. Some of the motions were wings and limbs struggling or gesturing their share of futility, but most of the movement came from their mouths, beaks, mouthparts, as they spoke.

John heard what they said but could make no sense of it. The world seemed thin here. With little effort he might rub right through it.

The dead want you to listen to them. That's all they want.

John walked into the dimness until he found the casket. It was empty.

It looks like the wheels have finally fallen off the bus my friend.

A pale form sat in a chair by the windows. It reached over and tapped hard on the pane. All the occupants fell, or flew away, clearing the glass. *I hate vermin, don't you?*

Del sat there in his nice blue coat, white shirt, red tie, in boxers, his feet bare. He held an unlit cigarette in his left hand. His face appeared oddly animated, even with his eyes closed. *Can you believe it? I hope my mother didn't pay for pants.* Del's voice was loud and clear in John's head, but Del's lips did not move.

John nodded but did not say anything.

I apologize. This must be hard for you, seeing me like this. Del swept his arm in a broad gesture, pointing with the cigarette.

'Would you like me to light that for you?' John went into his pockets looking for a lighter, hoping he had one. He didn't smoke himself, but he'd always carried a lighter or matches for Del.

Ha! The explosive noise was odd coming out of Del, who had never laughed that way. *It was in my coat. I can't smoke, John. He sewed my lips shut. You can't tell – the stitches are tucked inside. The tissues shrink, the gums and everything. I guess you already know how bad it looks, when the mouth hangs open like that.*

'Yes,' John said softly.

I can't open my eyes either – they put in these spiky plastic contacts. But I can still see you! Isn't that incredible?

'What's happening here, Del?'

I need to show you something. Come over here. It'll only take a moment. Del staggered over to the casket and pointed inside. *Do you see? Come closer.*

John gave him a wide berth and leaned over one edge of the casket. 'What am I looking for?'

He felt the pressure and then the lift. He was rapidly falling forward into a vast white hole. He twisted around and saw Del's face far above him. *Just look!* Del shouted before dropping the lid.

What came next was long and slippery, watching his arms and legs disintegrating into endless vacancy, and so full of regret for the smallness of his loss, after all he had not done.

After a prolonged period, John was sitting on the floor in front of the casket. Del hovered over him, the cigarette still in his hand. John wondered if he was even capable of letting it go.

'It was like nothing, like nothing at all.'

Then not much of a change for you.

John shook his head. 'I have a life. I do.'

Women will be out there today. Old single women. They come to these things. I've met women at these things. Some of my old girlfriends are likely . . .

'Stop it. I get your point.'

You told my sister you would speak at the service. I know it's a big step for you.

'Just tell me what you want me to say.'

Tell them something amazing! Tell them something they will never forget! Tell them what it was really like. And if you can't do that, make something up. They won't know the difference.

By the time the family and the others arrived, everything, including Del, was back in its proper place. John sat at the far end of the front row, turned around so he could watch everyone coming in. The large number of mourners surprised him, as did their variety. Del had many friends John never knew.

Several women of the right age were in attendance. He thought he'd seen one or two of them with Del. He couldn't be sure. He would say hello if they first said hello, and he would talk to them if they wanted to talk, but he would not be making any special attempts at conversation. John was old enough to recognize his story wasn't that kind of story.

Several people had their cell phones out, talking, texting, speaking to those around them while having a cell conversation at the same time. They did not have the decency, some of them, to keep the volume down.

As often happened, he was surrounded by conversations which did not involve him, both among groups of people and with their phones, and the best he could do was to ignore them, because to listen was to encounter troublesome fragments which became increasingly disturbing as he strained to hear.

He saw several older men he'd known from other funerals. They nodded at him respectfully.

The room was warm, and at one point Del's sister went to one of the windows for air. John panicked and almost stood to warn her about what lay outside, but the window cranked open without incident.

Many people spoke, including Del's younger brother. They revealed details John hadn't known about, and he wondered if they were even true. Most of us pass our lives as strangers, he thought, even when we believe we've confessed everything.

There was now so much talk, such a volume of conversation, John truly could not hear himself think. When it came his turn, he went to the lectern and stood a moment gazing at all these strange and exotic creatures. He tried to be tidy about it, but his mouth fell open into the most hideous gape, and all those wounded voices came spilling out.

John Keir Cross

'Happy Birthday, Dear Alex'

In the mid-20th century, in both the U.S. and U.K., a certain type of horror story seems to have been very popular, which we might term a conte cruel, *tales with a particularly wicked or cruel twist at the end. A number of Valancourt authors, including notably Charles Birkin, wrote in this style, but perhaps one of the best practitioners of this type of story was* JOHN KEIR CROSS (1914-1967), *whose excellent collection* The Other Passenger (1944), *published by Valancourt in 2017, features a number of such tales, including possibly the best ventriloquist's dummy horror story ever written, 'The Glass Eye'. The following story first appeared in an anthology in 1965 and is fairly typical of Keir Cross's work, with its engaging storytelling style, a fair amount of humor, and of course, an unexpectedly nasty denouement. It does not seem to have been reprinted in forty years, so we think it will be new to most of our readers.*

I AM, ESSENTIALLY, I THINK, A SIMPLE MAN.

I make the statement with no kind of false modesty: it is only something that has become apparent as my long life has gone on and I have failed so often, until it is too late, to comprehend the small complexities with which we are all surrounded from day to day.

I shall even be simple in setting down this particular incident in my life – I shall have no skill in any kind of story-telling about it, and so you will see through it all long before I may reach a particular point which someone more skilful in the art of writing would have been able to mask for dramatic effect.

You will see through Hare's terrible secret from the start, I daresay, where I never did till it all was almost over.

His shop was in a small side-street. From the start I should perhaps have suspected something sinister from the very air and atmosphere of the place, yet naturally, on such a quest, one hardly expected anything other than a slightly unusual flavour, shall I say. Certainly the other shops I had previously visited were also peculiar in one way or another, even the one that was very large and medicated in Marylebone. No doubt the association from the commodity I was seeking predisposed one to subjective impressions somewhat macabre.

The commodity in question was to be a gift for my young cousin Alex. It was, in fact, to be a birthday gift – how strange a birthday gift! – yet one that would be curiously welcome. One hardly quite knew where to begin – it is, after all, not the kind of gruesome relic that one is likely to wish to purchase every day; one had certainly no realization that there was even a positive shortage of the articles, with consequent visions of patient queues of earnest students assembled outside a supplier momentarily well-stocked. But it all was so; and after a while there came even to be a sense of mild excitement in the quest, as source after source was explored unavailingly, yet more and more clues were uncovered as to possible further milieux for enquiry...

You will note, no doubt – I realize it myself reading back this laborious opening of mine (laborious since, as I have said, I am no skilled writer) – that I have, probably from some lingering sense of delicacy, so far avoided any open mention by name of the commodity's nature. Let me come to it boldly and straightly, then: the object I sought to purchase was none other than a human skeleton! And the explanation for the horrid search is simplicity itself – as again you will plainly have guessed: my cousin was a medical student, engaged conscientiously in a meditation upon the mysteries of anatomy...

I do not exaggerate, incidentally, when I say that at the period of which I write so inexpertly, the objects in question were in great demand and short supply. I had even read a mildly humorous article in *The Times* not long before to that very effect – one of the inimitable fourth leaders of that notable journal which still, behind a façade of some light-heartedness, announced the undoubted fact that for one reason or another, skeletons for medical study purposes had become extremely difficult to obtain, and those that were available, even at third or fourth hand, as their owners progressed beyond the necessity of further study, were outside the purses of most young medicos. It was where I thought I might be of some assistance; Alex had been in the search for some time, only to find that indeed the prices were outrageous, where I, more fortunately endowed with this world's goods through a pleasing inheritance some years previously, might be able to be of some worthwhile family assistance – and with Alex's birthday not far in the offing, might also (if the mild jest may be permitted) kill two birds, as it were, with one somewhat costly stone.

My first difficulty, however, was to know even where to begin, as I think I have already stated. But by dint of some discreet enquiry among medical friends – even of Alex during a supposedly social visit only – I eventually found myself on the long trail, calling one bright spring morning at that large and distinguished-looking shop in Marylebone.

I was interviewed by a young man of superior smartness, with a curiously clean and – if I may say – a sterile look. As I moved forward to confront him, I found myself almost slipping on the excessively polished linoleum beneath my feet. All around me were glistening machines and implements of unknown medical functionalism – trays and boxes of neat cold forceps, curiously shaped scissors, small knives, contrivances spouting arrays of red rubber tubings. At the back, where the light – perhaps fortunately – was somewhat shady, there were some shelves of silent bottles, with nameless shapes afloat in their spirituous depths. About the whole place was an elusive odour of linoleum polish and formalin. I found myself oppressed, but the thought of young Alex's forthcoming pleasure sustained me.

The assistant inclined a somewhat oleaginous but courteous head, with a murmured request that I should state my requirement.

'I want,' I began, with some initial nervousness, ' – I want to purchase – ah – not for myself, you understand – for a friend – a cousin, in fact . . . I – ah – had wanted to enquire about the possibility of obtaining – '

At that moment, as I glanced somewhat timidly about me, I saw, calmly regarding me from a small pedestal, a prime specimen of the object of my very search. The disinterested glare of the hollow orbs unnerved me a little, then I was able to give a small exclamation of satisfaction as I gestured towards it.

'A skeleton, sir?' The young man's tone held a trace, I thought, of professional sorrow – as if, almost, I were a near relative of the deceased we both now contemplated, swaying a little on its suspending wires. I remember reflecting, even in the moment, how unexpectedly small we are untrammelled at last by flesh – those little spindly bones of ours, so frail-seeming against the might of the world: the perpetual grin of our hapless mouths behind whatever expression of grief or soft sentiment our lips might once have worn: our dry small cage of a chest enclosing hearts that once throbbed deliriously in joy or passion: our boxy little skulls within whose confines noble thoughts may once have raced, whole symphonies or epics been composed, the plans of great cathedrals limned . . . So went my simple thoughts, until I became aware that the young man was still speaking in his smoothly modulated way:

'Articulated, of course?'

'Of course,' I nodded. Unacquainted with the terminologies I assumed that the expert before me must have some profound purposes in his 'of course'. Besides, I recollected Alex having said something too about this need for 'articulation' in the article.

'Somewhat in this manner, perhaps,' went on the young man gravely, stepping forward towards our solitary companion and touching a wire stretched almost invisibly along the spine.

Instantly, with a small dry rustling – hardly more than a whisper through the antiseptic silence – He Who Once Had Been executed a deft brief convulsion of all his members simultaneously. He quivered and revolved with a delicate waving of arms, an inclination of legs, a pointing of slender toes. He engaged in a total arabesque, a chilly mechanical ecstasy of interrelated bones and silver pivotal pins, through all his tiny joints... and, as I started back a little, involuntarily apprehensive, the young man beside me said reverentially, in such a tone as I might once have used myself in my distant youth in a contemplation of Madame Pavlova, no less:

'Beautiful – ah, beautiful! Such poise, such balance, sir – such exquisite co-ordination!'

Then, with a further humble moment before the great dancer now slowly settling to no more than a lingering wavy tremor, he turned to me suddenly, briskly.

'I'm sorry, sir – deeply sorry. We are quite out of stock.'

'Nothing at all?' I asked, as one might ask in the normal course of day-to-day shopping when confronted with a shortage of, say, summer shirtings during the holiday season or warm underwear with the approach of winter.

'Nothing, sir. Our supplies are very limited – the demand of late has been quite remarkable.'

'To what,' I asked academically, 'do you attribute such a curious state of –' I had almost said 'trading', then changed to 'shortage in the line?'

'It's difficult to say, sir. At one time we carried almost more of the articles in our stock-rooms than we had space for – we frequently had to dismember them entirely so as to be able to find accommodation; for as you will understand, it is an easier matter to group, say, all the tibiae, all the fibulae, in one shelf, with all the metacarpals in another and so forth, than to pack the fully assembled items together with any . . . well . . . comfort.'

(I groped a little at his undoubtedly strange use of the word 'comfort', visualizing that unimaginable stock-room somewhere below and far away – beyond the shady bottles on the farther shelves, perhaps . . .)

'You haven't, by any chance – ' and I hesitated again, wondering how one might convey the possibility of an under-the-counter purchase, recollecting one's wartime habits in the acquiring of tobacco or whisky, for example.

'Nothing at all, sir,' he said severely. 'We think sometimes that it may all be due to the Health Service in some indefinable way – no doubt that people are living longer, perhaps – '

'No doubt,' I said vaguely.

' – or even that patients are tending to die in their beds rather than in the unnamed wards of hospitals. We had some useful connections in the better times with the riverside morgues, for an instance; but somehow suicides are less frequent than they were – or rather, should I say, the present-day practitioners tend to stay at home rather more. The genial sleeping-draught overdose has come somewhat to the fore; and so one is more in the position of being found by relatives or friends and given – as they say – a decent burial.'

He contrived to inject an odd flavour of distaste and even disapproval into his tone.

'These things move in trends, of course,' he concluded with a sigh. 'One can hardly predict or even comprehend the general movements in trade. And it was never, of course, the kind of commodity that could be . . . well, as one might say . . . made to measure. It is hardly a case for the assembly line.'

'Plastics?' I murmured tentatively, with visions of a fortune to be made in a factory established somewhere in the Midlands, the young men and women streaming to work each morning on bicycles, the staff canteens, the Sports Welfare Clubs, the whole great machinery of modern industry geared towards meeting the strange demand. Yet I realized on the instant that I had made an immense faux-pas. He regarded me with an ill-concealed pity.

'It would hardly perhaps serve, sir. In our profession we must observe the proprieties. We are dealing, I think, with Fundamentals. Plastics would be hardly ... well ... worthy, shall I say?'

There remained one more possibility. Small as he had made me feel, I screwed myself to the suggestion.

'Perhaps,' I said, with a somewhat forlorn gesture, ' – perhaps that model there – ?'

He froze to an immobility as marked as that of the now still subject of our whole discourse.

'I beg your pardon, sir! It is for exhibition only. It has been with us since the initial establishment of our whole business. It is in fact – and was bequeathed as such, so that, as he put it in his will, he might constantly be in a position to watch our progress – it is, in fact, our original Founder ... Good-morning, sir: I am sorry not to have been able to have been of more assistance.'

I crept into the bright sunshine. With one backward apologetic glance I saw him stare after me with an expression of supreme distaste on his face. I could have sworn, in the shadows there, that he then turned for a moment and bowed to that small dangling shape that once had trotted so briskly, so joyously, through the very medicated doorway from which I had that instant emerged ... I told you, I think, that I was – and indeed still am – an unsophisticated man. . . .

I will not weary you with a full account of my peregrinations. At every turn I met only frustration. I visited shops of a like nature to, but less opulent than, that veritable temple in Marylebone. But the tale was constantly the same – a hundred assistants, some sympathetic, some brusque, some positively rude, announced the identical dismal state of affairs. Skulls – yes, occasionally; isolated tibiae or fibulae, possibly; complete feet more rarely, but still at least remotely; pelvises – by some strange freak, pelvises by the score: but fully articulateds? – no, sir! One very aged proprietor of a small supplier off Holborn told me gloomily, being more courteous than most dealers that I encountered:

'I've been in the trade man and boy, sir, for sixty years and more; and I've known nothing like it, nothing, not since the days of the great 'Uman 'Eart shortage in '02.'

'And what was that?' I enquired, offering him a cigar, which he took with some absence of mind, his eyes fixed nostalgically on that distant past.

'Terrible times, sir, terrible. In the old days we done quite a trade on the side in 'Uman 'Earts – Aitch-Aitches as we used to call 'em. Pickled 'em in acid and such and used to put 'em up in handy little jars that we bought wholesale from the jam factory down the road – changed the labels, o' course. You won't remember them old times of the Pawning Days?'

I shook my head. By this time, you will comprehend, I had acquired a positive interest, if not a thorough fascination for the whole subject. The Pawning Days – the unimaginable Pawning Days!

'When you was down and out,' said my informant, leaning confidentially over a counter littered with second-hand syringes, scalpels, tweezers, stethoscopes and the like, ' – which I don't suppose you've never been in all your life, sir, nor never hope to ... but when you was down and out in them old days, and you'd pawned your watch and your overcoat and your spare elastic-sideds and such, and the old rolled gold medallion with your mother's picture inside and a lock of hair, there was still one thing left that you could pawn, and it was yourself.'

'Yourself,' I said non-committally.

'Yourself, sir. You went into St William's Orspital, like, and you said 'Ere I am, what's left of me. And they said Good, sign here. And they gave you a form, sir, and it said on it that in exchange for a five-pun note you hereby bequeathed your body to medical science for research when such time should arrive as you passed on, see. Now, if you signed another form which said as you'd never smoked or had a drink and never would, then you got another fiver, and that made ten. So off you went with your cash, see, and that was you fixed. But if times got better for you — if you maybe came into a fortune or such — you could always go and get yourself out again; and if you were a five-pound job that would cost eight, see, 'cos they had to have their profit, but if you was a ten-pounder it was eighteen, 'cos they reckoned that if you didn't smoke and didn't drink they'd have had longer to wait anyways, and so the interest was higher, like. But there wasn't many as was able to redeem themselves that way, and so they was the great times for Aitch-Aitches, and skeletons too, see.'

'And what happened in '02 to put an end to it all?' I asked.

'Reckon the Orspitals got wise to it, see. 'Cos after St William's started it, every other Orspital ran a scheme too. And there was chaps that made a regular living out of going round 'em all and signing papers right left and centre so that when the time came nobody knew what tibia belonged to who and what fibula belonged to t'other. So in '02 they all stopped simultaneous, and there we were — not an Aitch-Aitch in the place there weren't.'

He stayed gloomily contemplating that terrible period of slump, then shook himself.

'Ah well, times picked up a bit after all, in the '20s, I s'pose, 'cos of the fashionable suicide wave, see; but now they've settled back again, now that folk are more homekeeping and we've the Health Service and such — ' and in his more homely way he repeated the curious argument of my supercilious friend of Marylebone.

I left him at last with a desolate conviction that the day would never come when I would be able to provide poor Alex with a birthday present — particularly with that birthday looming constantly nearer and nearer. He gave me only one word of possible comfort:

'Take my advice, sir, and don't go round the medical suppliers. We're all in the same boat, see. Pawn-shops — that's the ticket.'

'Pawn-shops?'

'Yes, sir — them or the second-hand lads down side-streets. You see, the only time one of Them There comes on the market is when some young student chap like this cousin of yours you was telling me about gets hard-up sudden-like. So they round the corner to Uncle with Whats-'is-Name slung over their shoulder, and that's good for a tenner, you know, 'cos with things as they are Uncle can sell 'em again for as much as thirty and forty to chaps like you as is on the search, see. Mind you, mostly they're pretty old and falling to bits by the time they gets to Uncle, but even so there's sometimes something young and tasty like will turn up. So you just go on that tack, sir — there's a little shop in Camberwell I can give you the address of, that's been running Them-Theres for quite a time as a speciality — if you mention my name he'll see you straight...'

He gave me the address and I visited Camberwell. And so, eventually, the long trail drew towards its conclusion as I came in sight of Mr Hare....

— But not at first — not still for some little time. I had some further dismal rounds to perambulate. By this time the tension was rising within me to some positive degree of discomfort. The birthday was drawing closer and closer, yet still I saw little chance of success. And something else had arisen to occasion worry — something which might have held some element of the ludicrous were it not for the danger I saw in it that my whole scheme of a pleasant surprise for my young cousin might topple to desolate failure.

As I had moved from shop to shop on my quest, I had sometimes been aware of occasional faces becoming increasingly familiar — mostly of young men standing beside me at the various counters awaiting their turn, or approaching them as I withdrew. From a muttered remark once overheard, it one day dawned on me that these were none other than seekers like myself — young medicos who were also on the trail, chasing the elusive skeletons from shop to shop as I was. It was a simple step towards the further apprehensive thought that even Alex might be searching among those others — that there was consequently a chance, however remote a chance, that I might be forestalled!

The consideration quite appalled me. With the final examinations comparatively near at hand, Alex's need for a skeleton to study was growing quite imperative — it was why I had known from the first that my projected gift would be so singularly welcome to that studious cousin of mine. I had never disclosed my intention — in all gifts, I have always felt in my simple way, there should be an element of surprise. It was more than likely that in what little time could be spared from study, Alex would be seeking to obtain that curious heart's desire I also sought... and if our paths should cross — !

I had veritable confirmation of the danger on the very day of my visit to the little shop in Camberwell that had been recommended by the friendly dealer in Holborn. At the very moment of my approach to it I saw Alex's familiar figure hurrying out!

I concealed myself in a convenient doorway, then made my own way forward. The shop was small and dark — a misery of ancient junk of every description, the entire stock piled high in the single evil-smelling room — great heaps of soiled clothes, piles of cracked crockery, broken tables, crooked chairs... but as far as I could see, no skeletons.

'No, sir,' said the dealer gloomily, when I made my need known to him. 'Not in two years I ain't seen one. Old Joe up Holborn way was right, though — used to to deal in 'em regular. It's just that somehow they're so hard to come by now I've give it up.'

'Tell me,' I said hastily, ' — that young student who came in a moment before me . . . I think I know the face. As a matter of interest — '

The dealer smiled before I had completed the very sentence.

'Exactly the same, sir,' he said. 'I was just thinking how queer it was. Wanted one o' Them There too. In fact, there's several been in lately — might be worth my while to start up trade again, if I can even lay my hands on the stuff. Only thing is' — and he suddenly shrugged — 'I doubt if it would even be worth it. These young folk these days hardly have a chance, have they?'

'Why?' I asked.

'Cash, see. Even if I got one or two in I could hardly sell 'em under forty or forty-five smackers . . . and it ain't every younker of a student could lay hands on that amount of cash.'

He was right, of course — and I saw a sudden ray of hope. From my knowledge of Alex's resources it was only too plain that the purchase would be quite out of the question. Whereas I had only to trace the one physical object — one single skeleton in reasonable repair and, of course, articulated — poor Alex had to go further and find one at the very most costing ten or fifteen; and, with the demand as it plainly was, there was little likelihood of that.

I acquired a new confidence — yet still had a lingering far-off edge of apprehension. I sped from shop to shop — from Camberwell to Kentish Town, on an elusive trail thereafter to a pawnbroker in Cheapside who had been recommended — to a tangled junk yard in the Minories — to an aged surly crone almost invisible behind the ranked-high horrors of a used-clothing store in Rotherhithe.

It was she who gave me, with some reluctance at first, an address in Pimlico – then suddenly, peering closely at me, cackled quite hideously as she repeated it.

I found the side-street in a maze of crooked alleys and vennels behind Sloane Square – saw the name in blistered paintwork above the most wretched shop my eyes had ever confronted: 'W. Hare, General Dealer.' Having learned my lesson in Camberwell, I reconnoitred the neighbourhood with some care for a possible sign of Alex; then, satisfied, pushed forward and entered.

A cracked bell tinkled dismally through a musty dark silence. A small withered creature wearing a black skullcap came forward from the shadows. I babbled my request in some haste, anxious to escape from the whole unpleasant place as quickly as I could. I had even turned to the door again, so conditioned had I become to constant bleak refusal. But suddenly my distaste for my surroundings was swallowed in a great wave of relief as I heard Hare's thin and melancholy voice:

'Why yes, sir. I think I might be able to accommodate you. If you will give me a few particulars, perhaps...?'

For all his small repulsiveness I might almost in that exciting moment have embraced him!

He leaned closely to me across his piled counter. I perched as well as I could on a rachitic chair which, although plainly set out for the convenience of customers, still bore a price-ticket: seven-and-six.

With my eyes a little accustomed to the gloom I found myself gazing into the most horrible face I have ever seen. It was itself, almost, a skull. The lips were thin and cracked, drawn in a perpetual rictus-grin from teeth that were totally black. The skin stretched yellowly across his high cheekbones was so taut as almost to seem transparent – there was a momentary horrid temptation to set out a finger to poke through it bloodlessly, as if it were parchment. The eyes were pale and curiously glazed, with no spark of life in them, hooded beneath crusted and rheumy lids... the man was a living corpse.

And from him, or from the monstrous assembly of mysteries in that shop of his, there was a smell unconscionably repulsive. What its true nature was I had no notion – yet it was a condensation somehow of a smell I had encountered before: somehow animal – somehow associated with... with what? I am a simple man: perhaps, in that moment, if I had been a little more worldly-wise for all my years – however...

'You will realize,' he was saying in his soft toneless voice, 'that it may take a day or two before I can lay my hands on a specimen. I have none in stock, as it happens –'

'How long?' I asked impatiently. With my first relief now over I was only anxious again to escape from the oppressive atmosphere of that dark and evil corner of London.

'A week, shall we say? I must negotiate with my contacts.'

'A week! Great heavens, man,' I almost shouted, 'I can't wait a week! It's for a –'

Yet I hesitated. It seemed grotesque, suddenly, even in that place so grotesque itself, to announce that the object was required for a gift. I was mentally calculating dates – and realized that in all my general excitement I had had an impression of time more pressing than it actually was. A week from the 4th would be the 11th – the very day itself of the birthday.

'You could guarantee it in a week?' I asked.

'Most certainly – indeed quite definitely, sir. Articulated, of course?'

'Articulated,' I said.

'And... as to size? Would you require something on the larger side or the smaller, perhaps?'

The thing was absurd, of course. I could only stare at him for a moment. He spoke in his toneless way as a tailor might, discussing one's next suit. He had a small, much-fingered notebook on the counter before him – held over it the grimed stub of a pencil in fingers quite hideously crooked, all marked and burned with strange yellow stains.

'It ... it hardly matters,' I said — somewhat lamely I feel now — in something of an anti-climax after all my tension. My aim — my only aim — was to buy the thing: it was even absurd, after everything I had been through, to discover that there might be such a thing as a choice in the matter.

'I would suggest small, sir,' he said smoothly, writing carefully. 'They are somewhat easier for me to obtain — and are, of course, more portable. So. And male? — or female?'

Again I could only stare. The choice was still more bizarre. Was there even any difference? — Alex had never once suggested any kind of preference. Beyond a dim recollection of some Biblical lore about more or fewer ribs, I could not conceive of any vital reason why one sex should be more or less suitable for the purposes of study than the other.

He saw my hesitation and fluted quietly:

'Then if I may suggest again, sir, female. They also are a little easier for me to obtain. And besides, in the thought of the more delicate flesh once enclosing them — '

He broke off his intolerable leer as he saw the expression on my face. I believe I might almost have struck him!

'You will require it packed, sir?' he asked, even a little hastily, turning the dangerous corner. 'I have a consignment of suitable light-weight cardboard boxes I usually use for the purpose.'

The very question of transport had never occurred to me. I had had a far notion, in the earlier days of the search, of an arrangement with Carter Paterson or some such firm of conveyors of general merchandise. I saw now that if I was collecting the gift on the very day I was also having to deliver it, I would have to remove it and transport it myself. Were such things heavy, I wondered? — would the box fit comfortably into a taxi?

Again it was as if he read my thoughts.

'You will find it very light and easily carried, sir. If I might suggest a taxi-cab when you call –?'

I nodded again and rose.

'Yes – packed, then,' I said abruptly. 'But I should like to examine it, of course, before I take it.'

'Of course, sir. It was my intention. I shall have it ready a week from today, and it will be a matter of moments to enclose it in the box after your examination.'

He smiled with a hollow malevolence and shut the notebook with a snap.

'And the price, sir? Shall we say . . . fifty?'

It was larger than I had anticipated, even knowing the general situation. But I could ill afford a hesitation this time, with the end so happily at last in sight.

'Very well. Fifty.'

'Guineas, sir?'

'Guineas!'

'Thank you, sir. And if I may suggest it, since you will be taking the article away with you . . . cash, sir? – rather than a cheque?'

'Cash, Mr Hare!'

'Thank you, sir. I feel quite certain that you will be completely satisfied. Good evening, sir. A week from today – at shall we say eleven o'clock in the morning, perhaps, if that is convenient?'

I left him bowing across the counter, his yellow hands clasped tightly, the tassel of his skull-cap dangling over his thin hooked nose. I stumbled round silent heaps of rubbish – of monstrous vases set on pedestals, dead marble busts of no conceivable value, tall looming bric-à-brac stands in outmoded Victorian bamboo-work, poker-work, repulsively carved walnut . . . behind me the bell tinkled faintly as I achieved the blessed air away from the eternal smell and hurried from the shop as quickly as I could move. W. Hare – General Dealer!

It was the name, indeed, more than any other circumstance, that I found curiously lingering to haunt me. As the week passed by in a strange indolence after all the fury of my quest from that bare and antiseptic temple in Marylebone to the dingy horrors of the little shop in Pimlico, I found myself strangely repeating at odd moments simply: 'W. Hare, W. Hare, W. Hare...' and seeking some elusive association – as elusive in its different way as the odour from the man which had so oppressed me. Yet whatever I might feel about his unpleasantness – his positive evil, indeed, as I recollected his whole essence in that dusky place, leaning forward over his notebook – whatever I might feel, I had also to recognize that the man had saved me. And in that thought, as the week went on, I regained some measure of delight. I had exaggerated – my simple mind had grown infected through its piling disappointments, through the half-ludicrous gruesomeness of the whole adventure. When I encountered Hare again in the clearer light of day, his warped grotesqueness would reveal itself only as something subjective creeping through my own mind in a consideration of the macabre nature of the goods he purveyed. He was even, no doubt, a simple man like myself, of quiet tastes and lonely habits...

On the eve, my excitement mounted to a pitch where I could not sleep. I lay tossing for some hours, reflecting on the pleasure I was to give next day. I took a mouthful of brandy, and when it after all did not have the soporific effect I usually expect from it, I turned to my bedside bookshelf for consolation from my favourite Dickens.

It was when I read the passages referring to the nefarious secret occupation of the good Jerry Cruncher in the immortal *Tale of Two Cities* that I suddenly, with a small mortal chill, recalled the association in the name of that 'General Dealer' of mine in Pimlico. Jerry Cruncher the Resurrectionist – those other notorious real-life Resurrectionists in the old Edinburgh of a hundred and fifty years ago ... Burke and Hare – Burke and *Hare* ...

I almost laughed aloud in the suddenly realized folly of it all. The thing was a coincidence and an association, no more. Nevertheless, it made me lose for once my taste for the Master and I tossed the book aside, seizing instead another favourite – a volume of the enchanting short stories of the good O. Henry ... and opening it by another coincidence – an altogether happier one – at that famous little masterpiece about birthdays and birthday presents, *The Gifts of the Magi*.

In its lulling sentimental influence I fell asleep at last, and woke to a bright and cheerful morning, all horror vanished.

The mood still lingered as I directed my cab-driver to the little street in Pimlico. Indeed and indeed my fears and imaginings had been the merest shadows! The very shop in the bright sunlight was almost cheerful in its ridiculous window-display of old rugs and tarnished silverware, its shelves of outspread books at threepence and sixpence per volume. I entered it blithely, determined against any recurrence of the old oppression, and found Hare already awaiting me, his hands as always clasped before him, his skull-cap tassel dangling.

The smell was still about me but I hardly noticed it – was determined at least to ignore it. There was little time, indeed, to notice anything in the sudden contemplation in that magic moment of the object at last of all my searching – for there, set up against the end of the counter, was the beautiful thing itself!

And you know, in a curious way it even was quite beautiful to me at that moment, even apart from all the pleasure of its finding, the further pleasure it would give. In *itself* it had a strange beauty – the slightly yellowed bones so cunningly fitted, the gleam here and there of the tarnished silver articulation pins and wires. Not the face, perhaps – or the lack of face: a skull can never be beautiful ... but somehow the whole marvellous framework of it, once the supports of the very uttermost marvel of all God's universe!

The dealer had set it in one of those tall, specially made

cardboard boxes of his, the lid of it waiting in readiness on the floor. He asked if I wished to examine the articulation more closely but I shook my head – apart from my inexpertness, I knew at a glance that the thing was as perfect a specimen as could be obtained. I almost chuckled to little harmless Hare in my delight as he set to fitting the lid in position and tying the whole long parcel for me with white new string, strangely out of place in that shop of dingy second-handness. I counted out the notes I had obtained from my bank on the way to Pimlico – found I had no ten-shilling notes and cheerfully, as Hare fumbled in a pocket for change, cried:

'Leave it so, Mr Hare, at fifty-three! You deserve it!'

In its box the skeleton was smaller than it had even seemed before – I had a recurrence of my philosophic thoughts from Marylebone. And it was after all quite curiously light, as Hare had said – I could carry it with the greatest ease to the waiting taxi.

'I marked, sir,' he said, as he opened his tinkling door for me, 'a small H in pencil at the head end, so that you can keep it upright as you carry it, before unpacking. It will avoid damage to the articulation.'

It was a small and friendly touch, I felt, and I smiled to him as he stooped in a final bow to me on the pavement.

The girl who lived with Alex opened the door of the flat to me. She was an engaging, nubile young creature, I had always felt, named Miriam. I propped my box – head upwards, of course – against the lintel, smiling to her; yet noticing too that she wore an unexpectedly worried look.

'Alex isn't in,' she said; and my triumphant moment vanished. I had built so carefully to it – so carefully! In my simplicity it had never occurred to me to confirm that my young cousin would be available to receive my gift.

I had a thought to go away and come back – to ask if I might wait. It was essential that the presentation should be carried out by myself and not by proxy, after all that I had gone through. But Miriam was speaking again.

'It's been worrying me to death,' she said. 'Of course, we only live together, and I naturally can't be expected to be given a note of all Alex's movements; but to have gone away for so long without a single word –'

She broke off almost petulantly, regarding me in the gloomy small corridor.

'For so long?' I asked, dazedly a little.

'A week nearly enough – and not a single word. It's *too* bad.'

I wonder if I had my first inkling even then? – in my simplicity?

I gestured rather lamely to the tall package.

'It was to have been ... a birthday gift,' I said desolately. Miriam smiled.

'Of course! – I'd forgotten the date! Alex must surely come back home for that! Do you want to leave it?'

'Yes,' I said. 'I'll leave it.'

I turned away. There was no other immediate emotion in me, I think, but a great detached sadness – over my own inability, through my simplicity, to comprehend after all the years the ironic bitterness of the bright world in which we live. I reflected too, I believe, on the strangeness of coincidence – that of all the tales in the world I should have been reading, the previous evening, that sweetly melancholy one of O. Henry's about the people who all unwittingly give presents that can no longer be of any value to their recipients. . . .

'If you should see Alex,' cried Miriam after me, 'tell her to let me know at least when she's coming home.'

My foot, as I turned, had caught the edge of the package still leaning against the lintel. With a small whispering from its jostled contents it now fell forward into the hallway where Miriam stood, rocking gently for a moment at her feet.

'Alex,' I said, into infinity – 'has come home.'

Garrett Boatman

Rain

To borrow a music cliché, GARRETT BOATMAN, *author of* Stage Fright (1988), *a weird and wild paperback horror novel sporting a keytar-playing skeleton on its cover, was something of a one-hit wonder. His novel came out right at the end of the horror publishing boom, when the market was saturated with horror novels and publishers were moving onto other things; between then and now he never published any more fiction. So join us in welcoming him back to the fold with this brand-new tale, 'Rain', which is the first the world has heard from Boatman in quite a while, but certainly won't be the last.*

I DON'T GO TO THE BEACH ANYMORE. I don't go fishing and I get the cold sweats every time it rains. Which is why I took the boiler room job at the Lubco Industrial Laundry in Boulder. Five-thousand-three-hundred-forty feet above sea level. High and dry. (Relatively dry anyway: I don't mind the steam.) No windows and so much noise from the roaring furnace with its maze of feeder pipes rushing steam upstairs to the rows of hand presses and folders and the long speed ironer with its clanking rollers and acre of canvas belt that I wouldn't know if Armageddon were raging outside.

I got a cot down here. Ninety degrees in the middle of a Colorado winter. A hundred plus in midsummer. Fine by me. Rainy nights I sleep over. The only water I got use for comes from the cavespring used to make Jack Daniels so smooth.

Not that I'm drunk right now. Wish I was, but I ain't. Never been so sober in my life. I'd drive down to the Party Hour liquor store and get me a fifth of Tennessee sipping whiskey, but it's raining out. Raining like it ain't rained here since June of 1965 when a mile-wide section of city streets flooded and two boys on horseback were swept away by the South Platte River. So my radio tells me, anyway. Water up to the hubcaps in some neighborhoods. Two people dead from a mudslide. I ain't walked out to the loading dock to see for myself. Ain't going to either. I can't abide the rain.

I turned the radio off. Just hearing about the rain makes my guts seize up as if a snake had crawled in there and died. It ain't healthy to know too much, and the devil don't like nobody knowing his business.

The trucks won't be coming in tonight. The laundry's closed. I'm the only one here. Even Tony, the night watchman, who's on duty weeknights and who's generally as regular as a Swiss watch, couldn't make it in this evening.

I'm writing this down in this trucker's log because . . . well, I feel I gotta tell my story to someone and I ain't been able to talk to nobody about it since it happened and maybe the only way I can get it off my chest is to commit it to writing. I can always burn the log when I'm finished. Except that maybe an ornery part of my mind don't want to burn it. As if leaving my story lying around so somebody could read it might stave off death for a while. Maybe. Though I think death may be tapping me on the shoulder sooner than I'd like. I been getting pains around my heart tonight. Pains that got nothing to do with indigestion, if you take my meaning.

Got to be the rain doing it to me. Like I said, I can't hear the storm what with all the racket down here. But I hear it in my mind. Oh yes, I know the sound the rain makes when the sky opens up and an ocean pours down with no let up day after day and the swollen waters sweep off trees and houses and dogs and cats and people and you can't sleep for fear of drowning and when you do nod, exhausted by fear, you dream of drowning and wake up thrashing, gasping for air. Yeah, you could say I know that sound better than most.

I ain't never been to that Niagara Falls up in New York where the honeymooners go, but I seen it on the TV and I imagine it's as good an image as any to describe the kind of rain I'm talking about. Only flood rain ain't romantic, and it's not just over yonder where you can stand off safe and dry with your arm around your honey and ooh and aah at it; it's all around you, pounding the roof, carrying off everything that ain't tied down and some things that are. Killing waters.

One time when I was a lot younger I was working a coal barge down in Louisiana. It rained three straight days and nights and the Mississippi swoll up so bad the town had crews out shoring up the levies. Everybody threw their backs into it – me included. I remember the rain drumming so hard on my skull it gave me a migraine. First night I couldn't sleep for the rain drumming on the barge cabin's tin roof. But I got used to it and by the third night I slept just fine.

Point is I didn't fear the rain then. It was just a nuisance. Uncomfortable. Miserable. But nothing terrifying. Guess it ain't the rain I fear now – though even the thought of an April shower gives me the cold sweats. It's the flood and the memory of what happened the last time I got caught in one that really scares the bejesus out of me. But then its the rain that brings the flood, ain't it?

I know – I've spent enough time yakking. Time to get to the point. I'd like to put off writing down what happened until the rain stopped and the sun came out and I could destroy this log; but I keep getting these pains in my chest and the muscles over my heart and in my left arm feel all prickly like thousands of little needles stabbing and if I'm going to tell my story this may be my last chance.

Sorry about the shaky handwriting. A couple double-shots of bourbon might fix it, but as I said I ain't got any and it don't look like I'm going to get none. Maybe that's for the best.

Otherwise, after reading this log, you — whoever you are — might just say, 'Aw, he weren't nothing but a no good, lying drunk, telling stories that came out of a bottle!'

Well, I'm here to tell you I'm sober, friend; and this ain't no bottle story. Here's what happened.

My name's Frank Boeglin. I was born in Waterproof, Arkansas. ('Waterproof'! Ain't that a laugh! One of life's little ironies, considering.) Yeah, there's such a place. You can look it up. Just up and across the Mississippi River a little ways from Natchez.

About a year and a half ago (I been tending this boiler just over a year now), I had me a job down in Del Mar, Texas. Handyman in the Belle Starr Hotel. Same kind of work I been doing half my life. Tending the boiler, fixing the plumbing, changing light bulbs, putting the doorknobs back on. The Belle Starr was a big old gingerbread Victorian. Four stories, a musty lobby, a long narrow dining room and a creaking old elevator that kept me busy, I can tell you!

Because Del Mar's on the Gulf Intracoastal Waterway and near some fine beaches and bird watching, the Starr got its share of tourists during the summer. Not like Padre Island to the south or Galveston to the north, but fair considering she wasn't nothing but an aging, small-town hotel. Of course, when the storm came it was fall, hurricane season, and the vacancy sign was out with more than half the twenty rooms and suites empty.

It had already been raining for days. Nothing like the torrential downpour that was to come. No big winds like we got when a hurricane was cruising out in the Gulf. Just a steady rain, day and night, night and day. Warm Gulf rain, soaking everything. Air so humid it lay thick in your lungs and turned plaster walls into damp chalk.

For a Gulf storm to get tagged a hurricane, winds got to be at least 74 miles per hour. This mother of a rain storm never got anywhere near that. It was just another tropical storm. Tropical Storm Ella they were calling it on TV. Ella hung off the coast, meandering this way, then that, sometimes squatting in one spot for most of a day, not making her mind up where she intended to go and seemingly in no hurry to do so. Like she was content to be a tropical storm and not a hurricane. A monster of a storm, taking a monster dump the length of the Texas coast.

The day Ella made her move the tide in the bay was four feet above normal and the Matagorda River was running at flood capacity. The TV advised everybody to evacuate because it looked certain Ella was going to hit Del Mar dead on. Some did. I saw a few cars and trucks loaded up heading inland that day. Most stayed. I mean every Gulf Coast town from Pensacola to Corpus Christi has seen storms at one time or another. And plenty of bad ones have hit Texas. But Los Angeles don't turn into a ghost town every time somebody yells earthquake. You figure it ain't going to happen, not to your town, not to you. Know what I mean?

Besides, Ella wasn't even a hurricane. Winds only 40 to 50 miles per hour. Nothing like the 100 miles per hour winds of the hurricane that destroyed Galveston in 1900. I've heard it said that in that storm nearly as many people were decapitated and sliced to ribbons by flying glass and roof tiles as died by drowning. Or Hurricane Audrey's 105 miles per hour winds that ripped up trees and hurled cars for blocks in Cameron, Louisiana, leveling bayou villages and blowing thousands of poisonous reptiles and alligators into village streets. Nor was there anything resembling Camille's 25-foot-tall tidal waves that swamped the Mississippi coast in 1969.

People stayed put. Even when the police car drove by with its loudspeaker urging everyone to get while the getting was good, most of the old timers smiled and said, 'Looks like we're in for a speck of weather,' and tacked plywood over the windows, brought in the porch furniture, put in a few extra groceries, bottled some water and settled back to watch the show.

I went around the Belle Starr putting up sheets of quarter-inch plywood over the big picture windows downstairs and latching the shutters upstairs. Just in case the wind did pick up enough to start tossing trees. Made sure my provisions were stocked – two fifths of Jack Daniels. Did my share of smirking at the pussies who ran for higher ground.

People don't learn. It can't happen here. Not to me. Hell, you don't stop smoking in bed just because you heard somebody died doing it. People are funny that way. And I suppose – had the storm been the only thing I'd had to live through – I might have stayed on in Del Mar; Lord knows there was plenty of work for handymen afterwards. But the flood and the drownings weren't the worst things I witnessed that week. No, not the worst by a long shot. You know, I can close my eyes and still see that cop car with the loudspeaker cruising by, urging residents to evacuate. God, how I wish I'd heeded that policeman's advice!

There were fourteen people staying in the Belle Starr, including myself, the day Ella came ashore. Some opted to leave after the cop went by. By dinner time there were five.

The owner lives up in Houston and seldom gets down to Del Mar. But the manager – a tough old gal named Elma McKinny – stuck around, as did Franklin, the Belle Starr's black cook, who was getting up in years and had a room on the first floor in the back. Franklin had been serving a southern fried chicken dinner on Thursday nights and ham dinners Sundays for twenty-three years. That left me and two guests: a Mr Langforth, a businessman who owned a string of pie emporiums, and his young 'wife' Tina. Nobody believed Tina was his wife for a second, and frankly nobody cared. While Langforth was a bore telling how he just bet the Starr's dining room would be filled if Mrs McKinny put his pies on the menu, 'Mrs'

Langforth bored us telling anybody — whether they wanted to hear it or not — how much lovelier the Starr might be if Mrs McKinny had it painted a seashell pink and how Franklin's ham was delicious but how its flavor could be improved if Franklin would marinate the ham overnight in Coca-Cola.

Just before dinner the rain picked up. What had been a steady downpour, sounding like the white noise you hear on the TV when the station goes off, suddenly spun the spigot full pump. As if waves were tumbling from the sky, rain crashed against the Starr's shingled hide, roared on her striped awning.

While we were eating and Mr Langforth was bending Mrs McKinny's ear — raising his voice around a full mouth to be heard over the barrage of the storm as he hearkened back to his humble beginnings as a traveling Bible salesman — the bell out at the front desk rang. As it amused me to see Elma McKinny squirm before Langforth's oblivious swagger, I got up before she could excuse herself and went to see who had braved the rain.

The young man standing before the desk looked like a drowned rat. Long, shiny-black hair plastered to his narrow skull. Soggy, wide-shouldered jacket drooping over his skinny frame. A guitar case and a suitcase-sized, vinyl-covered amplifier sat beside him on the floor; a canvas rucksack slung over his shoulder. Had he been carrying only the rucksack and guitar I would have taken him for a hitchhiker, but anyone lugging an amplifier had to have wheels.

'Can I help you?' I said.

'Yeah, I want a room. Top floor. Facing the bay.' The kid (he looked to be about twenty) spoke with an up-north accent.

I asked him if his car had broken down. 'Naw,' he says. 'I drove down from Houston to see the storm.'

'To see the storm!' I says. I'd looked out when the rain picked up and you couldn't see more than half a block. And that was before the sun set! 'What in the hell would you want to do that for?' I asked him.

His dark eyes twinkled as he answered. 'I dreamed the world was going to end,' he said. 'And I figured I might as well be on hand to see it happen.'

It was my turn to smile. 'Good Lord, son. Rain ended the world last time. Don't you remember what the Bible says? Next time fire?'

'Don't believe everything you read,' the kid says with a look in his eye that told me he knew something I didn't.

I gave him a key, top floor bay front, (nobody else on the top floor anyway), told him he could settle up with the manager later and that, if he hurried, he could catch a bite to eat before the table was cleared. He signed the register Joe Wade.

I offered to help him with his gear, but he declined. The amplifier looked heavy, but he lifted it and walked over to the elevator like it was a suitcase containing nothing more than some socks and underwear.

I generally wouldn't take to a mop-haired, snot-nosed punk rock and roller, but the way he shrugged when I told him about the police urging everybody to evacuate, as if to say a little ol' tropical storm don't bother me, struck a chord in my flinty heart. Before long I would revise my opinion of the youngster, but at that moment I thought he was all right. Boy was I wrong, I can tell you!

Wade didn't come down for dinner and about two hours later I heard the most godawful racket. Over the roar of the storm you could hear him torturing his guitar, whipping it like it was a dog that shat in his boots. Drawn out, crashing chords that brought to mind an image of a mad dentist using a pair of pressure pliers on howling, unsedated patients.

Somebody was bound to complain, and sure enough, Langforth, who had retired to his room with 'Mrs Langforth', calls down and demands somebody put a stop to that caterwauling.

I went up. The racket was tremendous in the fourth floor hall. I knocked on the kid's door, but he either didn't hear me or didn't want to be bothered. I jiggled the handle, not so much to open the door as to let him know I wasn't going away. The door swung open.

There he stood, striking a wide-legged stance, dressed in shiny black leather, swaying in front of an open window, the shutters thrown wide and the rain driving in, soaking him and three quarters of the room. He seemed to be playing to the storm, and, in its own way, the storm was responding. I might have felt some dread, some gooseflesh or shiver that should have told me something weird and unnatural was going on; but I guess I was too PO'ed seeing the mess he'd made of the room — a mess I'd have to clean up! — to feel anything but anger.

I pointed my finger and opened my mouth, ready to order the kid out of the Starr, storm or no storm, if he didn't can the racket and close the window — when somebody bellowed, 'What the Sam Hill is going on?'

The music — if a noise like ten thousand live cats fed through a meat grinder can be called music — stopped. Me and the kid both turned at once.

Langforth and his 'missus' stood in the door. Langforth was glaring like somebody had said his pies tasted like cow flops. Tina whatever her name was had a big moony grin on her chops like one of those loony gals that used to go ga ga for Frank Sinatra.

Wade must've picked up on Tina's smile, because he ignored Langforth and me, didn't give either of us a nod or a howdy. Just looked at Tina with her tight sweater showing off those high tits and that tight ass squeezed into tight jeans and he smiled. There was something snake-like about his eyes, I thought later. Did I mention they were dark? Almost black? They were. So dark you couldn't tell the pupils from the irises. He smiled at her. Didn't say a word, just smiled like he knew she was his for the taking and the hell with Langforth even if he did have eighty pounds on him. Real arrogant. And his fingers started rippling over the guitar strings. The music that came out of the amplifier was low, throbbing, persuasive.

Tina started dancing, a slow sinuous weave, her body sort of rippling, breasts thrusting forward, then pulling back while her pelvis whipped out and ground around in a tight circle. It was a weird scene. This strange kid and airhead nympho making love to each other with music and motion while rain drove in through the open window and Langforth and me stood there gawking with our jaws unhinged.

I thought Langforth was going to bust a vein for sure, maybe lay into the kid. It didn't happen. The overweight pie salesman spun on his heel and stomped out of the room.

I wanted to say something, maybe tell the kid Del Mar had laws to deal with hotel guests guilty of willful destruction of property. 'Willful destruction' ... that's a laugh in light of what happened later. Anyway, I guess I was embarrassed, as if they already had their clothes off and were grinding away on the soaked sheets of the double bed. So I shut the shutters and window myself and got out of there lickety-split.

That low pulsing voodoo rhythm followed me down the hall, as did the image of that starry-eyed floozy doing some sort of fuck dance in front of that greasy-haired punk. I'd heard of people tossing their morals to the wind when confronted by catastrophe, but Christ! we're talking nothing but a little rain!

At that point anyway.

It wasn't until I was on my way down in the elevator that I noticed my arms were crawling with gooseflesh.

During the night, the first floor flooded. I had a dream I ain't had in going on half a century. I dreamed I pissed my bed. Not willful destruction, mind you. I dreamed I had to go something pitiful, but I was paralyzed. Not so paralyzed that I couldn't pee, but I couldn't get up and go to the john. Instead I just laid there whizzing away in my long johns.

I woke up and, sure enough, the bed was soaked. I mean soaked top to bottom. I sat up knowing there was no way I could have pissed the bed that much. Besides pissed sheets are warm and my covers felt like they'd been dipped in ice water.

I swung off the bed and found I was standing knee-deep in flood water. Something brushed against my leg and I reached down. It was the wicker clothes hamper I had; I'd just done my wash the day before and it was empty, buoyant. Swearing under my breath, I started across the room to throw the light switch ... and froze.

Just two years before, the basement in the bed and breakfast across the street flooded. The owner's son went down to check on the damage and somehow – nobody never did figure what exactly happened – got himself electrocuted. The very thought gave me the bejeebers, and I just stood there paralyzed by indecision like that Hamlet fellow until it occurred to me that the water was up to the outlets and if I hadn't fried yet I probably wasn't going to.

Franklin was in the hall when I came out. I could barely see him (the light was out) but I sure heard him cussing. I told him to stay put and groped my way back to the kitchen and got the big Ranger flashlight magnetized to the side of the fridge in case of emergency.

The Belle Starr's lobby was a weird sight. The flashlight beam threw a white shine over the black water. The flood was rising fast: minutes ago it was knee-deep; now it was lapping at my crotch. The water looked oily and it stank of river mud and sewage. I got two keys from behind the front desk and me and Franklin took rooms on the second floor. I didn't think Mrs McKinny would mind, considering the circumstances.

It seemed I would never sleep again with the shutters rattling and the rain hammering the Starr like water in a car wash pounding a car's steel skin. I kept worrying about the mess I was going to have to clean up when the rain let up in the morning. Toward dawn I dozed anyway. Loud as the storm was, it was a monotonous roar, seldom varying except for the occasional banshee shriek of gusting wind.

No sooner did I start to snore than a tremendous *crack!* like a big oak tree splitting lengthwise snapped me awake. I was on my feet blinking before you could say 'boo'. I thought the Starr's foundations had given way. But the floor seemed level enough.

Forcing one shutter open and leaning into the driving rain, I saw an amazing sight. The streets were flooded up to the tops of the first-floor windows. Cars had vanished. The roof of a white delivery truck stuck out of the water like the sleek back of a dead whale. Below, the Starr's blue-and-white striped awning drooped into the water.

Then I heard that sound again like a sequoia snapped over Paul Bunyan's knee and I looked up just in time to see the steeple of the Gethsemane Methodist Church two blocks away (a fuzzy gray triangle rising over the roofs) break off and collapse into the street. Despite the percussion of the rain beating the shutter beside my ear I heard the tremendous crash it made.

The previous summer the church had raffled off a Cadillac to raise money for renovations. Too little too late was my guess. I told myself the church was old, dating back to Civil War times. The fact didn't console me none, however. The Belle Starr was just as old.

I started to close the shutters and something caught my eye. I didn't want to believe I was seeing what I was seeing, but there was no denying I was looking at the nude corpse of a young woman. Her upper torso was caught in the lower branches of a tree two houses down. It was pitiful the way her legs thrashed in the rough current as if she were trying to swim.

I'm not an imaginative man, but I recall thinking what if, one day, the tide came in but didn't go out. It would be like in Noah's Ark: the end of the world. Or close to it.

All day it rained without letup. Thunder rumbled in the distance. I worried about the Starr's foundations. Electricity was out and the whole first floor was a swimming pool. Franklin was too old for the work, but me and Elma McKinny went swimming and hauled up enough canned goods and soggy dry goods to put together a decent lunch in a second-floor suite. It wasn't the most pleasant swim I've ever had: I ran into a school of disposable diapers and a reef of toilet paper down there. Seemed like all the crap (literally) the town had dumped over the years had come back to haunt us.

Langforth joined us. He was morose and gratifyingly untalkative, but obviously a man who found solace in food. (He polished off most of a canned ham singlehandedly.) He went back to his room soon as he finished. I guess I felt sorry for him, losing his 'Mrs' and all, even if he had made a fool of himself cozying up with a girl less than half his age.

Later, I took a plate up to Wade's room, enough food on it for two, rapped on the door. Rapped again when nobody answered. I'd set the plate on the floor and started to leave thinking maybe he and Tina were still wallowing in each other's juices, when Wade opened the door rubbing his eyes.

He looked unwell, I thought, pale, skin moist-looking, sweaty, a greenish-gray as if he'd been seasick. His eyes looked larger than I remembered them from the night before. Farther apart too. And his ears ... As I said, he had long hair and I hadn't paid any attention to his ears the previous evening; but his ears were tiny, almost nonexistent, and his hair seemed thinner, the hairline receding.

He thanked me when he saw the food, took it in. Up late last night, he said. My flesh crawling with gooseflesh, I asked if he and Tina needed anything. He surprised me by saying she'd left his room last night.

I went downstairs with a bad feeling in my gut. The corpse I had seen caught in the tree had been floating face down, but I thought I might recognize it if it turned over.

The guitar started before I was halfway down the stairs. A tortured high-pitched screaming note stretched out and out until you thought it would break then stretched some more, then suddenly plunging into grinding chords that crashed down and down and down to emerge as a pumping demonic bass that hurt my teeth and lifted the hackles on the back of my neck. I groaned. What a racket! Then a chill ran up my spine – *no electricity*! How could Wade play an electric guitar without electricity? A battery? Had to be. But that bad feeling ulcerated in my gut, bloomed like a rust flower eating a hole in a car's sheet metal.

I thought about going back to the kid's room and telling him to cut the racket. Maybe take a peek to see where he was getting his juice. But even as the thought shot through my head, I knew up was the wrong direction. Don't ask me how I knew; I just did. The way you know if you step out of a car moving seventy miles an hour you're likely to lose some body parts.

A long peal of thunder cracked overhead. The thunder that had boomed in the distance all day had arrived suddenly and with a vengeance. The building shuddered from the shock wave.

My heart pounded as I flew down those steps. I didn't know what I expected. Tina laid out on Langforth's bed with a knife sticking out of her chest? Texans can be nearly as violent in their jealousy as Mexicans. Perhaps that would be better. If she wasn't in the salesman's room ... I kept seeing that bobbing corpse caught in a tree.

I didn't have time to wonder much. Langforth's room was on the second floor. I burst from the stairwell in time to see water surge up from the lobby and roll down the hall in a three-foot wave. I thought crazily about Noah's flood and how it was here and I didn't have a boat.

Thunder *cracked*. Then a tremendous *crash* as something big slammed into the side of the Belle Starr. The floor tilted out from under me, dumped me in the water. I came up sputtering, noticed the floor was still tilted and somebody was screaming.

Wade's guitar was a locomotive running wild, railroading through my skull. But above the guitar's howl a man's high, pain-racked scream split the air. Coming from Langforth's room. Locked! I threw my shoulder against the door. Wood splintered. The door shot open.

The prow of a boat from the marina across the street jutted through a gaping hole in the wall. Big 38-foot Silverton sports fisher. Though its fly bridge and the roof of its cabin were sheared off, I recognized her by the double aqua-blue stripes around her hull. The *Lucy May*. Belonged to Lawrence Withers, retired pediatrician.

Langforth was wedged under the prow, only his face above the water. No longer screaming, he was sputtering, gasping for air.

I started into the room, but the *Lucy May* shifted, began to slide back out, fiberglass grating against wood as the boat freed itself. And then Langforth did scream as the boat squished the lower half of his body. The water turned a frothy red. The *Lucy May* wrenched free, was carried off by the current, creating a suction that pulled Langforth out through the gaping hole. I grabbed the door jamb and held on for dear life. The businessman screamed horribly as he clawed at a protruding board. Then he was gone, sucked under by the tide.

What if the tide came in and didn't go out? That was the thought that kept yelling over and over inside my head while I clung to the door jamb and the water rushing by sucked furniture out of the room.

Old Franklin hauled me out, closed the door. Then I noticed.

The guitar had stopped.

In at least one respect Mrs McKinny and Franklin were two

of a kind: surrounded by death and destruction, they braced up and took care of business.

Other than what we could see and hear we didn't know what was going on out there. Rooms at the Starr had TVs, but they were useless without electricity; and my transistor radio was down in my room, underwater. We were cut off from the news, but a lot of people in the area weren't so lucky to live in a four-story building. I was pretty certain there were more than a few corpses floating around out there.

We had retreated to the third floor. The second floor was flooded and the water was rising fast. One side of the hotel was leaning dangerously. We met in a suite on the level side. Franklin made me a cold cup of tea to quiet my nerves while I told them about the corpse in the tree and Langforth's death. They had both heard Joe Wade's guitar.

Mrs McKinny, who was an alderwoman at the now steepleless Gethsemane Methodist Church, spoke first. 'The young man is evil,' she said. 'Can't you feel it?'

I could. It felt like something dark and moldy that had nothing to do with the damp that bloated the carpet and peeled the wallpaper. Something rotten. A stink you smelled with your noggin and not with your nose, if you take my meaning.

Mrs McKinny showed us a small .38 revolver. She had it on her in case of burglars. Now she planned to use it to force Wade to give up his guitar.

Yeah, I know what you're thinking. This part sounds crazy. Every time the kid whips his guitar, somebody dies. And he's playing it without electricity to boot. Well, if you're having a hard time swallowing this, don't worry, it gets crazier. But like I told you when I started — I ain't crazy and this ain't no bottle story. What I've told you and what I'm about to tell you is God's own truth. Believe what you will. I'm not an imaginative man and I ain't a liar.

We left the room, Mrs McKinny with her gun, Franklin with a butcher knife and me with a flashlight. No sooner had we stepped into the dark hall than that damned guitar music started up again. Mrs McKinny groaned, clapped her hands to her ears, smacking herself with the gun butt.

The guitar riff charged up a spiraling steel stair that went up and up through the roof and into the storm, joining forces with the thunder and lightning to shake the night. And then it happened.

Like before, something hit the Starr: another boat or part of a building. Something big. The hotel lurched. I slammed into a wall, held onto the flashlight only by luck. I realized what was going on: the building was breaking up. The floor tilted precariously. Then dropped out from under us.

I landed on my back, stood. Water was surging all around, rushing over my calves, lapping at my knees. The first floor had caved in and the floors above had settled on the ruins.

My flashlight stabbed around. Franklin beside me. The beam found Mrs McKinny. On her knees, water swirling around her waist. Her hands were still clapped over her ears and I realized the kid was still playing.

'The Starr's breaking up!' I shouted at her. 'We got to get on the roof!'

'Something's inside me!' she screamed. Elma McKinny was not a woman you'd ever expect hysterics from, but she had lost it. Her left hand clawed at her throat, while with her right she scraped the butt of the gun against her cheek.

The floor shifted again. Big building like the Starr has got to weigh a lot, but it was no longer anchored to its foundation and the flood and the wind were conspiring to haul it off to God knows where. I reached for Mrs McKinny. She swung the revolver in my face and I pulled back in a hurry.

'Something inside!' she screamed again and I could see she was shaking bad. 'All over me! Like worms under my skin! I can't stand it!'

And you know, to this day I believe I did see her flesh writhing as if something were crawling in there, just under the skin. Me and Franklin stood there staring in horror a moment too long. Elma McKinny turned the gun and shot herself in the neck.

She collapsed in the water. Then a horrible thing happened. Not the worst thing I saw that night. No, the night was still young and the party had just started; but what I saw next will haunt me for the rest of my life – which (please merciful God!) won't last much longer.

As Elma McKinny's body went under, long worms – dead-white under the flashlight beam – poured out of her mouth and swam away.

As long as I'd known him, Franklin was always a soft-spoken man. He scared the bejesus out of me when he roared like some godawful piece of machinery starting up full crank.

'I'm gonna cut that son of a bitch!' he said, fisting his butcher knife. He started for the stairs.

I was right on his heels. There was danger up there, no doubt about it. But to stay down here was suicide.

Franklin (sixty-seven years old but spry, and big – two-twenty if he was a pound) bounded up the leaning stairs two at a time, burst into the hall, charged Wade's door. The Starr seemed to have come alive in her death throes. The floor heaved under my feet like the back of a waking monster.

Satan rock poured through Wade's door in thick molasses chords and wailing banshee notes that I felt in my bones. Music guaranteed to set your teeth on edge.

Franklin didn't slow. Twisted at the last moment, ducked his head, slammed his shoulder into the door. Metal screeched as the latch plate screws tore free from the wood. The door crashed into the wall, driving the white ceramic knob into the plaster.

The kid's looks had changed. The front of his face had pushed forward and his nose had receded so that his head seemed to slope sharply back from his big lips to his brow. His eyes — huge now and dead white with slitted black pupils — had slid around to the sides of his skull. His ears had shrunk to little stubs of ribbed cartilage and what hair remained on his mottled pate hung down in stringy clumps. The impression was fishlike. And the air *smelled* fishlike.

One time I was delivering a horse to a rich guy down in Mexico. Hauling a horse and trailer behind an underpowered six-cylinder Ford pickup. Going up a hill outside of Matamoros, I got stuck in a pile of fish that had fallen off somebody's truck. All mushed up and turning to jelly in the hot Mexican sun. Spinning my wheels, fish flying. The stink rising through the Ford's rusty floorboards. The smell in Joe Wade's room was like that. Thick, cloying, stinking of seaweed and marsh ooze.

Wade — or whatever he had become — ignored us. Kept crashing through those ungodly chords, rocking back and forth in time to his licks, the neck of the black and chrome instrument rising and falling like an ax. The window was open again, the shutters thrown wide. Sheets of rain drove in. Thunder beat a demonic bass to the kid's riffs.

I dreamed the world was going to end, Joe Wade had said. And staring at that monstrosity pounding out an unmelodious tribute to the god of discord with chaos howling at his back, I could believe it.

The building shivered, hitched lower into the flood. Water poured over my shoes. We were sinking. The outer wall was leaning inward. One of the shutters popped off. The window exploded, the rain driving the glass into the room.

'Shine your light over there!' Franklin shouted over the ruckus.

I aimed my light at where he was pointing — to where the amplifier was plugged into the outlet.

I'll never forget the chill that went through me. A cold hand closing over my heart. The outlet was dead, stone f—ing dead. And here this monster's guitar was howling away as if it had a direct line to the Matagorda County power house.

Franklin grabbed the cord. I guess he intended to unplug it. But he stiffened up and started jitterbugging with his eyes bugged out and his mouth open like he was fixing to scream only what came out was something like *unnnngh unnnngh unnnngh*. Green fire flashed from his eyes and mouth and ears. Green smoke rose off his clothes, his skin. Looked like he was cooking in some sort of hellish swamp gas.

I just stood there with my jaw hanging down to my chest, water rising about my knees, smelling burnt meat.

But Franklin was a tough old boy. Suddenly, he roared like he'd done in the hall downstairs, brought that big knife up pretty as you please and sliced the cord clean in two.

The kid's guitar was silent before Franklin's body hit the floor.

The tilt of the room grew steeper. Water surged around my waist. The noise of planks popping, beams snapping was deafening. The room bucked. I fell, lost the flashlight, but scrabbling to get up I found Franklin's butcher knife.

Crash! The twisting wall spat the window frame into the howling night. Then the roof tore free. I cowered in the water, covered my head as plaster and lathing showered down.

The floor dropped out from under me. I sank, came up sputtering. Rain churning up the water all around me, blinding me. My hand struck wood. I grabbed it, hung on. A section of roof, floating like a raft. I hauled myself onto it.

Lightning flashed. A giant forked bolt lit up the night and singed the air. The smell of ozone was as thick as the stink of cordite at a turkey shoot. I thought I would go deaf from the thunder.

I wasn't alone on the roof. Less than ten feet away, Joe Wade – or rather what Joe Wade had become – stood, naked as a jaybird, legs planted wide, a big shark-toothed grin on his fish face. The rain splashing off him created a sort of halo around him, a watery aura. He held one hand stretched in front of him steadying himself as the roof pitched in the flood; and in the instant before the lightning faded, I saw the hand was webbed.

I still had the butcher knife. Fact, I'd driven the blade into the roof and was hanging on for dear life. To tell the truth, I was paralyzed with fright and don't think I could have used it anyway.

Lightning sizzled and cracked. And the kid lets out this wild whoop of rheumy laughter. I tell you it wasn't no sound no human ever made. No *sane* human anyway!

The lightning couldn't have lasted more than a few seconds, but it seemed like I was staring at that impossible face for an hour before the world plunged into darkness. I think — *know* — I stared at that face too long, because I see it every night in my dreams. Every time I close my eyes. I know that face at least as well as my own. Guess you could say I'm haunted.

The last thing I noticed while I was studying that face — and I remember this clearly, as if I were seeing it now — was movement behind and below the ribbed stumps that used to be his ears. A glistening wet hole in the side of his neck, stuttering open in time to his laughter.

It took me a moment to comprehend what I was seeing. Darkness returned and I heard the splash of Joe Wade diving into the flood. And then I understood.

Gills . . . the son-of-a-bitch had grown gills!

The night passed. I kept waiting for Joe Wade to come for me. He didn't. And pretty soon the business of staying alive got to be so all-consuming I didn't have time to dwell on it.

Day came and the storm passed. The roof broke up during the night so that I wound up clinging to a little piece about four by six. The storm tore the clothes off my back so that I ended up with one boot, a sleeve and a hank of pants clinging to my belt. Just before dawn my raft beached, and when the sun rose I saw I was atop a pile of lumber.

At first I thought I had come to rest in a lumberyard, then I began to make out house beams and railroad ties and sections of walls and roofs and realized the Gethsemane Methodist Church and the Belle Starr weren't the only buildings in Del Mar to be reduced to kindling. There were corpses sticking out of the pile here and there, so I counted myself lucky and prayed like I ain't prayed since I was a boy.

Took a few days for the water to recede. I learned I'd ridden that slab of roof over three miles inland. When the water got low enough to travel, I went hunting.

Two days I searched. Didn't really think I would find anything, but I had to look. Do you understand? I mean, if you were absolutely certain you'd seen a flying saucer come down in a field one night, wouldn't you be driven to go take a gander come morning? You know — just to be sure? 'Course you would! And I went looking for Joe Wade.

Found him too . . . what was left of him.

Wish I hadn't. Should have left well enough alone. I mean, I was alive. I could have just run and kept on running. Could've told myself I'd been hallucinating. After all I'd been through, maybe I'd even dreamt the whole thing!

Yeah, lot of things I could've done. But I didn't. I went and looked. And now I know I wasn't hallucinating and I'll never forget what I saw. Like I said before, 'It ain't healthy to know too much, and the devil don't like nobody knowing his business.'

Some of the bodies I saw were cut up pretty bad. Glass, shingles, boards — all manner of projectiles were flying around during the height of the storm. I received a nasty cut on the forehead sometime during that endless night; something flying out of the dark. Others got crushed when driftwood they were hanging on crashed into buildings. It looked like both accidents had befallen Joe Wade.

I found him wedged under a roof beam amid a pile of bricks

and timbers, a strip of copper, green with verdigris, lodged in his throat. The jagged edge had sawn deep into his neck. The corpse was bloated and reminded me more than ever of those rotting fish I'd spun my wheels in that time in Matamoros. Puckered white wounds on his face and upper torso marked other cuts the body had received.

Wade had completed his transformation: his nose had disappeared completely, so that his chinless head sloped back from the wide gash of his mouth. But he hadn't made it to open water. I remember thinking God had been watching the young man's communion with Satan. And what the devil had granted, God had taken away.

I stared at those gill holes – no longer pulsing with the rhythm of life – for a long while. Then I went and found a shovel and came back and buried the monstrosity as deep as I could.

That's it. That's my story. Believe what you will. If these pains in my chest get any worse I don't think I'll see the end of tonight's rain.

I should never have gone looking. That's where I made my mistake. I could have endured the nightmares but not the reality. And now he's come for me. There's nobody here but me and I just heard the boiler room's steel door open and close. And now I can hear the wet squishing of Joe Wade's webbed feet on the steel floor up there.

Sweet Jesus! The pain in my chest! My left arm won't move! Pins and needles!

My God! There he is at the railing at the top of the steel stairs, the only way down to the boiler room. Just standing there under the fluorescents, staring down at me, dripping rain. Death's been none too gentle on him. His lips have rotted away and some of the shark teeth have fallen out, but the gills are working and his webbed hands look strong enough to do the job.

Joe Wade's come for me! Not Wade exactly, but whatever power's animating his corpse!

My heart! The pain!

No way out but up those stairs, and I can't move and I couldn't bear to go out into the rain anyway.

He's coming down! Please Dear Lord, take me now! Before those rotting hands touch my flesh!

I'd burn this log if I could, but ain't no time. I pray he destroys it. Better nobody reads it. Dangerous. It ain't healthy to know too much, and the devil don't like nobody knowing his business.

Our Father which art in Heaven, hallowed be Thy name. Thy kingdom come. Thy will be

Felix Timmermans

The Coffin Procession

FELIX TIMMERMANS (1886-1947) *was extremely popular in his day – not just in his native Belgium, but also worldwide – for his often lighthearted, rural-themed fiction, including* Pallieter (1916), *an uplifting book that was seen as an antidote to the grim misery of the World War One years. Curiously, though, at the beginning of his career, his outlook rendered rather pessimistic by a near-death battle with a serious illness, he penned a number of highly gloomy and macabre tales reminiscent of Poe. Several of these were featured in his collection* Intimations of Death (1910) *(published in English for the first time by Valancourt in 2019). 'The Coffin Procession' appeared in a 1924 collection by Timmermans and revisits the morbid themes of his earliest work. This is its first English-language appearance.*

THAT WINTER, WHEN HE WAS LIVING IN BORGERHOUT (he lived now in the Sint-Andries neighborhood), Piet Lawijd had promised that if his little Rose might be cured of her scarlet fever, he would make a pilgrimage on foot to Scherpenheuvel and there would make an offering of his dead wife's gold earrings and ten francs to the miracle-working statue of the Madonna.

The child was cured. Piet was firmly convinced that it was his promise that had brought about the miracle. And soon the little girl was playing once again in the street, in the clamor of the fertile, noisy neighborhood.

May, the month of Our Lady, came with its long days and blue skies, and the pilgrims went to the holy places, like Averbode, Scherpenheuvel, Edeghem, Lisp, and anywhere where there was a well-known statue of the Madonna to worship and call upon.

Piet Lawijd had forgotten his promise.

He toiled all day long at making shoes in his back room, behind the red geraniums and purple fuchsias that stood before the open window. He had to work hard to bring up his four children. He had no desire to remarry. His wife had been constantly sick for two years; he'd had his fill, he'd had enough.

Now and then he took a short break to watch his fancy pigeons or to look at his flowers by the little window, and on Sundays and Mondays he played cards from morning till night at the inn or on the doorstep of his house. You couldn't find a better player at klaberjass. He loved his children too much to let them want for anything, and only seldom was he able to eat until his own belly was good and full. But if the opportunity presented itself, like on Saint Crispin's day, he would stand aside for no man and would shovel down his rabbit with four pounds of potatoes like it was nothing.

But Piet Lawijd had forgotten his promise.

Yet one Monday evening his young daughter came dancing in, carrying a little pennant from Scherpenheuvel.

Piet was really shaken up by it.

'Where did you get that?'

'We practiced the music for the procession to Scherpenheuvel, and I got the little flag from the Pastor.'

Piet thought about his promise.

There was only one Sunday left in May for him to go with the procession to Scherpenheuvel. He could of course go alone, later in June, but alone was *so* alone, ten hours on foot from Antwerp! Prattling and chattering, the time passed quickly, but ten hours without even opening his mouth, no, that was only good for the blind men's pilgrimage.

Maybe put it off until next year? And if little Rose got sick again in the winter? For Piet wasn't at all superstitious, except when it came to death and sickness.

The question was whether there was still a procession going on Sunday, otherwise he could set out on his own.

That same evening he went to Mieke Mumbol, a little old lady who said prayers on commission, sat all day long in the church, and was well informed about the masses, novenas, octaves, holy days, and pilgrimages. He gave the old woman a penny and learned that the following Sunday the Coffin Procession was going to Scherpenheuvel; that was the final one this month, and this year, from Antwerp.

All he had to do was show up at the church of Sint Andries at three o'clock in the morning and join the party of pilgrims.

And on Sunday that's just what he did, without knowing, or asking, or thinking any further about what exactly the Coffin Procession was.

It was four in the morning, the streets were still empty and unobstructed, lonely and silent, and the houses like stone masks, when the procession got underway.

The undersexton went in front with the cross, then two choirboys with the candles, and behind them the band, a few men who'd been scraped together whom you might see again the following day playing at a dance. They played a slow, airy march composed by the sexton of Berlaer, with whose words the hundreds of pilgrims sang along:

> In Lourdes in the mountains
> there appeared in a cave,
> full of riches and luster,
> the mother of God
> Ave, Ave, Ave
> Ave Maria

Piet walked between two women, right behind the musicians, and shyly mumbled along with the song.

Everyone had a little basket or pail with them, well supplied with food and drink.

After the singing, a Hail Mary was said, read by the Pastor himself.

When they came out of the great city, through the Berchem Gate, the large, bright-orange sun shone so intensely over the milky-white landscape that they soon had to cover their eyes with their hands...

They walked now under the shade of two rows of tall trees, and the erratic sunbeams, which fell through the cracks in the foliage and danced up and down on their buttons and their bodies, played tricks on their eyes.

In between two Hail Marys, the woman walking to Piet's right said, after a heavy sigh:

'I'm a little curious who's going to die now.'

'What do you mean, die?' asked Piet.

'Well, yes, someone always dies on this pilgrimage, don't they?'

'I don't understand you,' Piet said, sniffling a little, and opening his eyes wide with fright, for he couldn't bear the thought of death.

'Don't you know that this is the Coffin Procession?... Just look behind you and you'll see the coffin being carried by two men.'

Piet turned around, and standing on his tiptoes, he peered over the hundreds of swaying heads and, indeed, in front of the yellow stagecoach he saw a white coffin dancing above the dark forms of the people.

'And what is that for?' Piet asked, stiff with terror.

'Well, I'll tell you the short version,' said the woman, but she told him the long one instead, how over the course of many years someone always died on this pilgrimage, and when people came to feel that this had to happen, that it was unavoidable, they had started bringing a coffin along with them, to make it easier to transport the dead person back home.

'Then why do you go with them, and why do the others go?' asked Piet, a shiver running through his body.

'Because of the great merit,' said the woman, 'there is, after all, more merit in taking part in a procession in which someone must die, whether it's me, you, or someone else, than in some other, ordinary procession.'

'Yes, there's more merit in it,' thought Piet, but he didn't say it. He chewed a wad of tobacco to calm his frightened nerves, and he started to think in a deathly terrified way about the procession and its obligatory death, beginning with: 'If I had known that, I would have gone with another procession, for that death could befall me just as easily as someone else,' and ending with, 'then I'll go on my own. After all, I didn't promise to be brought home between four planks of wood. I promised to make the pilgrimage on foot, on foot,' he especially emphasized 'on foot' and added, 'and to come back on foot as well! . . . I'm sticking to my promise, I'm doing it all on foot!'

And when they came to Lier, he said to the woman: 'I'm just going to go and buy a tart, I'll catch up with you shortly.'

But he only went and stood at the baker's shop window until all the pilgrims had passed by. He let the procession go on, and when they had disappeared over the tall bridge, he said: 'I'll just wait half an hour or so, otherwise I'll catch up with them again.' He wanted to put as much distance between himself and the procession as possible, as if to make clear to the invisible powers that he was no part of it, so that he wouldn't wind up in the coffin by mistake. 'I have nothing, nothing whatsoever to do with that procession,' he said with decision, and so as not to be bored during that half hour, he stepped inside a little inn, 'The Open House'. But the people there were playing cards just then, and presently he stood watching with his pint in his hand, and he forgot about the pilgrimage, got caught up in the card game, gave advice after each hand, and all of the men thought: that must be a good card player, and when the one who had lost the most money stood up, he took his place, and they played, earnestly, solemnly, full of silence and contemplation, until at the end of the game everyone shot up in amazement, and the players and the onlookers called out at the top of their voices, so that the tavern sang with the noise like a glass goblet.

Other players joined in, the best were called to play, but Piet won, won almost continuously, and none of them could do anything other than praise him. And Piet grew red-faced from glory and from the beer. More money was wagered, and each man played with a pounding heart and the tips of their noses white with emotion. The men stood around them in a tight, thick circle, with their pint glasses in their hands. They forgot their beers and their Sunday cigars.

Women came to call their husbands to eat, but the men snarled them away, or else the women came to join in watching and forgot about eating too.

It was one o'clock in the afternoon, and it was only with the cry that, 'The pigeons are there! they're there! At Teresa and Louis's son Jef's place, his witzwing[1] just showed up!' that relief came, and the card game languished.

Now that Piet had a thick sack full of money, he bought a couple of rounds for those who had stuck around, but all that drink tingled like steam heat up to his brain and his thoughts began to dance and spin. And at three p.m. he went outside on his wobbly beer legs and sang, supporting himself by leaning against the houses,

> 'In Lourdes in the mountains
> there appeared in a cave. . . .'

and thinking that he was going towards Scherpenheuvel, he set out in the direction of Antwerp, in the hope of finding

[1] A particular variety of fancy pigeon. The reference is to pigeon racing, then a popular practice in Flanders, in which breeders would release the birds – who would travel distances of 100 km or more – then measure how long it took them to return home. Their return after such a long journey was apparently, as here, a source of great local excitement. [Translator's note.]

something good to eat and still to make it to Scherpenheuvel by evening.

The procession had arrived safely in the holy place.

No one had died yet. And in the morning, after the mass and the communion, and after having bought a toy trumpet, a little pennant, cookies, and prints for the children, they once more left the rolling hills, which lie long and blue and supple around Scherpenheuvel.

The music sounded and they rushed through the Lord's Prayer, and fear settled on everyone's heart. Now someone was going to die, and each of them thought: 'It could be me,' and they prayed for it not to be them, and that it might be someone else. And those who walked in front looked behind them to see whether someone back there had died yet, and those in the back craned their necks to see whether in front of them someone's flame of life had been snuffed out, and those in the middle looked both forward and back. And louder, more pleading and more plaintively, did they pray that no one would die.

Death hung over them like an invisible cloud, targeting the one that it wanted, and every heart was pinched by fear to the size of a bean. Their faces were white with terror, and they hastened so as to be home as quickly as possible. That wouldn't help them much, of course, but it nonetheless lowered the chance of death a little. They passed through Aerschot. Not more than two times out of ten did they make it so far without someone having died.

Rikus, the sexton, with his chicken's head on which a single feather blew, who organized the procession and made all the arrangements for the masses, eating, and sleeping, walked in his tight black tailcoat, jittery from head to toe, constantly asking fearfully: 'No one's sick? No one's unwell? Oh, if just for once no one died!' He gave no thought to himself dying, he was of too great importance, for otherwise who would organize the procession?

Aerschot was already far behind them; from atop the last hill they could now see, far in the distance, the pepperpot tower of Lier, and still no one had died.

That had never happened before!

Fear squeezed more and more around their hearts, each of them held his soul in his body with an iron grip. And they raced forth as fast as they could, and no one felt pain in their legs or in their overworked knees. The whole procession was like a balloon that has been blown up too full and for whose approaching burst one sticks one's fingers in one's ears.

There were only two who were not afraid. The sexton, who for today was immortal, and the fat, jolly pastor, who said reassuringly to the people: 'What God keeps is well kept, and if they come for me, I'm ready, so you can feel free to pray that I'm the one they take.'

They came to Lier. As usual, they had to pass through a tight press of people, who always came with big, fearful eyes to watch the Coffin Procession curiously and ask who had died.

And now it was a real disappointment for the people of Lier, when they perceived that no one was dead.

'Should I leave my house unattended,' said Jef Verdicht, the book printer, 'to go and see an empty coffin? I'll stay home this time. I'm sweating like a watering can, and it's just a pilgrimage like any other.'

The happiness of the pilgrims made little cracks in their dark fear, and when they made it back to Oude-God without anyone dying, Rikus waved his long arms in the air like windmill blades and called out, 'We'll ring the bells! We'll light our windows with candles tonight!'

Just yonder was Antwerp!

Still no one dead!

'Faster! Faster!' went from mouth to mouth. And suddenly, because that procession of hundreds of people was like one person, they went faster, faster in order to outwit Death, and they broke out into a run! The undersexton in front with the cross, the two altar boys, the musicians, who weren't playing, the pastor, who had to keep up while at the same time smilingly and sympathetically urging the people to remain calm, and then all the women and men, the crippled, the blind, the lame, they ran, and the two coffin bearers ran, and the stagecoach tottered now behind them at a trot, and those who couldn't walk sat inside it, squashed together like herring in a tin, and some hung from the stairs, and those who couldn't get inside were carried along behind, pulled, dragged.

It was like a hunt after a deer by an invisible hunter. And they ran, just ran, and loudly and confusedly they began saying the Hail Marys, no one could pray one all the way through, and it rose to a cry, a howl.

And the townspeople in their Sunday best, who sat at the outdoor cafés along the Steenweg, drinking or playing cards, or else were bowling, had to laugh at the racing speed of that dressed-up crowd, and yelled, 'Fools! Fools! Fools!'

But when they heard what it was, they too got excited and they ran along with them to see if anyone would die before they reached the Berchem Gate, and there were some who took advantage of this to get out of paying for their beer.

And there was the fortress wall and the Berchem Gate with its bronze lions!

And people collided with each other, stormed through the wide gate, and those within the fortress had soon begun to cry out, to cheer, and to rave with joy. Everyone wanted to get through immediately, they squeezed, they pulled and pushed.

The pastor shouted: 'Now you're going to cause even more deaths yourselves!' A wild, mad desire to stay alive scorched their spirits, they didn't listen, and they gushed through the gate like a bag of peas that is shaken empty. They fell over one another, but they were inside the fortress! and they opened their mouths to cry out with joy.

And there came the packed stagecoach inside the fortress walls! They were saved, no one had died! And the band began to play the 'Flemish Lion' and some knelt and others danced.

The tears streamed down dirty, dusty, sweaty faces. They sang, they cheered. Every one of them was happy, not only because he was not dead, but because no one had lost their life. Unconsciously they felt like one whole, like one body with many limbs, like a chain of brotherhood.

They danced in a circle around the cross, they tossed their hats in the air and swung their canes!

At the pastor's command, the cross bearer started forward and now the pilgrims went arm-in-arm, dancing and singing behind him to the melody of the music:

> Where can we be better off
> than with our best friends.

And in the distance, in the day's fading gold, stood the tarnished green copper of the Sint Andries church tower, black against the sky.

And there were bells in the tower that swung gloomily back and forth, everyone could see it, and everyone could hear it.

'The death bells! The death bells!' they said in astonishment, 'and yet no one died!'

And there was a woman who came to meet the procession and went to the pastor and said something to him.

And the news flew over the heads of the crowd.

Piet Lawijd had died yesterday at an inn, where he had wagered he could eat twenty-four hard boiled eggs.

And soon everyone knew that he had accompanied the procession, but that in Lier he had fled out of fright.

The joy was dissipated at once, and terror struck like flames around their hearts.

Fate itched with cold fingers in their hair.

Translated from the Dutch by James D. Jenkins

John Metcalfe

Time-Fuse

JOHN METCALFE (1891-1965) *is one of a number of highly regarded horror writers of the early 20th century whose works are nonetheless seldom republished and often available only in expensive secondhand copies. His fame rests mainly on two collections of short stories,* The Smoking Leg and Other Stories (1925) *and* Judas and Other Stories (1931), *from which the following tale is taken. We have previously reprinted his brilliant horror novella* The Feasting Dead (1954), *and we included one of his stories, 'No Sin', in Volume 2. We regularly get reader requests for more Metcalfe, so here you go! 'Time-Fuse' (1931) has been reprinted in a couple of anthologies over the years and appeared in Ash-Tree Press's now out-of-print and very expensive 1998 edition of Metcalfe's stories, but seems not to have been reprinted since.*

MISS MOODY, WHEN EDDIE FISK HAD GONE, sat at her table in the sewing-room looking over the papers about Spiritualism which he had left.

She had large, masculine hands, knuckles slightly swollen by rheumatism, and heavy, painstaking thumbs. Her movements, as she shook the papers together into a neat pile on her left and transferred each, as soon as she had glanced through it, to an equally neat pile on her right, were methodical with a sort of restrained hopelessness. Now and again, however, her expression quickened. She breathed noisily and her eyes grew luminous with interest. Mr Fisk had given her an *Occult Review*, some copies of *Light* and a sheaf of propagandist broadsides entitled collectively *The Other Side*. There would not be time for her to do more than skim this literature during the week-end, yet Eddie would unreasonably expect her to know all about it before Monday evening's séance. She frowned vaguely and sighed, laying the last broadside carefully upon the pile. Her face was long, sombre, rather equine in cast, and with a look of despondent fidelity which certainly supported the resemblance to a horse. Mr Fisk, indeed, had made a more recherché comparison. Returning with his brother Gilbert from the north-west of Canada, he had decided that his former landlady reminded him of a bull-moose. Of this Miss Moody had suspected nothing.

Before the War, Eddie and Gilbert, with a third brother, Morris, had been her first 'guests' in the house on Gordon Square. Originally a dressmaker, Miss Moody, on her father's death, had been enabled to lease the entire premises of which she had till then inhabited a single floor, and that the highest and most inconvenient. Reserving these old apartments for her own continued use, she had converted the remainder into a boarding establishment, enlisting in this venture the cooperation of her widowed sister, Janet Phillimore, who performed the offices of cook. During some strenuous but modestly remunerative dozen years the two of them had entertained successfully (as the 'Remarks Book' in the hall would show) more than two thousand gratefully admiring gentlemen, and – by exception only it would seem, the difference in the totals being so pronounced – close on one hundred of their wives and families.

For 'Gentlemen,' indeed, Miss Moody's preference was fixed. She was large-hearted, awkward, incapable of finesse or any shade of cattiness. Her boarders, beginning usually by laughing at her raw-boned frame and at that curious, dark-muzzled looking face of hers, would end by feeling for her something like affection, at the least, respect. 'A good sort,' 'A good creature,' 'One of the best.' . . . A few of them, like the brothers Fisk, would even call her 'Ellen' and be admitted to the intimacy of the upper floor where she had practised, long ago, her trade of dressmaking. Here, in the sitting-room, there still remained a sewing-machine, and, by the window-seat, a pair of dress forms. These latter were a standing joke between Miss Moody and her visitors. Eddie, particularly, was used to swear at them. Their extreme air of tepid ladylikeness extending upwards till the neck was reached, but ending there in neuter horror of a black polished knob, would almost always move him to profanity. Janet, whilst generally approving of her sister's friends, could wish that Eddie's language were a little more restrained and, a more serious count, that he would cease to worry Ellen with those everlasting trashy books...

Unitarianism, Theosophy, the Ethical Church, Vegetarianism, the Yogi breathing system, Taoism and now Spiritism. Ellen was always getting bitten by the virus of some new and foolish cult and mazing her poor wits with it. She was vulnerable to strange religions as other people are to measles or to chickenpox, and Eddie, far from checking her or talking sensibly, persisted, on the contrary, in humouring her fantastic whims. He would laugh almost openly at all these fads himself, yet by some curious quirk of character appeared to find amusement in making her their dupe. Ellen meanwhile continued, muddled, yet dumbly confident of 'something in' these far-fetched creeds, constantly being disappointed in each one yet always hopefully proceeding to the next.

For Gilbert, Janet had far greater tolerance. Gilbert was tall, commanding, with a hearty breeziness, 'much more of a man,' she thought, than Eddie, who behaved clownishly and had a reedy voice. Neither Eddie nor Gilbert were 'boarders' any longer, having embarked on business in a hide and tannery concern which lay too far away at Kennington. Both of them, however, would drop in every now and then as time and opportunities allowed. Eddie especially, since he had taken up with Spiritism and found that he had mediumistic powers, was always coming with fresh tracts and booklets to the house.

Of the third brother, Morris, none of them, least of all Miss Moody, cared to speak. Amongst a long and constantly extending series of 'soft spots,' this one, and even after he was dead, remained the softest still. Unconfessedly, it was the obstinately painful memory of Morris Fisk which, more than anything, provided impetus for those researches into Spiritism which Janet so deplored. Morris, quieter than the other two, with a reserve and gentleness of manner likely at first to be mistaken for timidity, had come to say good-bye to Ellen before he went off to the War, and given her his photo. His eyes had held a dumb, startled look of suffering. As he was finally descending the front stairs and passing through the 'lounge' into the hall he had shaken hands with her three times, but whether out of absentmindedness or no she could not quite be sure.

Now, as Miss Moody finished the perusal of her 'literature' and slowly crossed the room to poke the fire, she wondered how it was that Morris had got killed. Nobody knew exactly, or, at any rate, Eddie, when she questioned him, had appeared loth to say. Eddie was disappointing in some ways. After the last séance, held some few days ago and in this very room, Ellen had asked him, had he, perhaps . . . had he got any message? And Eddie had looked curious, confused, almost displeased. Surely that was unreasonable. Surely with that miracle of disappearing flowers fresh in every mind it wasn't so preposterous that she should imagine he had heard from Morris. . . .

It was six o'clock. The March evening was cold. It was getting dark. She would have to go downstairs and look in on Janet in the kitchen. But before descending she returned to the table and glanced once more at one of the leaflets. It was an account of the life and mediumship of Daniel Home. Mr Home, as everybody knew, had been a genuine and wonderfully gifted medium, and carried glowing coals upon his head and held them in his hands. Her eyes lit and her breathing became rapid.

Somehow, though Ellen could not have explained this to herself, she felt that if she, too, could emulate this feat, if she herself could do a thing like that, then something in her brain that troubled her would be resolved and pacified, disproved or proved. She would feel better about Morris Fisk.

II

'Well,' said Janet, 'even if those flowers did vanish, and I'm not actually saying they didn't, what does it prove? It proves they vanished, that's all. And what good does that do? Does it help us to run this boarding-house any better, I should like to know?'

'Oh, but – it proves a lot of things, if you think far enough. It proves...' Ellen hesitated, suddenly losing what it had been in her mind to say. Whenever Janet 'pounced' on her like this she became flustered and unable to go on. She ended lamely: 'It proves that there are other laws we don't know anything about. Eddie was saying that it proved a fourth dimension.'

Janet was shorter than her sister, crisper and sharper tongued, with black hair, thick eyebrows, and a complexion harshly reddened by twelve years of cooking. She removed the stove-lid with a clatter, set a large saucepan in its place, then turned and said contemptuously: 'A fourth dimension, eh? When I can see and smell it I'll believe in it. What does it *do*? If it'd help to keep the oven hot, or stop my face from getting scorched...!'

Miss Moody, unequal to the contest, retreated sadly from the kitchen. Not only was she incapable of reasoning with Janet in these moods, but it was certainly not fitting that such arguments should be conducted before little Agatha, the scullery-maid. Besides, there had been something in her sister's last remarks which curiously discomposed her. It had been funny that she had said that about the fire scorching her!

Supper was over, and Ellen paused for a few moments in the

'lounge' to talk with Mr Brace. The Braces, man and wife, had now been 'permanents' for seven months. Mr Brace was a very old, bald-headed gentleman retired from the retail hosiery profession, but his wife was much younger, with blondined hair, hardly middle-aged, and occasionally quite pretty. Both had been present at the séance.

'Coming upstairs on Monday? Yes, of course we'll come, though, mind you, we don't swallow *all* we're told. Too highty-flighty in his ways, your friend, for me. Too joky. And those disappearing flowers . . . I'm too hardheaded, I suppose. Still, we'll be glad to come.'

Miss Moody passed upstairs to her own floor. The Braces, though still sceptical, were genial and not contemptuous like Janet. Talk with them had somewhat reestablished her. She took up some sewing from a chair and brought it underneath the light. Janet would come up presently to retire for the night, and Agatha, who now 'slept in' on a camp bed in the adjoining room, but for a while she had the evening to herself.

As she sewed, she thought over old Mr Brace's words concerning Eddie. His comments, she regretfully admitted, had upon the whole been just. Eddie, as an advocate, was not convincing. That was his way. His manner was too often flippant and facetious. Yet, if the thing were true, it remained true however Eddie acted, even if he did not entirely believe in it himself. One could have powers of which one was not worthy. But if you *were* sincere, if you *were* worthy, surely that would mean greater power still.

Miss Moody rose to fetch a thimble and caught her reflection in the glass. A darting remembrance of something which Mr Brace had said about her hair distracted her and made her smile. He had made some impudent though evidently complimentary remark for which his wife pretended to rebuke him. 'Goddiver,' what was that? Old sauce-pot – and at his age too! Ellen's hair was copious, brown and lustrous, her single beauty. She patted it, and her smile grew broader, emphasizing large teeth and rather exposed gums. 'Oo, hoo – he has a cheek – but he's a nice old thing!' A short, gruff laugh escaped her, and she performed an awkward pirouetting motion. Occasionally, when unexpected flattery made her bashful, she had a way of flushing suddenly and mildly teetering, tricks which although ingratiating and coquettish in her early girlhood, were now an inappropriate survival.

Presently she resumed her sewing. Up here it was usually very quiet, but to-night there was a wind, sprung up since supper-time, rattling the panes and making curious yawning noises round the eaves. It blew, all at once, down the chimney, puffing a cloud of smoke into the room. An ember fell into the grate. Ellen, sneezing violently, stared at it fixedly some moments. Its bright redness dulled, changed as she watched to a dead grey. Yet it would still be much too hot to touch.

Her thoughts turned once again to Mr Home. What had that booklet said? Though she had only scanned it cursorily she found that she was able to remember certain phrases word for word. 'Home, in the presence of witnesses whose probity and public records placed them beyond suspicion of collusion in any form of trickery, on several occasions thrust his hand amidst the red-hot coals and, withdrawing some of them from the fire, set them upon his head. This amazing performance was attended by no pain or other ill-effects and neither his hands nor scalp showed the slightest trace of any burn.' Miss Moody sighed sharply. Accounts of such an exploit captivated and at the same time terrified her. The mirror before which she had stood a few minutes ago to admire her hair was opposite her still, and for a second she could see a look almost of suffering on her face. To banish it she forced herself to smile, then dropped her glance and shifted her position slightly from the fire.

Faith, it was faith, she knew, that had enabled him to perform miracles like that. With enough faith one could do anything. Even she, Ellen ... Her lips parted and she caught her breath. She felt tortured. 'Oh God, give me faith ... !' That was all right, to pray to God for faith. The Spiritualists believed in Him. But fire – she was more terrified of fire than anything. And Janet's disbelief made it more difficult. It had been Janet all along who had prevented her from being what she might...

Suddenly she started, checking a cry. She had, whilst thinking about Mr Home, mechanically continued sewing, and now her glance, becoming less abstracted, fixed itself in surprise upon her needle. She stared at it frozenly. The threaded eye was visible outside the thumb of her left hand that held her work; the other end, the point, projected perhaps half an inch upon the inner side, towards the fingers.

Then she had pricked herself – driven the needle, seemingly, right through her thumb. Yet she felt nothing. She could not believe it. For some seconds she stared, and then, hesitantly, began to draw the needle out and backwards. Yes, true enough, it must almost have grazed the bone. It was out now, and blood was flowing, though not copiously. How was it that it didn't hurt?

She rose from her chair, conscious all at once of a peculiar numbness. But the numbness was not mere absence of sensation. It was something, a positive something, charging, filling her. She could feel it rapidly invading her, extending itself outwards from the centre of her body towards her head and hands and feet. In stages, like the beating of a pulse or like a clock ... As if, inside of her, numbers were being counted, very quickly, numbers that mounted up a scale to a predestined figure. And there was silence. The noise of the wind in the road had ceased, was lost to her. Within her brain as well was silence, more profound. When the counting was over and the final number reached, the silence would be absolute. Then, Ellen knew, she could do anything.

Now. She bent, put out a hand towards the fire.

She saw her fingers in the flames, moving among the coals.

She pulled out two or three of these, red-hot, transferred them to her other hand. Her sleeves were short, and for a while she drew the embers up and down her lower arms. Finally she pressed them to her cheeks, placed them upon her head.

The door was being slowly pushed ajar. Someone was peering in. Agatha. Miss Moody, though she had not heard the sounds of her approach nor yet her knock, could clearly see, at first, the look of wild incomprehension on her face.

'Come in, Agatha, and shut the door.' Ellen was not sure whether her voice, level and calm and reassuring as she hoped, were audible or no.

Agatha's eyes had now grown wide in horror. She was opening her mouth to scream.

III

Ellen, wrapped in her dressing-gown, was sitting up in bed. It was Sunday morning and nearly eleven o'clock, but she had no intention of rising till the afternoon. Janet, after her first bewildered 'What, not getting up? Do you feel ill?' had gone her way downstairs without another word, probably quite convinced that to account for this unprecedented state of things her sister must have something seriously wrong with her. She had ascended later with the breakfast tray. 'Well, anyhow, your appetite's quite good. It seems I needn't fetch the doctor after all...' She was evidently prepared to be indignant and sarcastic, but on meeting Miss Moody's glance thought better of it. Her own eyes, usually so sharp and menacing under their thick brows, had lowered suddenly as if she were afraid.

No, certainly, Miss Moody didn't need the doctor. All that she wanted now was rest, and leisure to think over what had happened on the previous evening, that miracle of which the only witness had as yet been Agatha, but whose reality would presently be wonderingly admitted by the world. Meanwhile she sat and listened to the church bells ringing down the road, their peals confused and muted, at moments altogether silenced by the still unabated clamour of the wind.

'I, Ellen Moody, am possessed of superhuman powers.' She had tried to explain as much to Agatha when the latter had recovered from her faint, though rather unsuccessfully, she feared. After replacing the embers on the fire she had lifted the little scullery-maid from the floor where she had fallen by the door, laid her upon the sofa and hastened to fetch brandy from the cupboard.

But Agatha, when with difficulty revived, had only stared at her in horror for an instant and then mutely turned away, upon the verge, as was too obvious, of a fresh collapse. She had been sick three times since then, so Ellen learned, but had, it seemed, said nothing of what she had seen to Janet or to anybody else.

That was as well. Janet, though curious as to the cause of Agatha's indisposition, would certainly not credit it if she were told. She had come up, grumblingly, a little later, as Ellen had been getting into bed and rated her for 'pampering' people in hysterics. And now, this morning, left short-handed in the kitchen and with nobody but herself to superintend the running of the whole establishment, her temper would undoubtedly be worse than ever.

But before long Janet would know. She, too, like Agatha, would understand. Not yet, not till to-morrow evening at the séance. Miss Moody raised herself against the pillows, took a long, deep breath. She would attempt nothing till then. That, something told her, would be wise, respectful of the power given her. She must have time to think, to know this different self that now she was, to fit herself again ... And, while she waited, she was anxious to be undisturbed, not have to talk to anyone, not even Agatha. Indeed, for some obscure reason that evaded her, she wanted Agatha the least of all.

Later in the day, after dinner, she got up and came downstairs. There were concerned enquiries from the Braces, from all her other boarders. Had she been ill, and was she better now? Janet, upon the point, she saw, of bursting into protest, looked at her curiously and changed her mind. Ellen knew why. She knew now that she was different. Already they as well could apprehend this difference, all of them. She felt a confident languor, expanding, filling her. She was shining at them, at everybody who came near to her.

Tea over, she once more retired to her bedroom and spent the remainder of the evening in looking over Eddie's papers. Poor Eddie, he was in some ways to be pitied, yet he, too, had powers. She must not forget that. She must be grateful to him even in his ignorance and flippancy, for showing her, for pointing out the path. It was only after she had seen him make those flowers disappear that she had had the faith...

And for the sake of Morris...

She looked at herself intently in the mirror. 'I, Ellen Moody...'

IV

Agatha had packed her trunk and left. Miss Moody could still see her small, scared face as she had passed her on the stairs. Janet had been outraged. What was wrong with the girl? She must be made to stop another week at least, to give notice properly. But Ellen, though she was sorry to see Agatha depart, said no. Let her go. It was no use to keep her if she didn't want to stay.

That had been early in the morning, and now it was afternoon. Monday afternoon, and not so very long before the séance. Miss Moody went about her work as usual, saw that the tea, for such as wanted it, was set out on the little copper-covered tables in the lounge, added accounts, made out a bill or two, and interviewed the plumbers who had come to fix the wash-bowl taps in number eight. At supper she presided with her customary cheerfulness, rallying Mr Brace upon the vaunted 'hardness' of his head. 'Well, well, we'll see. I'm not that bigoted. If the thing's not a fraud I'm quite agreeable to be convinced. Look here – if I could only get a line on Sammy Price, who got his ticket in a motor smash last year ... He owed me forty pound ...'

Old Mr Brace was really terrible, and Ellen should not have encouraged him. His wife didn't like it, nor, it was plain, did Janet, who, though responsible for preparation of the meals, was usually able to sit down to them beside her sister. Her frowns, however, were without effect upon Miss Moody. Ellen had hitherto refrained from talk of Spiritualism or other cults in public, but for to-night felt careless of offence. What if it *were* 'bad taste' or impolitic – what if some of them didn't like it? Perhaps a few, who hadn't heard of it, might become interested, wish to join the séance.

Shortly after half-past eight a thunderous tattoo on the front door, executed in the the rhythm of the 'Policeman's Holiday,' indicated the arrival of Eddie. He entered, carrying a large, box-shaped object, something like a botanical press, bound with two leather straps. When he had exchanged greetings with Miss Moody he humorously extended a little finger towards Mr Brace, who had walked out with her into the hall. Mr Brace, having gravely shaken the finger, tapped on the box. 'Family keeping well I trust, sir?' he enquired waggishly. 'Not giving any trouble?'

Eddie smiled and shook his head. 'No, thank you, Grandad. Family's OK. Sophronia gamma's got a little flighty since she's been acting as control to Gertie Gush the movie star, that's all. Otherwise in the pink.'

Mr Fisk was short, fair and dapper with a tiny blond moustache. He had sharp, restless eyes of a shallow grey and was a little overdressed, wearing a blue silk waistcoat with enamel buttons, and cloth-topped, patent-leather shoes. His feet were very small.

'All of us ready?' he asked Ellen, casting a glance beyond her towards the lounge. 'Gilbert's so sorry that he couldn't come. He's got a cold.'

'Yes, we're all ready.' Miss Moody had turned and made a signalling motion with one hand. Mrs Brace and four or five others had detached themselves with an attempted air of casualness from the remainder of the company and now were wending their way rather sheepishly into the hall. Two of them — gentlemen who had not assisted at the previous séances — Mr Brace introduced very carefully to Mr Fisk, as if he thought that Eddie might explode. Somebody uttered an embarrassed laugh.

'Well, shall we go upstairs?' Miss Moody headed the procession, with Janet, more than usually sour, bringing up the rear. Mr Brace, the irrepressible, offered to carry Eddie's box.

'Oh, no, you don't. My ladies don't like strangers...' Ellen, hearing this badinage behind her, turned and spoke rebukefully. 'Now, please, we must be serious...'

Eddie, as soon as they were all collected in the room, briskly began to tell them off upon his fingers. 'Eight of us, four ladies and four gentlemen. That's very nice. We'll sit the same as we arranged last week, alternately. Miss Moody here, by me, Miss Winter there, then Mr Tharp and Mrs Phillimore... We want another chair or two, I think...' He distributed the company in a circle round the table. 'Now ... well, we might as well begin. P'r'aps Mrs Phillimore would be so good as to turn off the light.'

With the extinction of the light Ellen was conscious of a thrill. It was dark, but not entirely so, for a dull glow shone redly from the fire. Young Mr Simpson, one of the two newcomers, spoke diffidently: 'Hadn't we better put a screen in front? How rapidly the general atmosphere of eeriness had told on him was evident in his voice. His tones were almost reverent.

'Oh no, it's not enough to matter ... but we ought really

to have music, a piano or something ... I get started easier ... it's a pity ...' Mr Brace gave a sudden cough, and then, as if afraid that it had sounded sceptical, repeated it more sympathetically. Miss Moody was just able to see Eddie's face. Though not, as he was careful to explain, a 'trance' medium in the strictest sense, it was his custom to 'go off' a little at the commencement of a séance. He had now closed his eyes, was fidgeting upon his chair. 'You know, it takes a little while to come. Some nights I'm good and some I'm bad. It all depends upon conditions. I mean, it's more than simply turning on a tap...' Ellen had heard all these preliminary remarks before. Presently he would begin to sway slightly, and his thin voice would take on a sing-song quality. Yes, it was getting like that now.

'Oh ...' He sat up, drew in his breath sharply. 'Mrs Brace, do you mind giving me your hand? Thank you, I— The name George is given me. Elderly man, well past the middle age, medium height, eyes very dark ... Passed over several years ago ... I get a fullness here, a sort of tightness, painful...' Eddie had placed his other hand upon his chest. 'Was it pneumonia – or bronchitis?'

'No, lung trouble, consumption. He passed over seven years ago, in 1920.'

'Then you recognize the name and the description?'

'Well, yes, I think so. Only his name was Geoffrey – and he wasn't very old.'

'An elder brother, perhaps?'

'Well, no,' said Mrs Brace, confused, 'he was younger, a younger brother ...' After a short pause she enquired timidly, 'Does he ... is there any message?'

'Yes,' replied Eddie. 'He says ... wait, I must catch it clearly – he says, what you are passing through just now is only for a time, not long. You are to have strength and courage.'

'Oh, thank you.' Mrs Brace withdrew her hand, retired gratefully into obscurity.

It went on. Next Mr Simpson, after him Miss Winter, Mr Brace ... Eddie had messages to-night it seemed for everyone but Ellen and her sister. That there were none for her Miss Moody was not sorry. Usually she would be breathlessly absorbed in all that Mr Fisk would say and do, but now ... She was nervous, impatient, wished he would 'get on.' She was looking forward to and yet half dreading what was to happen after he had done. None of them knew, not Janet and not Eddie, what she had got in store. Morris perhaps? Her throat grew dry. Perhaps ... ?

Mr Fisk was talking, this time in his natural voice. The light had been turned on, and he was smiling guardedly, wiping his face at intervals with a blue handkerchief. The sitting had exhausted him. Janet, endeavouring to look at him sarcastically, blinked suddenly and gave a formidable sneeze.

'And now,' said Eddie, 'we're just going to try the slate trick.'

Ellen wished that he would not be so profane, and that his manner and appearance were less 'chirpy,' sparrow-like. Of course, his calling things a 'trick' was just his way, but Mr Brace, for instance – he would be certain not to understand. He would be sure to think ...

Mr Brace, however, had to confess himself completely mystified. From his box Eddie produced what seemed to be an ordinary school slate and fragment of slate pencil. He and Mr Brace, now sitting opposite each other, held up the slate securely pressed against the table's under side, the pencil having first been introduced between the two. Mr Simpson had previously been persuaded to write a 'question' on a slip of paper which he had folded up and put into his pocket. After a few moments a faint scratching sound was heard which continued for perhaps half a minute. When it ceased the slate was removed and the writing on it compared with that upon the paper. Mr Simpson's question had been, trivially, 'How many buttons are there on my suit?' to which the answer ran: 'Add the numbers of the year of your birth.' As Mr Simpson had been born in 1899 this gave the total twenty-seven, a figure which, if trousers were included, he admitted to be accurate.

'There then,' said Eddie, beaming, 'you got more than you asked for, didn't you? You see, it's extra proof to answer you that way. None of us knew the year when you were born.'

''M,' muttered Mr Brace. 'It's very clever, very clever. I'll admit you've got me shaky. And it's been most interesting. I'm sure we're all exceedingly obliged.'

'Oh, but,' said Ellen. 'We aren't going yet. It's hardly half-past nine. I was so hoping that you'd do the flower tr— experiment again.'

She flushed, annoyed that she herself had barely escaped saying 'trick'. But that was Eddie's fault. 'I'm sure we've lots of time,' she went on hastily to cover her confusion, 'and I was so looking forward . . .'

In her own voice she caught a strange anxiety, excitement. Eddie, too, for some reason, appeared all at once put out of countenance and ruffled, unwilling to comply with her request. ''Fraid it'll make me a bit late. You know I'm right across the river now.'

V

Ellen faced him, feeling her cheeks grow hot. 'Oh, but it wouldn't take so long as that. Hardly a minute.'

She wondered. Why did she insist so vehemently? Was it because that miracle of disappearing flowers had first persuaded and convinced her, given her the faith to do what she herself had done two days ago?

Eddie was still demurring. 'Rather rushed to-night. There's Gilbert ill. And then, I haven't got the apparatus handy . . .'

'Tut, tut,' said Mr Brace, although benevolently, 'his "apparatus"! Really, that sounds bad.'

'Nonsense,' said Eddie, reddening. 'We wanted apparatus

for the thing we did just now, if you call slates and pencils apparatus. That doesn't make it any less — less genuine. Next time we'll do the flower stunt and everything. And the direct voice, too — if you don't call a trumpet too much of an apparatus.'

' 'M,' said Mr Brace again, now slightly less benevolent and evidently inclined to grow contentious. 'All right, young man. No doubt you know what programme suits you best. But all the same if I remember right all that you needed when you worked that little piece of mystery before was just an ordinary cut-glass vase and three geraniums. At least, that's all that anybody *saw* . . .'

'All right!' Eddie was now exasperated, smiling but finding it a little difficult to keep his temper. 'Of course . . . if you intend to *challenge* me . . . Of course, to you, I suppose, there's nothing in conditions. A vase is just a vase and flowers flowers . . . I'll try it, but if it doesn't happen to come off, then don't blame me.'

He had resumed his seat, lips pursed. Janet had brought a vase containing six carnations from the adjoining room.

'Lights out, I s'pose?' said Mr Brace sardonically.

'Yes, please, at first.'

Darkness, and once again, for Ellen, that peculiar thrill. She was still next to Eddie, could see his lowered profile, dimly, at intervals, infer the motions of his hands. He was, she thought, somehow a little nervous, and this troubled her, made her more anxious that he should succeed. Then Mr Brace would see! And she — she too would then have strength to do as she had planned, repeat *her* miracle before them all, play with the red-hot coals. Her breath caught chokingly.

The seconds passed. What was delaying Eddie? On the last occasion, she remembered, as soon as the lights were turned on, the flowers had been discovered, no longer in the vase, but shut up in her workbox in a far corner of the room. Then, in the sight of all, they had, as they were watching, disappeared.

They were there, and then they were just not there. It was a double wonder.

But to-night the first part seemed to take much longer. That was Mr Brace's fault for talking as he had and making the conditions adverse. Presently, however, he would be confounded as before, and —

Her thought halted abruptly, went on again next instant with distressed intentness. Uncanniness, now mounting to acute alarm, had for some seconds anticipated recognition of its cause. Then, when she understood, her heart turned over sickly. She felt faint. It was Eddie. Something was wrong. She heard the noise of shivered glass, an object falling to the floor, a muttered curse. Oh, *what was Eddie doing? What —*

The light! Suddenly and like a blow, blinding, making them wince, exclaim. Janet, who had crept to the switch and turned it on, standing indignant, pointing at the broken vase. Her voice, trembling with scorn: 'Faker! There, that'll show you all. The faker! Look at him!'

And Eddie — Eddie discovered, groping, searching apparently beneath the table for whatever he had dropped, emerging presently, his face white and dejected as if he were about to cry, blinking and stammering ... 'There, then, just look at him! Look at that thread wound round his hand! I'm sorry to have had to do a thing like this ...'

But it was not upon the abject spectacle of Eddie, however dismally engrossing, that their attention remained fixed for long. Something far worse and far more discomposing than the belated and well-merited exposure of a blundering charlatan was going forward in this room. It was at Ellen that they looked.

Miss Moody had risen from her chair, her mouth open, though for a time no sound emerged. Terror or pain or both seemed to have checked her speech. She held up her arms, swayed, tottering. At last her voice was heard, ending upon a shriek: 'Fire ... the fire ... !'

To Janet only did her words appear to carry any meaning. 'Quick, she's – she must have burnt herself somehow...' She sprang across the room towards her sister, dragging the cloth off the table on her way and sending Eddie's paraphernalia crashing to the floor. 'Run quick – the tablecloth's no good – too thin – blankets – in the next room – she's burnt herself!'

Burnt! Ellen, before her anguish had become too great, could realize that. Ellen alone – it might be Agatha as well if she were here – could for some tortured seconds understand ... The fire! That fire she had scorned two days ago now had its way with her, unchecked. Upon her face, her head, her arms and hands, wherever she had held the coals, the scars appeared. Her flesh was blackening. She could apprehend no more. Her mind faded, dissolved in an inordinate agony. She began to run, wildly, in small circles, hither and thither, trying to cool herself, uttering shriek upon shriek.

'Blankets – fetch *blankets*!' Finally, perceiving that the rest were still too stunned and horror-struck to be of any help, Janet was forced to run for them herself into the bedroom, tear them from off the bed. But, though she made what speed of it she could, returning with a couple almost instantly, her efforts were in vain.

She was, she found, too late. The screams that filled the room a moment since had ceased.

Francis King

A Scent of Mimosa

Beryl Bainbridge hailed FRANCIS KING *(1923-2011) as 'one of our great writers, of the calibre of Graham Greene and Nabokov'. King, a modest man, was embarrassed by the blurb and hated to see it emblazoned on his books. He was prolific, publishing some fifty volumes over an incredible career that spanned from 1946 to 2009. At his best, as in novels like the gay-themed* Never Again *(1947) and* An Air that Kills *(1948), both republished by Valancourt, and in later books like* A Domestic Animal *(1970) and the horror-tinged* Act of Darkness *(1983), King is very good indeed and deserves a much wider readership and recognition. But though best known as a 'serious' novelist and a theatre critic, King was also sometimes drawn to the horrific and macabre: the ISFDB database credits him with eight horror stories. One of these, 'School Crossing', appeared in Volume 1. The story behind the following tale is an interesting one. In 1975, London's* The Times *newspaper held a ghost story contest, receiving thousands of entries. The judging panel was formidable: the famed comic novelist Kingsley Amis,* Strangers on a Train *and* The Talented Mr Ripley *author Patricia Highsmith, and Hammer Horror great Christopher Lee. 'A Scent of Mimosa' took second prize in the contest. This very quiet, subtle ghost story involves the writer Katherine Mansfield (1888-1923) and the writing prize named in her honor, which (fun trivia fact) Francis King had also won.*

I T WAS LONG PAST MIDNIGHT when the municipal Citroën dumped the four of them outside the Menton hotel. Tom, the youngest and most assertive of the Katherine Mansfield

Prize judges, grabbed Lenore's arm and helped her up the steps. It was Lenore, thirtyish and thinnish, who had that year won the prize, given by the municipality. Though they had never met until the start of their journey out to the South of France together, he was always touching her, as though to communicate to her some assurance, at the nature of which she could still only guess. As they followed behind, Theo and Lucy, the other two judges, maintained a cautious distance from each other. There had been some acrimony, many years before, about an unsigned review in *The Times Literary Supplement*. Lenore could no longer even remember which of the two had written it and which had felt aggrieved.

In the hall they all stared at each other, like bewildered strangers wondering what they were doing in each other's company so late at night, in an unknown hotel, in a foreign town.

Tom broke the silence, swaying back and forth on his tiny feet: 'Well, what's the programme for tomorrow? Christ, I'm tired!'

Lucy hunted for one of three or four minuscule, lace-fringed handkerchiefs in the crocodile bag that dangled from her wrist. When travelling with her stockbroker husband, she was used to more luxurious hotels, more powerful cars and more amusing company. 'Apparently we're going to be taken up into the mountains for another banquet.' She held the handkerchief to the tip of her sharp nose and gave a little sniff.

Theo, who was almost as drunk as Tom, wailed, 'Oh, God! Altitude and hairpin bends always make me sick.'

'Well, there'll be plenty of both tomorrow,' Lucy replied, with some relish.

Lenore gazed down at the key that she was balancing on her palm. 'The Ambassador told me that he would be placing a wreath on some local war-memorial. Tomorrow's armistice-day, isn't it?'

Lucy, who had been affronted that the prizewinner and not

she had been seated on the New Zealand Ambassador's right, exclaimed, 'What a dreadfully boring man! Nice, but oh so boring!'

'Oh, I thought him rather interesting.' Lenore was still secretly both frightened and envious of Lucy, who was older, much more successful and much richer than herself. 'Some young New Zealander's going to meet us up there, the Ambassador told me. In the village. He's coming specially for the Katherine Mansfield celebrations.'

'I suppose if your country's produced only one writer of any note, you're bound to make a fuss of her,' Tom commented.

'Well, we'd better get some sleep. If we can.' Lucy began to walk towards the lift. 'The beds here are horribly hard and lumpy.'

Tom again held Lenore by the arm, as he shepherded her towards the small, gilded cage. So close, she could smell the alcohol heavy on his breath.

Lucy got out first, since on their arrival together she had managed to secure for herself the only room on the first floor with a balcony over the bay. Bowing to Lenore, she sang out, 'Bonne nuit, Madame la Lauréate!'

Lenore gave a small, embarrassed laugh. 'Goodnight, Lucy!'

Theo got out at the next floor, tripping and all but falling flat, with only Tom's arm to save him. He began to waddle off down the corridor; then turned as the lift-gates were closing. 'Bonne nuit, Madame la Lauréate!'

Lenore and Tom walked down their corridor, his hand again at her elbow, as though once more to assure her and perhaps also himself of something that he could not or dared not put into words. They came to her door.

'Well ...' He released her and clumsily she stopped and inserted the key. 'Tomorrow we'll drive up into the mountains and watch poor Theo being car-sick and meet the Ambassador's young New Zealander. And, of course, hear lots and lots of speeches.'

She opened the door; and at once, as though frightened that she would ask him in, he backed away.

'Well, bonne nuit, Madame la Lauréate!'

'Bonne nuit, Monsieur le Juge!'

She shut the door and leant against it, feeling the wood hard against her shoulder-blades. Her head was throbbing from too much food and drink, too much noise and too much French, and her mouth felt dry and sour. What would each of the others be doing now that they had separated? She began to speculate. Well, Lucy would no doubt be taking great care of each garment as she removed it; and then she would take equal care of her face, patting and smoothing, smoothing and patting. Theo, drunken and dishevelled, his tiny eyes bleary and his tie askew, would perch himself on a straight-backed chair – he always seemed masochistically determined to inflict the maximum of discomfort on himself – and would then start work on the pile of postcards that he had rushed out to buy as soon as they had been shown into their rooms. The postcards would, of course, arrive in England long after his return. Someone had told Lenore that he had a wife much older than himself and a horde of children and step-children – six? seven? eight? – to all of whom he was sentimentally devoted. And Tom? Tom, she decided after some deliberation, would walk along to his room, wait there for a few minutes and then take the lift downstairs again and go out into the night, wandering the autumnal streets in search of a – well, what? She did not know, not yet; any more than she knew the nature of the assurance that constant touching was designed to convey.

The bed was soft, not hard and lumpy at all as Lucy had complained, too soft, so that its swaying was almost nauseating. Perhaps poor Theo would be bed-sick and would have to take to the floor ... She shut her eyes and yawned and yawned again ... She was asleep.

When she awoke, it seemed as if many hours had passed, even though the dark of the room was still impenetrable.

Her body was on fire, the sweat pouring off it, her head was throbbing and she had an excruciating pain, just under her right ribs, as though a knife had been inserted there and was now being twisted round and round. The central heating was always turned too high in these continental hotels; and after having eaten and drunk so much, she ought not to be surprised at an attack of acute indigestion. She threw back the sheet and duvet and then, after lying for a while uncovered with none of the expected coolness, she switched on the bedside lamp and dragged herself off the bed. For a long time she struggled with the regulator of the radiator that ran the whole length of the window; but the effort only made her sweat the more, it would not budge. She would have to open the window instead. Again she struggled; and at last the square of glass screeched along its groove and she felt the icy air enfolding her body.

From her suitcase she fetched a tube of Alka-Seltzer and padded into the bathroom. It was as she was dropping two of the tablets into a tumbler of water, the only light coming through the half-open door behind her, that suddenly she felt a strange tickling at the back of her throat, as though a feather had lodged there, coughed, coughed again, and then effortlessly began spitting, spitting, spitting.

Giddy and feeling sick, the sweat now chill on her forehead and bare arms, she stared down at the blood that had spattered the porcelain of the basin and was even dripping from one of the taps. She felt that she was about to faint and staggered back into the bedroom, to fall diagonally across the bed, her cheek pressed against the thrown-back duvet. Oh God, oh God . . . She must have had some kind of haemorrhage.

She lay there, shivering, for a while. She would have to see a doctor. But how could she call one at this hour? The best thing would be to go along to the room of one of the others. But she shrank from appealing to either Lucy or Tom. It would have to be Theo.

She got off the bed, still feeling giddy, sick and weak, and went back into the bathroom to wash away the blood. This time she turned on the light. The two tablets of Alka Seltzer were now dissolved; but, with an extraordinary hyperaesthesia, she could hear the water fizzing even when she was still far away from it. She approached the basin slowly, fearful of what she would find in it: the trails and spatters of blood on the glistening porcelain and over the tap. But when she was above the basin and forced her eyes down, there was, amazingly, nothing there, nothing there at all. Porcelain and tap were both as clean as she had left them after brushing her teeth.

It was cold and damp by the mountain war-memorial, a lichen-covered obelisk, one end sunk into the turf, with a stone shield attached, bearing names that for the most part were Italian, not French. The Mayor, cheeks scarlet from the many toasts at the banquet and medals dangling from his scuffed blue-serge suit, stood before it and bellowed out an oration to which Lenore did not listen, her gaze tracking back and forth among the faces, mostly middle-aged and brooding, of the handful of villagers huddled about her. Lucy had retreated into the back of the municipal Citroën, saying that she was certainly not going to risk a cold just before she and her husband were due to set off for the Caribbean on a holiday. Theo was holding a handkerchief to his chin, as though he had an attack of toothache, his tiny eyes rheumy and bloodshot. Tom, who had been chatting to their dapper young chauffeur in his excellent French, now stood beside the man, faintly smirking.

At last the oration ended and the Ambassador, grizzled, grey-faced and grave, walked forward with his wreath, stooped and placed it against the tilted obelisk. An improbable girl bugler, in white boots and a mini-skirt that revealed plump knees at the gap between them, stepped proudly forward and the valedictory notes volleyed back and forth among the mountains. Again Lenore felt that tickling at the back of her throat; but now it was tears. She always cried easily.

Suddenly she was aware of a smell, bitter and pungent, about her; and she wondered, in surprise, what could be its source. It was too late in the year for the smell to come from any flower at this altitude; and it seemed unlikely that any of the village women – with the possible exception of the girl bugler – would use a perfume so strange and strong. She peered around; and then, turning, saw the tall young man with the mousy, close-cropped hair and the sunburned face, his cheekbones and his nose prominent, who was standing a little apart from the rest of the gathering. A khaki rucksack was propped against one leg. Their eyes met and he smiled and gave a little nod, as though they already knew each other.

The ceremony was over. In twos and threes the people began to drift away, for the most part silent, and silent not so much in grief as in the attempt to recapture its elusive memory. The young man, his rucksack now on his back, was beside her.

'Hello.' The voice was unmistakably antipodean.

'Hello.'

'You won the prize.' It was not a question.

'By some marvellous fluke. I've never had any luck in my life before. Everything I've achieved, I've had to struggle for.' She gave an involuntary shudder, feeling the cold and damp insinuate themselves through the thickness of her topcoat. 'You must be the New Zealander.'

'*The* New Zealander? Well, *a* New Zealander.'

'We heard that you were coming.'

'I always try to come.'

The Ambassador was approaching, still grey-faced and grave. 'Your New Zealander has arrived,' Lenore called out to him.

'*My* New Zealander?' He looked at the young man, who held out his hand. The Ambassador took it. 'So you're from back home?'

The young man nodded, at once friendly and remote. 'Wellington.'

'What brings you here?'

'I wanted to be present at the ceremonies. I was telling Miss Marlow, I always have been.'

'Then you're a fan of K.M.?'

'Oh, yes.'

Lenore was becoming increasingly bewildered. She turned to the Ambassador. 'But didn't you say . . . ? Didn't you tell me last night – at the banquet – that you were expecting a New Zealander?'

'I?'

'Yes, surely . . .'

'But I'd no idea that this young man would turn up, none at all.'

'But I'm sure . . . Didn't you . . . ?'

'We've never set eyes on each other. And we know nothing about each other. Do we?' He appealed to the other man.

'Nothing at all.'

'Anyway' – cold and tired, the Ambassador began to move away – 'it's been nice to meet you. What's your name?'

'Leslie.' It might have been either surname or Christian name.

'We'll be seeing you again?'

'Oh, yes. I'll be at the prizegiving ceremony tomorrow. As I said, I've been at every one.'

Lenore and the young man were now alone by the lopsided war-memorial. Far down the road she could make out Theo, shapeless in his ancient overcoat, a cap pulled down over his bulging forehead, as he urinated against a tree that soared up into the gathering mist and darkness. Tom was climbing into the car beside Lucy; Lenore could hear his laugh, strangely loud.

'How are you going to get down to Menton? Would you like me to ask if we can give you a lift?'

'Oh, that's very kind of you. But I think I'd like to stay here a little longer.'

'Here?' She could not imagine why anyone should wish to stay on in this cramped, craggy village, with all the inhabitants drifting back into their homes and nothing to see in the coagulating mist and dark and nothing to do.

He nodded. 'She came up here. She was driven up here by Connie and Jennie.'

'Oh, yes, they were the ones who let her the Villa Isola Bella, weren't they? Connie was the aunt.'

'Well, cousin really.'

'I didn't know she'd ever been in this village. I know the journals and the letters pretty well but obviously not as well as you.' Suddenly she did not wish to let him go; this imminent parting from a total stranger had become like the resurgence of some deep-seated, long-forgotten sorrow. 'Can't we really give you a lift? We can squeeze you into our car.'

He shook his head. 'I want to stay here a little. But I'll be down. We'll meet again?'

'Perhaps this evening you might join us for dinner? We have the evening free and we thought that we might all go to a fish-restaurant in Monte Carlo. Lucy – she's one of the judges – says that Somerset Maugham once took her there and it was absolutely fabulous.' 'Fabulous' was not Lenore's kind of word; it was Lucy's. 'Do try to join us.'

'Perhaps.'

'Please! We'll be leaving the hotel at about eight-thirty. So just come there before that. It's the Hôtel du Parc. Do you know where it is?'

He nodded.

'How will you get down to Menton? There can't be a bus now.'

'Oh, I'll manage.'

'Lenore! Time we started back!' It was Tom's peremptory voice.

'I must go. They're getting impatient. Please come this evening.'

He raised his hand as she hurried away from him, in what was half a wave and half a salute. Then he remained standing motionless beside the war-memorial.

Lucy said fretfully, 'We want to get down the mountain before this mist really thickens.'

'I'm sorry. But that was... He was from New Zealand.'

'Is that the one you told us about last night?' Theo asked, wiping with a soiled handkerchief at eyes still streaming from the cold.

Lenore nodded. 'Yes, I did tell you about him, didn't I?' She all but added, 'But the funny thing is that the Ambassador pretended that he'd said nothing to me at all about his coming.' Then something made her check herself.

It was as though, walking over sunlit fields, she had all at once unexpectedly found ahead of her a dark and dense wood; had hesitated whether to enter it or not; and had then turned and in panic retraced her steps.

'Well, he's obviously not coming.' Lucy drew her chinchilla coat up over her shoulders and got to her feet. The two men also rose.

Lenore sighed. 'No, I suppose not.'

'He probably decided there were more amusing things for a young man to do on the Côte,' Theo said.

'I can think of less amusing things too,' Lucy retorted tartly.

'Perhaps he hadn't got the money for a slap-up meal.'

Of course, of course! Tom was right. Lenore saw it now. What she should have said was, 'You must be my guest, because I want to spend some of my prize-money in celebration,' or something of that kind. She had spoken of the 'fabulous' restaurant to which Lucy had been taken by Maugham – enough to put off anyone who was travelling on a slender budget. Of course!

Once again Tom tried to take her arm as they emerged into

the soft November air; but this time she pulled free with a sharp, impatient jerk.

The next morning they were driven out to Isola Bella, the villa on the steep hill where Katherine Mansfield had lived for nine months in a fever of illness and activity. The villa itself was occupied; but the municipality had made over a room on the lowest of its three levels into a shrine. A bearded French critic, who was regarded as an authority on the English writer, explained to Lenore that an outhouse had been converted into a lavatory and shower, in the hope that some other English writer might soon be installed in what was, in effect, a tiny apartment.

'But Katherine Mansfield herself never lived here?'

He hesitated between truth and his loyalty to his hosts. Then: 'Well, no,' he agreed in his excellent English. 'Katherine lived above.' (He invariably referred to the writer merely by her Christian name).

'And probably she never even came down here?'

Again he hesitated. 'Possibly not.'

Lenore wandered away from the rest of the party, up the hill to the rusty gates that led to the main part of the house. Ahead of her, as she peered through the curlicues of wrought iron, stretched the terrace on which the invalid would lie out for most of the day on a chaise-longue spread with a kaross made of flying-squirrel skins brought home from Africa by her father. Oh, and there were the mimosa trees, like elongated ferns – Katherine Mansfield had described how she would lie awake at break of day and watch the shafts of the rising sun shimmer through them. All at once, Lenore could smell the tiny yellow flowers still hanging from the fragile racemes. Though infinitely fainter, a mere ghost, it was none the less that same odour, pungent and bitter, that had enveloped her up in the mountains. But surely, so high up in the mountains, no mimosa could grow or, if it did, could come to bloom in November? As she breathed in the scent, deeper and deeper until her lungs began to ache with it as they had done that first night in the hotel, she thought once again of the New Zealander and wondered what had happened to him. She had hoped to see him in the town early that morning as she had wandered alone about it, pretending that she was in quest of presents but in reality in quest of him; but he had been nowhere. And now he had not turned up at the villa, as she had also hoped that he would do. Perhaps he had already moved on, with his exiguous rucksack, farther up the coast; perhaps she would never see him again.

Suddenly she wanted a spray of the mimosa. She rattled the gate and the rusty padlock swung from side to side, with a dry sound of scraping against the bars. The occupiers of the house must be away. But she tugged at the bell, hearing it tinkle from somewhere out of sight. No one came. She thought, If he were here, he could climb over for me. He'd find some way. She hoisted herself up with both hands, feeling the flaking metal graze a palm. But it was useless.

'Can I help madame?'

It was the French critic, stroking his beard with a narrow, nicotine-stained hand.

Lenore explained what she wanted; and then he too tugged at the bell-pull and even shouted out in French. No one came. Oddly, she could no longer smell that pungent, bitter odour, not since he had come.

He shrugged. 'I'm afraid that I am too old and too fat to climb over for you. Perhaps if you come tomorrow, the owners will be here.'

'We're leaving tomorrow morning.'

'Then . . .' Again he shrugged. When he had first seen her, he had thought her a dowdy, insignificant little woman, and had hardly bothered to speak to her. But now he experienced a sudden pull, as though a boat in which he had long been becalmed had all at once felt the tug and sweep of the tide.

Now he too grabbed her arm just above the elbow, as Tom had kept on doing until that rebuff of the previous night. 'Let me assist you down the hill.' How thin the arm was, how pathetically thin and fragile – the arm of a child or invalid. He felt excited at the contact.

'I have given most of my life to Katherine,' he told her, as they began to descend. It was not strictly true, since he had given much of his life to other things: to the editing of a magazine, to the collection of Chinese works of art, to women, to eating and drinking. But at that moment, when his fingers felt the delicate bone inside its envelope of flesh, he not only wished that it had been so but believed that it had been so. 'In a strange way you remind me of her, you know.'

In the town hall the audience for the prize-giving ceremony was composed almost entirely of elderly men in dark suits and elderly women in hats. Lenore had been told that she would have to make a small speech of thanks in French after Lucy had spoken, also in French, on behalf of the judges. Lenore had never made a speech in her life, let alone a speech in French, and she dreaded the ordeal. The hall was stuffy, its radiators too hot to touch even on this autumn day. She felt headachy, sweaty and vaguely sick, as she listened, in a kind of trance, first to the orotund platitudes of the Mayor, then to the clipped phrases of the Ambassador and finally to Lucy's few witty, lucid comments. In rising panic she thought, If he were here, if only he were here! In one hand she was clutching the typescript, the French of which Lucy had corrected for her.

She heard her name and then one of the French officials was giving her a little push from behind, his hand to her shoulder. She rose and, as she did so, she felt the room revolve first gently and then faster and faster around her. She clutched the back of her chair, staring up at the face of the Mayor on the dais above her. All at once she could smell, far stronger than ever before, that pungent, bitter odour of mimosa. It was all around her, an enveloping cloud. She moved forward and then up the steps, the French critic putting out one of those long, narrow hands of his to help her.

She was handed an envelope, cold and dry on her hot and damp palm and then she was handed a red-leather box, open, with a bronze medallion embedded in it. Whose head was that? But of course – it was Katherine Mansfield's, jagged prongs of fringe across a wide forehead. She looked down and read: 'Menton c'est le Paradis d'une aube à l'autre.'

The Mayor was prompting her in a sibilant whisper, perhaps she would wish to say a few words?

She turned to face the audience; and it was then, as she raised the sheet of typescript, that all at once she saw him, standing by himself at the far end of the hall, one shoulder against the jamb of a closed door and his eyes fixed on her.

She began to read, at first all but inaudibly but then in a stronger and stronger voice. Her French was all but perfect; she felt wholly calm.

In the premature dusk, they talked outside the Town Hall, pacing the terrace among the stunted oleanders.

'You saved my life,' she said. She felt the euphoria that precedes a bout of fever. 'I can't explain it but I was, oh, petrified, I felt sure I could not say a word, and then suddenly I saw you and all at once...'

'I like that story of yours. Very much.'

'Oh, have you read it?' She was amazed. The story had appeared in a little magazine that, after three issues, had folded and vanished.

'Yes. It was – *right*. For her, I mean. It's the only story that she herself might have written, of all the ones that have ever won the prize.'

'That's a terrific compliment.'

'I mean it.'

'I'd hoped that perhaps you'd have joined us last night.'

'Well, I wanted to,' he said, with no further excuse.

'And then I thought that I might see you at the villa.'

'I've been there many times.'

'But not this time?'

He did not answer; and then she began to tell him about the mimosa on the terrace – how she remembered reading about it in the journals and the letters and how she had wanted a spray, just one spray, but there had been no one at the house and the gate was padlocked. 'If you'd been there, perhaps you could have climbed over. But none of our party looked capable of doing so.'

'I'll get you a spray.'

'Will you? Can you?'

'Of course.' He smiled. His teeth were very white in the long, sunburned face.

'But we leave early tomorrow.'

'What time?'

'We must leave the hotel at ten for the airport.'

'Oh, that'll give me time. Don't worry.'

Boldly she said, 'Oh, I wish there were no banquet this evening! I wish we could just have dinner alone together.'

'There'll be other times,' he said quietly. 'Anyway, I won't forget the mimosa.'

'Promise?'

'Promise.'

After that Tom was again calling and the cars were starting up and people were shaking her hand and saying how glad they were for her and that soon she must come back to Menton again.

When she looked round for the New Zealander, she found that he had vanished.

Lenore was back in her dark, two-roomed Fulham flat. At the airport Lucy had been whisked off by her husband in a chauffeur-driven Daimler, barely bothering to say goodbye. Theo had explained that it would be impossible to fit any more passengers into his battered station-wagon, already packed with his wife, a number of children, a dog and a folding bicycle. Tom had said that it looked as if the friend who was supposed to meet him must have got held up and he'd wait around for a while. So Lenore had travelled alone on the bus. She had felt chilled and there was again that pain, dull now, under her right ribs.

She shivered as she stooped to light the gas. Then she remained kneeling before it, staring at the radiants as the blue light flickering up from them steadied to an orange glow. He had failed to keep his promise and she had no idea of where he might be or even of what he was called – other than that either his surname or his Christian name was Leslie. It was hopeless. She got up, with a small, dry cough, and went into the bedroom. There she hauled her suitcase up on to the bed and began to unpack it, hurriedly, throwing things into drawers or jerking them on to hangers, as though she did not have a whole empty evening ahead of her and a number of empty days after that. At the bottom of the suitcase she came on the typescript of her speech – she crumpled it into a ball and threw it into the waste-paper basket – and the red-leather box, containing her trophy. She pressed the stud of the lid and lifted it upwards with a thumb; and, as she did so, it was as if she were releasing from it the smell pungent and bitter, that soon was all around her. She gave a little gasp; the pain in her chest sharpened. Looking down, she saw the spray of mimosa that lay across the medallion.

She took the spray in her hand; but it was dry, dry and faded and old as though it had lain there not for a few hours but for many, many years. 'Leslie.' She said the name aloud to herself and then, with no shock and no alarm but with the relieved recognition of someone lost who all at once sights a familiar landmark, she remembered that yes, of course, Leslie had been the name of the beloved brother killed in the war, whom Katherine Mansfield had always called 'Chummie'.

She touched the arid, dead raceme and some of the small, yellowish-grey blossoms, hard as berries, fell to the carpet at her feet. They might have been beads, scattering hither and thither. Three or four rolled back and forth in her palm. She felt a tickle at the back of her throat; it must be pollen, she decided wrongly.

Then suddenly the concluding lines of Kathleen Mansfield's sonnet on the death of her brother, read long ago and forgotten, forced themselves up within her, like the spurs of a plant, buried for years, all at once thrusting up into the light of day,

> By the remembered stream my brother stands
> Waiting for me with berries in his hands...
> 'These are my body. Sister, take and eat.'

She gave another little dry cough, and tasted something thick and salt on her tongue. The scent of mimosa was already fading as those blooms had long since faded. But she knew that it would come back and that he would come back with it.

Simon Raven

Remember Your Grammar

It's unfortunate that the considerable professional accomplishments of
SIMON RAVEN (1927-2001) *have always been overshadowed by his
notorious personal life. Most infamously, he abandoned his wife and
their infant child, and when she sent a desperate telegram to say they
were starving, Raven suggested she eat the baby. He was known as a cad
and a bon vivant, a heavy drinker, reckless gambler, and a debauchee
who claimed to enjoy going to bed with boys who looked like girls and
girls who looked like boys. But he was also a very fine writer, with such
classics as the gay-themed war novel* The Feathers of Death (1959)
and the much-admired vampire novel Doctors Wear Scarlet (1960)
*to his credit. He was also something of a scholar, studying Classics at
Cambridge, and knew Greek and Latin well. He uses that knowledge
in the following story, which must surely be the only horror story ever
written whose twist depends on the translation of a Latin defective verb.
It's the sort of antiquarian-themed story that fans of M. R. James will
surely enjoy, and the kind of tale that (sadly) could probably never be
published today, when many horror writers lack a grasp of the intricacies
of English grammar, let alone Latin* . . .

I WAS RATHER PLEASED when James Lauderdale turned up in Venice last month. Late November has never been a time when one's friends go there, least of all these days with so many of the hotels closed. So I was glad to see James's familiar face, and happy to have him with me on the walks we went. Often in November the weather in Venice is clear and blue, more beautiful than at any other season of the year; but even on the brightest of days, a sudden mist will creep down a passage from the *Laguna Morta,* making the best known campos murky and alien, distorting angles and falsifying distance, gathering round you in dumb hostility, compelling you to look behind for the man who is never there ... and then, on one's walks, one is glad of company.

James Lauderdale was staying out on the Zattere, in a *pensione* which he swore Ruskin had patronised, but which I knew had not existed before 1920. Typical of James to be so inaccurate. A passionate amateur antiquarian, he had never yet got anything entirely right. His Norman doorways always turned out to be 19th-century restorations, and clumsy ones at that; his gold was always silver-gilt. But his curiosity and exuberance made him tremendous fun to be with, particularly in a place like Venice; and every morning I would wait impatiently in my hotel by the Rialto bridge for James to come rattling over from the Zattere and cart me off on whatever expedition he fancied.

One day, the last day of November, he suggested a stroll up through the old Jewish quarter to the church of the Madonna dell'Orto. He wanted to see its cloister. As it happened, the cloister was closed (as it often is) and there was no one around to let us in; so since it was still too early for lunch, we loitered a bit on the way home. We took a different route from the one by which we had come. We walked along a *rio,* which came out into the larger canal of the Misericordia, and we stood on a bridge for a while: in front of us were the waters of the Misericordia, to our left the tiny campo of the Abbazia, to our right the huge building, like a kind of urban barn, that had once been the school of the Misericordia. And then I drew James's attention to something which I had often noticed before. In a small alcove, between the vast school and the *rio* above which we were standing, there was and is a patch of rough grass, much of which is covered with nettles and bramble. Among the nettles, if you look carefully, there are two or three square white stones, set there in the manner of tombstones in an overgrown cemetery, and yet unlike most tombstones for being too squat ... neither long and flat, as horizontal tombstones are, nor tall and thin like the vertical ones.

'I've often wondered about these stones,' I said. 'Odd, a little wilderness like that in the middle of Venice.'

As I might have known, James Lauderdale had an instant and romantic theory to propound.

'Private graveyard,' he said. 'Used by the School in the old days to dispose of unwanted bodies, suicides and so on.'

'The stones don't look right,' I told him. 'Anyway, suicides and so on shouldn't have had stones at all. They should just have been put away out of sight.'

'Then perhaps it was a regular cemetery. Perhaps it was pukka hallowed ground which the School had permission to use. In any case, it's certainly an oddity, as you say, and it requires investigation.'

'How are you going to get into it?' I said.

I should explain that the alcove was between two massive buttresses that projected from the east end of the School right down to the edge of the *rio*. There was thus no way into it from the bridge on which we stood, or from the Fondamenta, the large quayside, which marched along the south wall of the Misericordia, between it and its eponymous canal.

'By boat?' said James.

But the level of the *rio,* I pointed out, was too low. There was a good nine feet of slimy stone between the surface of the water and the grass verge of the alcove above it. There were no steps; and no one could possibly have clambered up from a boat.

'Then there must be a way through the School itself. There must be a door out of this end of the School and into that little wilderness. There's something which might answer half-hidden in that angle there. We'll go into the School now,' he said, with his usual immediacy, 'and inquire.' The entrance to the School, which these days is used as a youth centre, is at the west end, i.e., at the opposite end from where we now were. We walked off the bridge, along the Fondamenta, eventually found a large door and in it a janitor who was about to lock it up. James bombarded him with enthusiastic and vile Italian.

No, said the janitor when he was allowed to speak, he could not show the *signori* the way to the garden (for that was what he called it). To start with, it was time he went home for his *pranzo*; secondly, the door was a special door and only the director of the centre had a key. Ah, said James Lauderdale; could we come back and see the director later? Had we not noticed, said the janitor, that the day was Sunday? The centre was closed on Sunday from noon onwards, and all of Monday, too, of course. If we came back on Tuesday . . .

'Garden?' said James as we went on our way towards our own lunch. 'Why should he call it that?'

I pictured in my mind the square stones among the nettles. I remembered the bare brambles and the long, damp grass. I thought of those nine feet of slimy stone plummeting down from the verge of the grass to the surface of the *rio* below, and of the massive buttresses which guarded the alcove on either side.

'Why should he call it a garden?' James repeated.

'Euphemism,' I said. 'In Latin countries you call unpleasant things by a polite name in case the wrong person is listening. I'm glad, now I come to think of it, that we can't get in.'

'We can – on Tuesday.'

But as you shall hear, we got in sooner than that.

That evening, we went to the winter casino in the Palazzo Vendramin. Casinos do not close on Sundays in Italy, whatever youth centres may or may not do; they simply increase the stakes. James had an infallible system of play, which cleaned him out of all the cash he was carrying with remorseless brevity. Much the same happened to me. And so, when we had perforce finished our gaming, it was still too early to go straight home.

'We'll walk a long way round,' James said. 'Up to the lagoon and back by Zanipolo. Do us good after this frowsty hole.'

'There's a heavy mist,' I said. 'Let's stick to the main streets and have a few drinks *en route*.'

'Never mind your dipsomania, Simon. We need exercise.'

So we went a long way round. But the mist, swirling over us at some vital junction, must have tricked us. For, suddenly, we emerged from a passage, not into a cross passage as we should have, but onto a quayside along a broad canal. The canal of the Misericordia. We were approaching the west end of the School. The door was open and there were lights inside.

'Open,' said James.

'That janitor said it was closed after midday on Sundays.'

'You can see for yourself.'

We stepped in out of the fog, some of which was hanging about in the small atrium which we found we had entered. At first, it was difficult to see; then I distinguished a desk, and, sitting behind it, a small, lean man who was wearing a black beret. James at once started banging on about the wilderness over the *rio*.

'The garden,' said the man. 'You wish to go there?'

'Yes,' said the unstoppable James.

'Now?' said the man indifferently.

'Why not?'

'Why not indeed? You will need the key and a torch.' He handed both to James.

'Which way?'

'Through the gymnasium and into the changing-room. There's a low door next to the WC.'

Without rising, the man in the beret waved towards a curtained archway in the wall to our right. We went through the curtain and into the gymnasium. This was more brightly lit than the atrium, but not brilliantly; a few youths were playing ping-pong or billiards; they made none of the raucous and quarrelsome babble typical of Italians who are engaged in such pursuits; indeed, they were silent, except for a low and general murmur among them, and ignored us totally. We passed into the changing-room, found the low door, unlocked it without any trouble, and came out into the alcove which one of the buttresses made with the main building. The fog concealed the bridge on which we had stood that morning, but was not at all thick over our patch of grass.

At once, James Lauderdale took the torch to the most prominent of the square stones among the nettles. I stood apart. I had not wished to come, I had been sucked in, so to say, in the wake of James's enthusiasm – which would soon, I hoped, exhaust itself and let us both leave.

'An inscription,' called James.

Hell, I thought; that will delay us.

'Bloody nettles,' James said. 'What one goes through in the cause of knowledge.' Then 'AUGUSTUS LARI,' he spelt out. 'Ouch, bloody nettles. *Sepultus hic Kal Dec MDCCXXV.* "Buried here on the Kalends of December, i.e. the first of December 1725." There's something more.'

Hell; more delay.

'An epitaph,' called James. *'Qui novit semper noluit.* "Anyone who knew him always wished he didn't." Witty Latin but not very charitable. And more of it: *Noli novisse.* "Do not wish to have known him" – that is, "Be glad you didn't," I suppose. And I think there's even more underneath. Funny I didn't spot it at first.'

A puff of wind scattered the fog; briefly I saw the *rio* below and the bridge over it; then the fog re-formed, blotting out the bridge and the *rio* but staying almost clear of the wilderness. Cut off, I thought; cut off on this little patch.

'Come on, James. I'm cold. Time to go.'

'I tell you there's something else carved here. In smaller letters, down near the grass.'

'For Christ's sake! We can come back again when it's light.'

I almost ran through the gymnasium. The sullen boys still murmured over their games. James caught me up by the desk in the atrium.

'Can we come tomorrow?' he said to the man in the black beret.

'Tomorrow they're closed,' I said.

'Monday.'

'You can come,' said the man, half ignoring, half answering my objection.

'Come early, and the door will be opened to you.'

As we left the School, the fog lifted. We made our way without difficulty towards the Rialto bridge.

'Lucky they were open after all,' said James.

'It's all wrong,' I said, remembering something.

'What is?'

'Sepultus hic on that stone. "Buried here" ... *with the date.* It shouldn't give the date of the burial but that of the death. It should have said *obiit* or *mortuus* ... one of the words meaning "died".'

'Don't be so pedantic. Perhaps Signor Augustus Lari was buried the same day he died. That would support my theory about the place being used for suicides.'

'There is another possibility.'

'Not that I can see. Do you want to come with me tomorrow morning?'

'No,' I said.

'Very nervy all of a sudden. Just because of *sepultus hic?*'

'There's something else wrong with that inscription. I can't place it yet, but there is.'

We came to the Rialto bridge. James crossed it, on his way to the Zattere. I went to my own hotel. We had agreed that he would call for me there the next morning, as soon as he had finished his early visit to the garden of the Misericordia.

That night I dreamed continuously. I was thirteen again,

doing my scholarship examinations. Latin. Long proses, some verses, some unseens. Every now and then I woke, when I slept again I was still in the examination room. Greek now. Mathematics. Then Latin once more. Grammar. Question: What is a Defective Verb? Answer ... answer ... but no answer would come – until I woke once more, remembering it. A Defective Verb is a verb which lacks one or more tenses and uses others to replace them. Classic instance: *noscere,* to know. Which never uses the present tense, but substitutes its perfect or aorist *novi* (which should mean 'I have known' or 'I knew') to express the present 'I know'. *Qui novit semper noluit,* that stone had written on it. 'Whoever knew him always wished he didn't,' James had translated: an unkind epitaph. But it did not mean that. *Novit* stood for the present tense and *voluit,* by the rules of sequence, must be perfect and not aorist. Thus: 'Whoever *knows* him *has* always wished not to.' And *noli novisse:* not 'Do not wish to have known him', i.e., 'Be glad you didn't', as James had rendered; but simply, since *novisse* stood for the present infinitive, 'Do not wish to know him.' i.e. 'Shun him.' Not an epitaph, then: a warning. Spelt out: Do not wish to know him, because he is someone or something which those who know him have always wished they would never know. And what would that be? The nursery terror, I thought confusedly as I huddled on my clothes, the creature of the night which one has always suspected of existing and has always wished never to know for certain, never to meet face to face.

It was half past eight. 'Come early,' the man in the beret had said. I must hurry to James's *pensione,* to prevent him. But he was not there. He had gone out very early, the porter said. By the quay in front of the *pensione* I found a water taxi. To the School of the Misericordia. The door was closed, I rang the bell, the janitor of yesterday appeared. No. He had not seen James.

'I told you yesterday,' he said, 'the centre is closed on Sundays from noon and all of Monday. Which is today. I have just arrived and no one is here but me.'

Disregarding his protest, I ran through the atrium, through the gymnasium, through the changing-room to the little door by the WC. The key was in it. (Had James left it there? Who had let him into the building?) I stepped out into the enclave. Nobody. That stone square James had examined – the nettles had been trampled for some distance around it. By James last night, of course. No; *newly* trampled. By James this morning? Then where was he? I looked at the stone itself. There was the epitaph, which he had read to me. And there, in smaller letters, down near the grass, was the further inscription which I had not let him stay to read.

JACOBUS LAUDERDALE
Sepultus hic Kal. Dec. MCMLXXV

'James Lauderdale, buried here on December the first 1975.'
But that's today, I thought, this very morning.
'James,' I called stupidly. 'Oh, James.'
And had no answer.

Lisa Tuttle

The Other Room

LISA TUTTLE has been publishing top-notch speculative fiction for a long time (indeed, she won the John W. Campbell Award for Best New Writer as long ago as 1974), but she is also an author who hasn't ever received the full attention she deserves. This is perhaps owing to the somewhat sporadic availability of her books, at least in the U.S.: her masterful collection A Nest of Nightmares *(1986) remained unpublished here and a legendary rarity among horror collectors until our reissue this year, while a projected series of her collected short fiction from Ash-Tree Press in 2010 fizzled after the first volume, itself now almost unobtainable. So we're pleased to be doing our part to bring Tuttle's work to a wider audience, with reissues in 2020 of both* A Nest of Nightmares *and her first novel,* Familiar Spirit *(1983), as well as a forthcoming volume of previously uncollected and rarely seen tales,* The Dead Hours of Night. *The author tells us that the following piece, which first appeared in* Whispers, *vol. 5 (1982), was originally slated to appear in* A Nest of Nightmares, *but another story was substituted in its stead at the last moment. This is its first appearance in print in the U.S. in over thirty years.*

IT WAS SOMETIME PAST MIDNIGHT when Charles Logue mounted the front steps of the house he still thought of as his grandfather's.

His grandfather had been dead thirty-five years: Charles had never known him. The house, unlived in, had been his own property for ten years. Still, Charles thought of it, when he thought of it, as his grandfather's house.

The house had been built solidly of wood in the days when families required a lot of room. The front porch was long and deep, and there had once been a screened veranda above it. Grandly pillared and gabled, it was an imposing, old-fashioned house in a once-gracious neighbourhood now gone to commerce. It had been stripped, gutted, and subdivided to hold small businesses in the early '60s.

Charles Logue stood on the porch, remembering evenings spent reading comic books on the splintering wooden steps in the last light of the day, until his mother or grandmother scolded him for ruining his eyes and sent him running across the street to join in a game of kickball or fox-and-hounds. He remembered the sound of cicadas, the sudden flare of fireflies in the deep shadows under the oak trees, the smell of freshly cut grass and baking cookies.

The keys jangled together – an adult sound – as Logue found the correct one and unlocked the front door. He entered uncertainly, trying to recall the present floor plan. The old one was still clear in his mind, and he knew he would have to superimpose new walls and spaces over the rooms of his memory.

There was a health-food store and a lawyer's office on the first floor; upstairs, he knew, was a record store and something called 'Woman/Space'. It might have been much worse – next door was a beauty parlour/fortune-telling operation, and a few houses down was a gift shop Logue had heard was a cover for more illicit business.

Something – broken glass? – ground and slipped beneath his feet as he walked slowly into the high-ceilinged hall, gazing at the health-food store's display window. Bands of white light from the street revealed dim shapes, boxes of tea, bags of nuts, and bottles of vitamin tablets. But Logue didn't see the present display, nor the ghost of the parlour once in that space. He was caught up in his misery again, thinking the thing he could not forget, the central fact of his existence for the past year:

His daughter was dying.

There had been room and time for hope, once. There had been an operation that was supposed to save her. But it hadn't. It hadn't helped at all. There was nothing any of them could do but watch her, every day, draw a little closer to death.

Already she had gone so far that it was hard for the living to talk to her, hard to pretend or to say anything that had meaning, impossible to comprehend her experience.

There was the barrier of physical pain, and the agony of observing, without being able to lighten or share, her suffering; there was the fuzzy, sense-numbing wall of drugs around her; but highest and sternest of all the barriers was death, which she approached steadily, leaving her family and friends helpless in the distance.

He sat for hours beside her bed, holding her bony little hand until his arm was numb, trying to pull her back by sheer force of will. He tried to pray. He would have made any bargain with god, devil, or doctor, but everyone told him there was nothing, now, that anyone could do. Nothing he could do but hope for a miracle or wait for the end.

Beyond tears, beyond hope, standing in the heart of the old house, Charles Logue pressed his hands to his face and shuddered.

Charles Logue first came to the house when he was eight years old, at the end of a long journey, late at night. The reason – although his parents did not tell him – was that the old man was dying. It was a uniting of the family, a last chance for togetherness and forgiveness at the end.

Under ordinary circumstances Charles's mother would have noticed he was 'coming down with something'. But in her own excitement and worry about her father, she was impatient with the boy's whining and fidgeting, and saw them as signs only of childish restlessness with a long car trip. To keep him entertained, she told him stories about her childhood in the house they were now going to, including the information that the house contained a secret room, accessible through a hidden door.

'I won't tell you where it is,' she said mysteriously. 'I'm not sure anyone in the house remembers it nowadays. I discovered it myself when I was a girl. You can have fun looking for it, and using it as a hideout.'

The prospect cheered Charles almost to the point of forgetting his discomfort, and he passed much of the trip in fantasies about finding the room and putting it to good use.

It was very late indeed by the time they reached the house, and Charles was bundled off to bed in a room filled with the lurking shapes of strange furniture. He wasn't made to take a bath, or even to brush his teeth, and he was put to bed – the grown-ups talking all the while over his head, oblivious to him – in his underwear, then left alone.

He lay quietly for a few moments, hearing the voices and footsteps move away from him and down the stairs. He gazed at the rectangle of light which was the doorway, blinking his eyes, which, like the rest of him, felt sore and hot.

Irritably, he kicked the covers off. The rasp of the sheet against his bare arms and legs annoyed him, and the air was so close he could hardly draw a satisfying breath. He got up and padded softly to the door.

The upstairs hall, he saw, was long and narrow, lit by a chandelier which hung above the landing at the turn of the stairs. It hurt his eyes to look at it – it seemed all fiery, faceted crystal, shooting light in all directions – so he turned his face away from the stairs to the winding hall to the left. It made a sudden turning after a few feet, and he could not see past the projecting corner.

As he stepped out into the hall, Charles suddenly wished he had not left his bed, however uncomfortable it was. His body ached, his throat hurt too much to swallow, and now, after having been so hot, he was shivering uncontrollably.

He called for his mother in a plaintive voice. But there was no reply. No one came. Charles realized that he could hear no one in the house, which surely meant that, wherever his parents had gone, they could not hear him, either. He could call until he had no voice left, and no one would come. Helplessly, because he felt so very sick, Charles began to cry.

But not for long: he was a brave, sensible boy and knew crying wouldn't bring his mother if she couldn't hear him. He would have to go look for her.

He turned to the stairs again and stopped short. They seemed to be moving, like the steps on an escalator he had once been afraid of in a department store. They crept back and forth between shadow and light. They taunted him with hidden teeth: step on me and I'll suck you under and chew off your legs.

Charles moaned softly, closing his eyes against the dizzying back-and-forth motion. He dared not go near those treacherous stairs. He leaned against the door-frame, calling for his mother in a hopeless whisper. Tears seeped from his eyes and rolled down his face.

Gradually, through his pain, Charles became aware of voices. Soft voices, muffled by a wall, but they were somewhere nearby, upstairs. He stopped sobbing and held his breath to listen, to be sure. It might not be his mother, but that didn't matter – any grown-up would do. Someone to take him back to bed, make him comfortable, and climb safely, carelessly down the stairs to fetch his mother back to him.

He turned and began to make his way down the hall, away from the stairs and the light. His legs were weak, so he leaned against the wall for support. He could feel the voices through the wall, a slight vibration, but when he paused to listen he could not make out any words. But the voices went on rising and falling, a comforting, natural sound. Behind this wall he would find a room with people sitting and talking together.

Yet when he finally came to a room, the door gaped on

black emptiness. Charles stared, disbelieving, into the silent darkness. Where were they, those people he had heard through the wall? Had he missed a previous door?

Shoulders slumping, head reeling with dizziness, Charles turned back and pressed his ear against the wall. Yes, the voices were still there. They were clearer now: he heard a woman say his name.

Excited now, he hurried, certain he had only missed the first door in his weariness. But he came back to the room he had started from without finding, in the long, empty stretch of corridor, any entrance to a room where people sat together and talked about him.

There had to be a door, Charles knew. He did not see how he could have missed it, open or closed.

Unless it was a hidden door.

He remembered then, with another surge of excitement, that his mother had told him this house had a secret room, behind a hidden door. That must be it!

He retraced his steps, leaning against the wall now less from weakness than from the hope of finding some difference in the surface, some bump or indentation or crack which would indicate the hidden door.

And at last he found it, just as he had imagined.

There was nothing more than a light depression, a smooth dip in the wood about the size of a grown man's thumb. Charles put his own thumb in the spot and pressed. There was a clear, distant click, and then a long, straight crack appeared in the wall, expanding as the door swung open.

The room was surprisingly large for a hidden room, Charles thought as he entered it. It was long and furnished like a waiting room or hallway with wooden chairs and dark oil paintings in heavy gilded frames. The floor was a dark, polished wood, and a rug patterned in maroon and brown made an aisle down the centre of it. Covering the far wall – or perhaps hiding a doorway – was a straight, heavy curtain.

Charles gazed around at this unexpected room and, suddenly, felt frightened.

'Charles.'

A whisper in the empty room.

'Who's there?'

Behind him he could hear the smooth, latching sound of a door falling shut. The faint echoes of his high, frightened voice hung in the air. The heavy curtain ahead of him moved slightly, although the air was perfectly still.

He could not go back, Charles told himself. He must be brave. He had come here to find someone, and he would. He had heard their voices. His mother knew about the secret room, perhaps she was waiting for him on the other side of that curtain.

Bravely, he walked the length of the room, and took hold of one corner of the stiff, heavy fabric. As he raised it, he felt a gentle waft of scented air against his face. Breathing it in made his heart beat a little faster, but he didn't know why. It was a sweet, slightly musky smell, strange to him, but exciting.

The newly revealed room was enormous, with an immensely high, airy ceiling that made Charles think of churches. The room was filled with a pale, blue-white light that seemed to have no particular source but simply was, like the air. The walls and floor were made of a highly polished white stone which had within it flecks which caught the light in a silver gleam.

There were people in this room, and the sight of them terrified Charles.

He had been looking for people – had heard their voices and come expecting to find someone, but he was not prepared for what he had found. These people were certainly not his relatives – they did not look like any people Charles had ever seen before.

Most startling was their colour. They were white: bone, chalk, dead white. They looked as if, instead of flesh, they were made of porcelain.

They were unnaturally thin and tall, with elongated necks and arms. When they moved — as now, they moved towards him — they undulated.

Charles didn't dare run — he felt too weak to escape them, and the idea of being caught by them was far more horrible than merely confronting them. So he held his ground, braced himself, and prayed they would not touch him with their dead-white hands.

'Dear boy.'

It was a woman's voice, gentle as music. He looked up into a narrow, elegant face. It wasn't human, but there was something beautiful about it all the same. Charles stared at her, his fascination winning over his terror. Her face seemed to glow with a faint light, and her long, narrow eyes glittered like blue ice.

'Come with me, dear boy, and rest yourself. I'll make you comfortable.'

Before he could think to pull away, she had rested her pale hand on his head, and immediately Charles felt soothed and cooled. He was no longer feverish or sore, and his initial terror of these strange people had been lulled. They looked strange, but they seemed so kind . . .

'Let the boy alone!'

It was a loud, coarse shout, completely out of place in this ethereal room. Charles was vaguely irritated by it. As he turned in the direction of the sound, he saw a large, angry man bearing down upon him. The man, like his voice, was equally an intruder here. He was an ordinary man, old and fleshy. His face reminded Charles of an old hound-dog, and he wore a red-and-white striped robe which was garish in this place of muted colours.

Charles shrank away from the stranger, against the woman who had offered to comfort him.

With surprising strength, a bony, freckled hand pulled Charles from his refuge. 'Get out of here, boy!'

Then the ugly old face swooped in close. 'Who are you, boy? You look familiar, somehow.'

Charles craned his neck to see how the white people were taking this intrusion. There were perhaps a dozen of them gathered around, all standing quietly, with no readable expression on their thin, still faces. He turned back to the old man. 'My name is Charles Logue, sir.'

'Charles. Logue. My name is Charles, too.' His voice quickened with eagerness. 'Logue . . . Are you Elaine's boy?'

'Yes, sir.'

'But what are you doing *here*?'

'We came to see my grandfather.'

'Bless you, son, I'm your grandfather. I mean how did you come *here*?'

'Through the secret door. My mother told me there was one. I heard voices through the wall, and looked until I found it. They said my name.'

'*My* name,' the old man said softly. 'You shouldn't be here, boy. It's no place for you. You go on back now, and find your mother.'

'You come with me,' Charles said.

The old man closed his eyes and shook his head quickly. 'Go on, now.'

Charles looked up. The lady who had offered him comfort was smiling at him. He had a glimpse of small, pointed teeth, like a cat's.

'Please,' whispered Charles to his grandfather.

The old man straightened to his full height. 'Let the boy go,' he said. 'You have no business with him.'

The encircling crowd did not move or speak. The old man bent down and spoke softly to Charles: 'We'll walk towards the curtain. The first chance you get, you must run for it, without looking back and without waiting for me, understand?'

Charles nodded and put his hand trustingly into his grandfather's. They began to walk, slowly, and the white people gave slightly before them. But they moved at a snail's pace – Charles realized that his grandfather did not want to touch, even to brush against, these people, and, not understanding why, he grew more frightened.

Finally they came near the curtain. The white people did not seem anxious to be close to it, and moved away, making a gap in the circle through which Charles saw he could escape.

His grandfather gave him a push, then, and Charles ran as he had been told to, without pausing or looking back. As he slipped behind the heavy curtain, he heard a woman's voice right at his ear, as if she ran at his side, saying, 'You'll come back. When you understand, you'll come back to me.'

Now a grown man, standing in the house he owned, Charles Logue was afraid to go upstairs. He didn't know which he feared more: finding the room, or not finding it.

Thirty-five years before, when he had recovered from his long illness, young Charles had begun to search again for the hidden door. The adults had told him that his grandfather was dead and buried in the ground – and what a pity they'd never met – but Charles knew better. He knew where his grandfather was, and he meant to find him, to save him, somehow, from the strange people who kept him prisoner.

But no matter how many times he walked the length of the hall, no matter where he pressed or knocked or scratched, he could not find the door again. His efforts were noticed, the object of amused speculation by the adults, and finally his mother had taken pity on him and told him that the secret room was downstairs. She had even showed him what she called the secret room – a stuffy little cave beneath the stairs, accessible through a door at the back of a closet.

It made no difference: Charles knew what he had seen. He refused to believe it had been only a dream, and, for the rest of the summer that he stayed in the house, Charles continued to look in vain for the door, the room, his grandfather.

Would it be any different this time, Charles wondered. Could it? Leaving aside the question of dream or reality, why should he succeed now when he had failed so many times as a child? Was it enough that he was an adult now and fully aware of what he proposed to do? That he was willing to sacrifice himself to save his daughter? He would try to leave the room with his daughter, but if a life was called for, he would give up his. All he asked was the chance.

He pressed his hand to his forehead, checking his fever like a key or a weapon. Would it be enough to get him in? But his hands were cold, and he could not tell if his face burned or not.

Coming down with this virus, three nights before, tossing restlessly in his bed, Charles had had a dream. In the dream he had gone again to that hidden room and there had seen his daughter, surrounded by those thin, white people. The look of mute terror on her face as she sought to find a familiar human being in that place had torn his heart, and he had woken crying and calling her name.

He knew she was there — he had heard her speak to them. He had seen the blue shadows of that room in her eyes. He'd heard her initial fear turn to a weak fascination as, in a drugged half-sleep, she begged them to touch her with their cool, white hands and take away her pain.

I come with pure heart and clear intentions, thought Charles, only half ironically. His mouth was dry. Please, let me save her.

He began to mount the stairs. The banister was new and ugly, but the steps beneath his feet seemed to be the same ones he had climbed as a boy, so old that a shallow depression was worn in the centre of each broad step by years of footsteps.

He heard voices above his head. Dimly, through a wall, he heard them.

Charles froze, holding himself perfectly still and silent, and listened intently. The murmur of voices came again, a distant, familiar rhythm.

He let out his breath in a sigh and continued to climb. He had been right to come here, after all. They had let him hear them; they would let him find the door again.

But the upper hall was not empty, as it should have been. He was not alone. There were others here, dark figures moving swiftly towards him, harsh human voices; he scarcely had time to realize that something was wrong and he was in danger before the sudden, intense pain took him into a suffocating blackness.

When he came to, he was standing in the antechamber with the dark oil paintings on the walls and the wooden chairs lined up beneath them. So he must have found the door, although he did not remember how or when.

His head ached abominably, and his shirt was wet — with blood, it seemed. He didn't stop to reflect on it, but hurried towards the tapestry hanging at the end of the room.

As he lifted one corner of the heavy curtain that rich, strange, musky scent came to him again for the first time in years. He breathed it in, feeling pleasure and nostalgia so sharply that he wanted to weep. He still did not know what the smell was, but it was beautiful.

The other room was just as he remembered it. His eyes went to his daughter at once, picking her out easily amid the strange, pale people. She sat on the floor beside a chair, and the person in that chair encircled her loosely with a bone-white arm.

Charles called out her name, and she turned her face towards him. The helpless, drowning look she gave him nearly broke his heart. She was almost past saving; she would have to be pulled away. But he would; he would do it, he would make her leave, thought Charles, and, hunched against the pain growing in his side, he began to walk towards her.

'You've come back at last. I've been waiting.'

It was the woman who had spoken to him during his first visit. She had not changed at all. She was still beautiful in the non-human way of stone or statue or insect with her dead-white, faintly glowing skin, her frozen eyes, her oddly elongated limbs. The sight of her made him shiver with something much more profound than cold or fear.

Before he could think to avoid her, she touched his side and then his head with the white branch of her hand.

'Let me make you comfortable,' she said.

The pain vanished instantly. Despite himself, Charles felt weakly, slavishly grateful to her. He had not realized how badly he was hurting until the pain had gone.

'Come and sit with me and let us talk together,' she said. 'It's what we've both been waiting for since you were just a boy.'

Charles could not imagine why he had ever wanted to run from her. She was so beautiful, and her touch was so soothing. Her voice was music that he wanted to listen to forever.

He knew now why he had come here, why he had dreamed of coming back and searched for the hidden door for so many years. His daughter – sad little thing – had never been more than incidental in his decision.

He put his large, rough fingers into her smooth hand and let her lead him away.

Robert M. Coates
The Fury

ROBERT M. COATES (1897-1973) *was best known in his lifetime as a writer and critic for the magazine* The New Yorker, *in which the following tale first appeared in 1936. He is the author of* The Eater of Darkness *(1926), an odd mixture of murder mystery and science fiction, complete with experimental typography, that has been called the first Surrealist novel in English, and* Wisteria Cottage *(1948) (republished by Valancourt in 2020), a noir psychological thriller with an unexpectedly bloody climax. 'The Fury' was one of Coates's most frequently anthologized stories, and though we're not sure it quite falls under the rubric of a 'horror story', it could certainly be given the recently coined label 'horror adjacent', and its subject — the actions of a deranged pedophile and their aftermath — is certainly horrific enough.*

THE LITTLE GIRL'S FACE, when she looked back, was white and convulsed with terror. Mr Flent bent his bright, his compelling gaze on her, and for a moment she stood there transfixed, her eyes never leaving his.

No one else, in the darkness and the general stir as the feature picture neared its end, had noticed anything; packed in between the guard rail and the last row of seats, everyone was moving inchingly this way and that, maneuvering for the dash down the aisle when the picture was over. Even the woman whose hand the little girl was clasping hadn't noticed anything. She too was too busy watching the picture.

Mr Flent remained where he was, holding the little girl's gaze tensely and surely, letting the feeling of pride and power and bright white imperious vengeful majesty rise up within him.

But it never crested and overflowed as it should have done.

Without warning, the little girl's glance wavered slightly, her cheeks tucked up towards her eyes and her eyes began to pucker; she was starting to cry, but Mr Flent had been alert for that. Instantly, his eyes lost their persuasive glitter, his face slid into its normal, noncommittal folds. His hands dropped to his side and he stepped back, drawing his raincoat more closely about him.

Someone else, pressing forward, took his place; others moved in from either side; expertly, with a minimum of disturbance, Mr Flent let them thrust him out behind them and into the cleared space at the rear. Here he was free. There were a few girl ushers in tight-fitting tunics standing against the wall, and a dribble of people coming in through the big entrance doors. None of them paid any attention to him.

He kept his ears cocked for a cry, a commotion, the sound of a woman's angry voice behind him, but none came. He moved slowly – tantalizing himself now with his own slowness, dallying with the dangers he still ran – under the amber-tinted lights toward the door. Inside the hot, airless raincoat wrapped incongruously about his thin frame he felt his body grow warm and sticky. 'Let them come!' he thought defiantly, and then found that he must have spoken the thought aloud, for one of the ushers turned to look at him. He twisted his wide, loose-muscled mouth into a deprecatory grin and moved a little faster. There was no pursuit.

In the street he stood a moment, dazed by the transition from darkness to mid-afternoon, too excited still to remember at first where he was. Then he saw that it was Fourteenth Street, and the street was tramping with people. 'The little devil!' he thought. 'The little devil. She knows what it's all about, all right!' His mouth tasted dry and there was a feeling of pressure behind his eyes. He set out walking blindly, the sights and sounds around him coming thumpingly against his consciousness yet never quite penetrating it, like seas breaking against a wall.

'Then she puts on the frightened act,' he thought. Across the street was the Consolidated Gas Company building. He had been here before. On his right was a sandwich bar, its busy interior wide open to the street, the sidewalk in front of it clotted with loitering men. He stared at them as he passed, wagging his head balefully. 'At that age, too,' he muttered, still thinking of the little girl.

He laughed, his thin giggling laugh, and a woman glanced at him. He looked away nervously; then, a pace or two past her, turned to stare after her. A plump piece, all right, in her thin spotted dress sticking tight to the hips. And under that only the swelling naked body. 'And they walk the streets!' he thought, and then suddenly the heat, the noise, the little girl and the men and the glancing woman all fused to form one emotion. 'Filth!' he exclaimed fiercely aloud, and stretching his arm straight out before him, he clenched his hand into a fist.

Then he opened his hand gently, tenderly, and let his arm drop slowly to his side. Abruptly, all his self-possession had returned, and he walked now so unctuously at ease that he seemed to move in an atmosphere of his own, from within which he looked out shrewdly and tolerantly on the hurrying figures around him. 'With the kindest intentions in the world,' he thought.

He paced onward slowly, feeling the sun, the summer air, watching the passers-by present themselves casually before him and disappear. A young man and a girl walking side by side, saying things and laughing together. Two women just entering a delicatessen store. A man in a drugstore doorway, lighting a cigar. Another man, leaning against an areaway railing, reading a newspaper. There was no harm in any of them; or what harm there was he could control, he could palliate, as if by a personal shiningness, just by being there.

Behind him he could hear the developing roar of an 'El' train. It passed over him, rushed onward. He was on Third Avenue, then. Or maybe it was Sixth. Anyway, he had been here before.

When he looked about him again, the Elevated structure still filled the street beside him, but he seemed to have gotten into a region of warehouses and factories. He had the feeling that he must have been walking for a long time.

But the little girl, at first glance, looked almost as if she might be the same one. Then he realized that it couldn't be, though the light cotton dress she had on was much the same color. This little girl seemed shorter and chunkier. She was bouncing a ball, solemnly and tirelessly, against the wall of a wooden shedlike structure a little way down the side street from the corner on which he stood. There was no one else about. Slowly, very slowly, he started walking towards her.

As he approached he could hear her counting. 'Thirty-four, thirty-five, thirty-six, thirty-seven,' she said, then she dropped the ball. She scurried to retrieve it, and began bouncing and counting again. 'One, two, three, four, five, six —'

Mr Flent put on his kindliest smile. He knew how easy it was to frighten these little ones. 'Hello,' he said.

The little girl stopped and looked up in surprise at the strange voice, and the strange face bending over her. But she was not frightened. 'Hello,' she said.

'What are you doing?' said Mr Flent.

She looked up at him seriously, impressed by this adult interest in her game. 'Practicing,' she said.

'Oh, practicing,' said Mr Flent. She was delicious, really delicious. 'Practicing what?' he asked, but before she could answer he went on. 'And doesn't it make you thirsty?'

She considered that. 'No,' said the little girl.

Mr Flent made his large eyes look wider. 'Oh, doesn't it?' he said. 'Well, now, you're the first little girl I ever did see that wasn't always thirsty for a nice ice cream soda. Most little girls are always thirsty for a nice ice cream soda.'

He paused and stared down at her, smiling compellingly. Her eyes had grown large and wistful, and when she spoke her voice was a little muffled, as if it came from some well of innocence. 'I like ice cream sodas, too,' she said.

'Do you now?' said Mr Flent, and giggled roguishly. She was a cute little thing, all right. 'Well, then, you shall have one,' and suddenly brisk and authoritative, he held out his hand for her to take. 'Come along, then,' he said. 'We'll just skip down to the corner together and have one. A nice, big strawberry ice cream soda.

'Come along,' he said as she still hesitated. 'If we hurry, nobody will ever know. Mamma needn't know. Nobody'll know. Maybe we'll have two,' he said. 'If we hurry.'

'I want pineapple,' she said, and put her hand in his. As they started away, however, she stopped suddenly. 'Oh, where's Dixie?' she said. 'I can't leave Dixie.' Mr Flent stared at her. The touch of her hand, her confidingness, had worked on him until now he was trembling almost visibly. And here she was, pulling the delaying act. Or maybe she really only needed coaxing. He couldn't be sure. The vengefulness, the fierce knowledge of the earth's iniquity, was rising in him now; and even as he looked down at her, her face and her expression seemed to fluctuate as if seen in an uneven mirror, changing from innocence to guile, from trustingness to sly coquetry – changing faster and faster, faster even than his breathing, until he almost lost sight of her features in the blur.

But he mustn't frighten her. Whatever her game is, he thought, I can play it; let her play her game, I'll play mine. He brought his smile to bear on her.

'We haven't time,' he said cajolingly. 'If we want to get that nice ice cream soda.' He still held her hand tightly, but not too tightly, in his and kept drawing her gently after him down the street.

'We must hurry,' he said, and pulled a little harder, but she still hung back and he could see that she was getting frightened, so he stopped. These young ones, he thought, you must handle them delicately; young, but the youngest of them as touchy as a queen. Down the street, he saw a woman in a gray wrapper standing watching him intently. 'Well,' he said, and the little girl looked up obediently into his wide bright smile. 'Well. Who is Dixie?' He made his eyebrows arch very high.

'He's my dog,' said the little girl, so seriously that Mr Flent was convinced of her innocence all over again.

'Your dog, is he?' he exclaimed, and – he couldn't help it – he squatted down beside her, his tight-buttoned raincoat flopping out awkwardly around him on the sidewalk, his face close to hers. He couldn't help laughing.

The little girl stared at him, a little dismayed by his sudden gesture. 'He isn't really my dog,' she said. 'He belongs to Mr Kramer, the delicatessen-store man. But he lets me play with him. I told him I'd be careful of him.'

This was delicious. Down the street he could see the woman in gray talking to another woman, and both of them looking up his way, but Mr Flent couldn't help it: he put his two hands on her shoulders and gave her a playful little shake, then let his hands slide affectionately down over her body. Under the thin dress he could feel the small bones, the flesh soft as wax. It made him feel young again. 'Mr Kramer's dog, then,' he said, and he couldn't help laughing louder. Then he sobered suddenly and made his eyes get wide.

'But we can't bring a dog into a candy store, you know,' he said, and got up to his feet and took her hand again. Down the street, the two women had started walking slowly towards him. He began speaking a little faster. 'We'll have to leave him behind this time, I guess,' he said, and made his eyes twinkle. 'What would a doggie want with an ice cream soda, anyway?' And he bobbed his head down at her quickly, so that his nose would have rubbed against hers if she hadn't drawn back a little. 'This time,' he said, with an almost lover-like cadence in his voice, 'it will be just us two alone.'

He could see the awe and the fearful fascination growing in her eyes. 'Think you'll like that?' he asked, and gave her a moment to let it sink in. 'Come along, then,' he said and, still holding her hand, started down the street.

But instead of obeying, she hung back. He could feel the weight of her, with her feet planted stiff on the pavement; without looking at her, he could feel her eyes, and the fear in them, fixed staring on his face. Not one thing but many things had combined to confuse her – the touch of his hands on her body, the strange bobbings up and down, the face held so close to hers, the reasonless laughter – and now the sudden tug on her arm brought them all to focus and before he had made three steps she burst out with a cry of pure terror. 'No, no,' she screamed. 'I won't go with you. I won't. I won't.'

Mr Flent's first feeling was one of high rage. He had been tricked again, he had been played for a fool, and, the smile gone, he bent down again face to face with her. 'You bitch!' he cried, almost beside himself. 'You think you can get away with that,' and seizing her about the waist he actually succeeded in heaving her up under one arm, feet kicking, arms flailing, mouth screaming; he had been ready to run with her, but when he straightened again one glance around told him he could never get away with it.

Behind him, the two women were running and yelling something. On the stoop of a house across the way a man in shirtsleeves had thrown down his newspaper and was starting down the steps. At the other end of the street, two men at the curbstone had stopped, surprised by the commotion; soon they would be running. And beyond them he could see others, still moving this way and that, unconcernedly, but they were his enemies too, and soon they too would be running, running to rend him.

He dropped the girl, giving her a cuff as he did so that sent her sprawling. 'Filth!' he screamed at her, and ran a few steps forward, then turned and ran back the way he had come. He was in a strange world in that narrow block, and it was a world full of his enemies, but the fury had taken hold of him, and he knew that his wrath was greater than theirs, he knew that he was invincible. It was to punish such as these that he had been placed upon the earth.

The girl had crawled hastily out of his path. Shaking his fists and screaming, he charged straight at the two women; the mere impact of his madness was enough to scatter them. 'Filth! Filth all of you!' he yelled, and ran past them so close he could feel the flap of his raincoat against their skirts. They didn't touch him; they dared not, but the moment he had passed them he heard them begin their shouting again. Like a white flash in the red haze around him he saw the face of a man just coming out of an area entrance as he passed. There was a louder shout behind him and an arm reached out for him but he struck it aside; something whizzed past him and landed on the sidewalk ahead of him. Then he was running free, with the bare street between him and the corner.

He reached the corner, and doubled it. He was under the 'El,' where he had been before, and only a block or two down the street he could see the steps of a station. Behind him, he could hear the shouting feet of his pursuers, but behind that he heard another sound, the sound of an 'El' train, far down the tracks, but approaching. He knew he could outwit them yet.

There were only a few people waiting on the platform. They saw him – a thin, long-nosed, disheveled man, with a face streaming sweat and a raincoat that flapped wildly about his legs as he ran – come scrambling up the steps, pause a moment before the turnstiles and then, as the train's approach grew louder, vault clumsily over them and come bursting out on the platform. They heard the man in the change booth give an angry shout.

Mr Flent heard it, too. Though he did not know it, the chase had stopped at the foot of the elevated stairs, but the shout meant only pursuit to him, and even if he had not heard it, it is doubtful if he could have stopped now. He had become an automaton; fear was all around him and he a mere running thing, escaping; all he saw was the white faces on either side of him and, down at the end of the platform, the blunt front of the 'El' train, approaching. Blindly, he ran towards it.

Those on the platform saw him do it, but they never knew what he was doing until it was too late. They saw him run to the edge and run off it, and then – his legs and arms still working frantically, his raincoat flattened against his scrawny back – they saw his body thump, in mid-air, against the front of the train. It seemed to hang there a moment, as if impaled; then his head snapped back, the face white, but the forehead bloody where it had slammed against the metal; his knees jerked upward and outward; the body began to fall.

The brakes were on, and the whole train was shrieking and shuddering under the drag of them; but it had coasted halfway into the station before it came to a halt. Long before that, the body was under the wheels.

Michael Arlen

The Gentleman from America

MICHAEL ARLEN (1895-1956) *is in some ways the archetypal Valancourt author, a writer who at one time was extraordinarily popular and well regarded but who subsequently fell into near-total oblivion. His novel* The Green Hat (1924) *was a huge success on both sides of the Atlantic, adapted for plays on Broadway and London's West End and filmed in 1928 starring Greta Garbo. Almost overnight, Arlen became an international celebrity, rich and famous, and even appeared on the cover of* Time. *Though he continued publishing, his work eventually fell out of critical favor, and he quit writing altogether after his loyalty to England was unjustly questioned during World War Two. 'The Gentleman from America' (1924) is written in Arlen's trademark style and features the same odd, disconcerting tone he strikes in his later supernatural novel* Hell! said the Duchess (1933), *a mixture of wry hilarity and rather grim horror. The latter work was reissued by Valancourt in 2013 and appears on Karl Edward Wagner's list of the best supernatural horror novels of all time. 'The Gentleman from America' was often anthologized in the mid-20th century and was adapted three times in the 1950s for television, including once for* Alfred Hitchcock Presents, *but seems not to have been reprinted for many years, an omission we're happy to correct here.*

I T IS TOLD BY A DECAYED GENTLEMAN at the sign of *The Leather Butler*, which is in Shepherd's Market, which is in Mayfair, how one night three men behaved in a most peculiar way; and one of them was left for dead.

Towards twelve o'clock on a night in the month of November some years ago, three men were ascending the noble stairway of a mansion in Grosvenor Square. The mansion, although appointed in every detail – to suit, however, a severe taste – had yet a sour atmosphere, as of a house long untenanted but by caretakers.

The first of the men, for they ascended in single file, held aloft a kitchen candlestick, whilst his companions made the best progress they could among the deep shadows that the faulty light cast on the oaken stairway. He who went last, the youngest of the three, said gaily: –

'Mean old bird, my aunt! Cutting off the electric-light just because she is away.'

'Fur goodness' sake!' said the other.

The leader, whose face the candlelight revealed as thin almost to asceticism, a face white and tired, finely moulded but soiled in texture by the dissipations of a man of the world, contented himself with a curt request to his young friend not to speak so loud.

It was, however, the gentleman in between the two whom it will advantage the reader to consider. This was an unusually tall and strongly-built man. Yet it was not his giant stature, but rather the assurance of his bearing, which was remarkable. His very clothes sat on his huge frame with an air of firmness, of finality, that, as even a glance at his two companions would show, is deprecated by English tailors, whose inflexible formula it is that the elegance of the casual is the only possible elegance for gentlemen of the mode. While his face had that weathered, yet untired and eager look which is the enviable possession of many Americans, and is commonly considered to denote, for reasons not very clearly defined, the quality known as Poise. Not, however, that this untired and eager look is, as some have supposed, the outward sign of a lack of interest in dissipation, but rather of an enthusiastic and naïve curiosity as to the varieties of the same. The gentleman from America looked, in fine, to be a proper man; and one who, in his early thirties, had established a philosophy of which his comfort and his assurance of retaining it were the two poles, his easy perception of humbug the pivot, and his fearlessness the latitude and longitude.

It was on the second landing that the leader, whose name was Quillier, and on whom the dignity of an ancient baronetcy seemed to have an almost intolerably tiring effect, flung open a door. He did not pass into the room, but held the candlestick towards the gentleman from America. And his manner was so impersonal as to be almost rude, which is a fault of breeding when it is bored.

'The terms of the bet,' said Quillier, 'are that this candle must suffice you for the night. That is understood?'

'Sure, why not?' smiled the gentleman from America. 'It's a bum bet, and it looks to me like a bum candle. But do I care? No, sir!'

'Further,' continued the impersonal, pleasant voice, 'that you are allowed no matches, and therefore cannot relight the candle when it has gone out. That if you can pass the night in that room, Kerr-Anderson and I pay you five hundred pounds. And vice versa.'

'That's all right, Quillier. We've got all that.' The gentleman from America took the candle from Quillier's hand and looked into the room, but with no more than faint interest. In that faulty light little could be seen but the oak-panelling, the heavy hangings about the great bed, and a steel engraving of a Meissonier duellist lunging at them from a wall nearby.

'Seldom,' said he, 'have I seen a room look less haunted – '

'Ah,' vaguely said Sir Cyril Quillier.

'But,' said the gentleman from America, 'since you and Kerr-Anderson insist on presenting me with five hundred pounds for passing the night in it, do I complain? No, sir!'

'Got your revolver?' queried young Kerr-Anderson, a chubby youth whose profession was dining out.

'That is so,' said the gentleman from America.

Quillier said: 'Well, Puce, I don't mind telling you that I had just as soon this silly business was over. I have been betting all my life, but I have always had a preference for those bets which did not turn on a man's life or death —'

'Say, listen, Quillier, you can't frighten me with that junk!' snapped Mr Puce.

'My aunt,' said young Kerr-Anderson, 'will be very annoyed if anything happens and she gets to hear of it. She hates a corpse in her house more than anyone I know. You're sure you are going on with it, Puce?'

'Boy, if Abraham Lincoln was to come up this moment and tell me Queen Anne was dead, I'd be as sure he was speaking the truth as that I'm going to spend this night in this old haunted room of your aunt's. Yes, sir! And now I'll give you good-night, boys. Warn your mothers to be ready to give you five hundred pounds to hand on to Howard Cornelius Puce.'

'I like Americans,' said Quillier vaguely. 'They are so enthusiastic. Good-night, Puce, and God bless you. I hope you have better luck than the last man who spent a night in that room. He was strangled. Good-night, my friend.'

'Aw, have a heart!' growled Mr Puce. 'You get a guy so low with your talk that I feel I could put on a tall-hat and crawl under a snake.'

II

The gentleman from America, alone in the haunted room, lost none of his composure. Indeed, if anything disturbed him at all, it was that, irritated by Quillier's manner at a dinner-party a few nights before, and knowing Quillier to be a bankrupt wastrel, he had allowed himself to be dared into this silly adventure and had thus deprived himself for one night of the amenities of his suite at Claridge's Hotel. Five hundred pounds more or less did not matter very much to Mr Puce: although, to be sure, it was some consolation to know that five hundred pounds more or less must matter quite a deal to *Sir* Cyril Quillier, for all his swank. Mr Puce, like a good American, following the Gospel according to Mr Sinclair Lewis, always stressed the titles of any of his acquaintance.

Now, he contented himself with a very cursory examination of the dim, large room; he rapped, in an amateurish way, on the oak panels here and there for any sign of any 'secret passage junk', but succeeded only in soiling his knuckles, and it was only when, fully clothed, he had thrown himself on the great bed that it occurred to him that five hundred pounds sterling was quite a pretty sum to have staked about a damfool haunted room.

The conclusion that naturally leapt to one's mind, thought Mr Puce, was that the room must have something the matter with it, else would a hawk like Quillier have bet money on its qualities of terror? Mr Puce had, indeed, suggested, when first the bet was put forward, that five hundred pounds was perhaps an unnecessary sum to stake on so idiotic a fancy; but Quillier had said in a very tired way that he never bet less than five hundred on anything, but that if Mr Puce preferred to bet with poppycock and chickenfood, he, Quillier, would be pleased to introduce him to some very jolly children of his acquaintance.

Such thoughts persuaded Mr Puce to rise and examine more carefully the walls and appointments of the room. But as the furniture was limited to the barest necessities, and as the oak-panelled walls appeared in the faint light to be much the same as any other walls, the gentleman from America swore vaguely and again reclined on the bed. It was a very comfortable bed.

He had made up his mind, however, that he would not sleep. He would watch out, thought Mr Puce, for any sign of this old ghost, and he would listen with the ears of a coyote, thought Mr Puce, for any hint of those rapping noises, rude winds, musty odours, clanking of chains, and the like, with which, so Mr Puce had always understood, the family ghosts of Britishers invariably heralded their foul appearance.

Mr Puce, you can see, did not believe in ghosts. He could not but think, however, that some low trick might be played on him, since on the honour of *Sir* Cyril Quillier, peer though he was – for Mr Puce, like a good American, could never get the cold dope on all this fancy title stuff – he had not the smallest reliance. But as to the supernatural, Mr Puce's attitude was always a wholesome scepticism – and a rather aggressive scepticism at that, as Quillier had remarked with amusement when he had spoken of the ghost in, as he had put it, the house of Kerr-Anderson's aunt. Quillier had said: –

'There are two sorts of men on whom ghosts have an effect: those who are silly enough to believe in them, and those who are silly enough not to believe in them.'

Mr Puce had been annoyed at that. He detested clever backchat. 'I'll tell the world,' Mr Puce had said, 'that a plain American has to go to a drug-store after a conversation with you.'

Mr Puce, lying on the great bed, whose hangings depressed him, examined his automatic and found it good. He had every intention of standing no nonsense, and an automatic nine-shooter is, as Mr Puce remembered having read somewhere, an Argument. Indeed, Mr Puce was full of those dour witticisms about the effect of a 'gun' on everyday life which go to make the less pretentious 'movies' so entertaining; although, to be sure, he did not know more than a very little about guns. Travellers have remarked, however, that the exciting traditions behind a hundred-percent American nationality have given birth in even the most gentle citizens of that great republic to a feeling of familiarity with 'guns,' as such homely phrases as 'slick with the steel mit', 'doggone son of a gun', and the like, go to prove.

Mr Puce placed the sleek little automatic on a small table by the bed, on which stood the candle and, as he realized for the first time, a book. One glance at the paper-jacket of the book was enough to convince the gentleman from America that its presence there must be due to one of Quillier's tired ideas. It showed a woman of striking, if conventional, beauty, fighting for her life with a shape which might or might not be the wraith of a bloodhound but was certainly something quite outside a lovely woman's daily experience. Mr Puce laughed. The book was called *Tales of Terror for Tiny Tots*, by Ivor Pelham Marlay.

The gentleman from America was a healthy man, and needed his sleep; and it was therefore with relief that he turned to Mr Marlay's absurd-looking book as a means of keeping himself awake. The tale at which the book came open was called *The Phantom Footsteps*; and Mr Puce prepared himself to be entertained, for he was not of those who read for instruction. He read: –

The Phantom Footsteps

The tale of The Phantom Footsteps is still whispered with awe and loathing among the people of that decayed but genteel district of London known to those who live in it as Belgravia and to others as Pimlico.

Julia and Geraldine Biggot-Baggot were twin sisters who lived with their father, a widower, in a town in Lancashire called Wigan, or it may have been called Bolton. The tale finds Julia and Geraldine in their nineteenth year, and it also finds them in a very bad temper, for they were yearning for a more spacious life than can be found in Wigan, or it might be, Bolton. This yearning their neighbours found all the more inexplicable since the parents of the girls were of Lancashire stock, their mother having been a Biggot from Wigan and their father a Baggot from Bolton.

The reader can imagine with what excess of gaiety Julia and Geraldine heard one day from their father that he had inherited a considerable property from a distant relation; and the reader can go on imagining the exaltation of the girls when they heard that the property included a mansion in Belgravia, since that for which they had always yearned most was to enjoy, from a central situation, the glittering life of the metropolis.

Their father preceded them from Wigan, or was it Bolton? He was a man of a tidy disposition, and wished to see that everything in the Belgravia house was ready against his daughters' arrival. When Julia and Geraldine did arrive, however, they were admitted by a genial old person of repellent aspect and disagreeable odour, who informed them that she was doing a bit of charing about the house but would be gone by the evening. Their father, she added, had gone into the country to engage servants, but would be back the next day; and he had instructed her to tell Julia and Geraldine not to be nervous of sleeping alone in a strange house, that there was nothing to be afraid of, and that he would, anyhow, be with them first thing in the morning.

Now Julia and Geraldine, though twins, were of vastly different temperaments; for whereas Julia was a girl of gay and indomitable spirit who knew not fear, Geraldine suffered from agonies of timidity and knew nothing else. When, for instance, night fell and found them alone in the house, Julia could scarcely contain her delight at the adventure; while it was with difficulty that Geraldine could support the tremors that shook her girlish frame.

Imagine, then, how differently they were affected when, as they lay in bed in their room towards the top of the house, they distinctly heard from far below a noise, as of someone moving. Julia sat up in bed, intent, unafraid, curious. Geraldine swooned.

'It's only a cat,' Julia whispered. 'I'm going down to see.'

'Don't!' sighed Geraldine. 'For pity's sake don't leave me, Julia!'

'Oh, don't be so childish!' snapped Julia. 'Whenever there's the chance of the least bit of fun you get shivers down your spine. But as you are so frightened I will lock the door from the outside and take the key with me, so that no one can get in when I am not looking. Oh, I hope it's a burglar! I'll give him the fright of his life, see if I don't.'

And the indomitable girl went, feeling her way to the door in darkness, for to have switched on the light would have been to warn the intruder, if there was one, that the house was inhabited; whereas it was the plucky girl's conceit to turn the tables on the burglar, if there was one, by suddenly appearing to him as an avenging phantom; for having done not a little district-visiting in Wigan, or, possibly, Bolton, no one knew better than Julia of the depths of base superstition among the vulgar.

A little calmed by her sister's nonchalance, Geraldine lay still as a mouse in the darkness, with her pretty head beneath the bedclothes. From without came not a sound, and the very stillness of the house had impelled Geraldine to a new access of terror had she not concentrated on the works of Mr Rudyard Kipling, which tell of the grit of the English people.

Then, as though to test the grit of the English people in the most abominable way, came a dull noise from below. Geraldine restrained a scream, lay breathless in the darkness. The dull noise, however, was not repeated, and presently Geraldine grew a little calmer, thinking that maybe her sister had dropped a slipper or something of the sort. But the reader can imagine into what terror the poor girl had been plunged had she been a student of the detective novels of the day, for then she must instantly have recognized the dull noise as a dull thud, and what can a dull thud mean but one thing?

It was as she was praying a prayer to Our Lady that her ears grew aware of footsteps ascending the stairs. Her first feeling was one of infinite relief. Of course Julia had been right, and there had been nothing downstairs but a cat or, perhaps, a dog. And now Julia was returning, and in a second they would have a good laugh together. Indeed, it was all Geraldine could do to restrain herself from jumping out of bed to meet her sister, when she was assailed by a terrible doubt; and on the instant her mind grew so charged with fear that she could no longer hold back her sobs. Suppose it was not Julia ascending! Suppose... 'Oh, God!' sobbed Geraldine.

Transfixed with terror, yet hopeful of the best, the poor girl could not even command herself to re-insert her head beneath the sheets. And always the ascending steps came nearer. As they approached the door, she thought she would die of uncertainty. But as the key was fitted into the lock she drew a deep breath of relief — to be at once shaken by the most acute agony of doubt, so that she had given anything in the world to be back again in Wigan, or, even better, Bolton.

'Julia!' she sobbed. 'Julia!'

For the door had opened, the footsteps were in the room, and Geraldine thought she recognized her sister's maidenly tread. But why did Julia not speak, why this intolerable silence? Geraldine, peer as hard as she might, could make out nothing in the darkness. The footsteps seemed to fumble in their direction, but came always nearer to the bed, in which poor Geraldine lay more dead than alive. Oh, why did Julia not speak, just to reassure her?

'Julia!' sobbed Geraldine. 'Julia!'

The footsteps seemed to fumble about the floor with an indecision maddening to Geraldine's distraught nerves. But at last they came beside the bed — and there they stood! In the awful silence Geraldine could hear her heart beating like a hammer on a bell.

'Oh!' the poor girl screamed. 'What is it, Julia? Why don't you speak?'

But never a sound nor a word gave back the livid silence, never a sigh nor a breath, though Julia must be standing within a yard of the bed.

'Oh, she is only trying to frighten me, the beast!' poor Geraldine thought; and, unable for another second to bear the cruel silence, she timidly stretched out a hand to touch her sister – when, to her infinite relief, her fingers touched the white rabbit-fur with which Julia's dressing-gown was delicately trimmed.

'You beast, Julia!' she sobbed and laughed. Never a word, however, came from the still shape. Geraldine, impatient of the continuation of a joke which seemed to her in the worst of taste, raised her hand from the fur, that she might touch her sister's face; but her fingers had risen no farther than Julia's throat when they touched something wet and warm, and with a scream of indescribable terror Geraldine fainted away.

When Mr Biggot-Baggot admitted himself into the house early the next morning, his eyes were assailed by a dreadful sight. At the foot of the stairs was a pool of blood, from which, in a loathsome trail, drops of blood wound up the stairway.

Mr Biggot-Baggot, fearful lest something out of the way had happened to his beloved daughters, rushed frantically up the stairs. The trail of blood led to his daughters' room; and there, in the doorway, the poor gentleman stood appalled, so foul was the sight that met his eyes. His beloved Geraldine lay on the bed, her hair snow-white, her lips raving with the shrill fancies of a maniac. While on the floor beside the bed lay stretched, in a pool of blood, his beloved Julia, her head half-severed from her trunk.

The tragic story unfolded only when the police arrived. It then became clear that Julia, her head half-severed from her body, and therefore a corpse, had yet, with indomitable purpose, come upstairs to warn her timid sister against the homicidal lunatic who, just escaped from an asylum nearby, had penetrated into the house. However, the police consoled the distracted father not a little by pointing out that the escape of the homicidal lunatic from the asylum had done some good, insomuch as there would now be room in an asylum near her home for Geraldine.

III

When the gentleman from America had read the last line of *The Phantom Footsteps* he closed the book with a slam, and, in his bitter impatience with the impossible work, was making to hurl it across the room, when, unfortunately, his circling arm overturned the candle. The candle, of course, went out.

'Aw, hell!' said Mr Puce bitterly, and he thought: 'Another good mark to *Sir* Cyril Quillier! Won't I Sir him one some day! For only a lousy guy with a face like a drummer's overdraft would have bought a damfool book like that.'

The tale of *The Phantom Footsteps* had annoyed him very much; but what annoyed him even more was the candle's extinction, for the gentleman from America knew himself too well to bet a nickel on his chances of remaining awake in a dark room.

He did, however, manage to keep awake for some time merely by concentrating on wicked words: on Quillier's face, and how its tired, mocking expression would change for the better were his, Puce's, foot to be firmly pressed down on its surface, and on Julia and Geraldine. For the luckless twins, by the almost criminal idiocy with which they were presented, kept walking about Mr Puce's mind; and as he began to nod to the demands of a healthy and tired body he could not resist wondering if their home-town had been Wigan or Bolton and if Julia's head had been severed from ear to ear or only half-way....

When he awoke, it was the stillness of the room that impressed his sharply-awakened senses. The room was very still.

'Who's there!' snapped Mr Puce. Then, really awake, laughed at himself. 'Say, what would plucky little Julia have done?' he thought, chuckling. 'Why, got up and looked!'

But the gentleman from America discovered in himself a reluctance to move from the bed. He was very comfortable on the bed. Besides, he had no light and could see nothing if he did move. Besides, he had heard nothing at all, not the faintest noise. He had merely awoken rather more sharply than usual....

Suddenly, he sat up on the bed, his back against the oak head. Something had moved in the room. He was certain something had moved. Somewhere by the foot of the bed.

'Aw, drop that!' laughed Mr Puce.

His eyes peering into the darkness, Mr Puce stretched his right hand to the table on which stood the automatic. The gesture reminded him of Geraldine's when she had touched the white rabbit-fur. Aw, Geraldine nothing! These idiotic twins kept chasing about a man's mind. The gentleman from America grasped the automatic firmly in his hand. His hand felt as though it had been born grasping an automatic.

'I want to tell you,' said Mr Puce into the darkness, 'that someone is now going to have something coming to him, her, or it.'

It was quite delicious, the feeling that he was not frightened. He had always known he was a helluva fellow. But he had never been quite certain. Now he was certain. He was the regular.

But, if anything had moved, it moved no more. Maybe, though, nothing had moved at all, ever. Maybe it was only his half-awakened senses that had played him a trick. He was rather sorry, if that was so. He was just beginning to enjoy the evening.

The room was very still. The gentleman from America could only hear himself breathing.

Something moved again, distinctly.

'What the hell!' snapped Mr Puce.

He levelled the automatic towards the foot of the bed.

'I will now,' said Mr Puce grimly, 'shoot.'

The room was very still. The gentleman from America wished, forcibly, that he had a light. It was no good leaving the bed without a light. He'd only fall over the infernal thing, whatever it was. What would plucky little Julia have done? Aw, Julia nothing! He strained his ears to catch another movement, but he could only hear himself breathing – in short, sharp gasps! The gentleman from America pulled himself together.

'Say, listen!' he snapped into the darkness. 'I am going to count ten. I am then going to shoot. In the meanwhile you can make up your mind whether or not you are going to stay right here to watch the explosion. One. Two. Three. Four...'

Then Mr Puce interrupted himself. He had to. It was so funny. He laughed. He heard himself laugh, and again it was quite delicious, the feeling that he was not frightened. And wouldn't they laugh, the boys at the Booster Club back home, when he sprung this yarn on them! He could hear them. Oh, Boy! Say, listen, trying to scare him, Howard Cornelius Puce, with a ghost like that! Aw, it was like shooting craps with a guy that couldn't count. Poor old Quillier! Never bet less than five hundred on anything, didn't he, the poor boob! Well, there wasn't a ghost made, with or without a head on him, that could put the wind up Howard Puce. No, sir!

For, as his eyes had grown accustomed to the darkness, and helped by the mockery of light that the clouded, moonless night just managed to thrust through the distant window, the gentleman from America had been able to make out a form at the foot of the bed. He could only see its upper half, and that appeared to end above the throat. The phantom had no head. Whereas, Julia's head had been only half-severed from – aw, what the hell!

'A family like the Kerr-Andersons,' began Mr Puce, chuckling – but suddenly found, to his astonishment, that he was shouting at the top of his voice; anyhow, it sounded so. However, he began again, much lower, but still chuckling: –

'Say, listen, Mr Ghost, a family like the Kerr-Andersons might have afforded a head and a suit of clothes for their family ghost. Sir, you are one big bum phantom!' Again, unaccountably, Mr Puce found himself shouting at the top of his voice. 'I am going on counting,' he added grimly.

And, his automatic levelled at the thing's heart, the gentleman from America went on counting. His voice was steady.

'Five . . . six . . .'

He sat crouched at the head of the bed, his eyes never off the thing's breast. Phantom nothing! He didn't believe in that no-head bunk. What the hell! He thought of getting a little nearer the foot of the bed and catching the thing a whack on that invisible head of his, but decided to stay where he was.

'Seven . . . eight . . .'

He hadn't seen the hands before. Gee, some hands! And arms! Holy Moses, he'd got long arms to him, he had . . .

'Nine!' said the gentleman from America.

Christopher and Columbus, but this would make some tale back home! Yes, sir! Not a bad idea of Quillier's, that, though! Those arms. Long as old glory . . . long as the bed! Not bad for *Sir* Cyril Quillier, that idea . . .

'Ten, you swine!' yelled the gentleman from America, and fired.

Someone laughed. Mr Puce quite distinctly heard himself laughing, and that made him laugh again. Fur goodness' sake, what a shot! Missed from that distance!

His eyes, as he made to take aim again, were bothered by the drops of sweat from his forehead. 'Aw, what the hell!' said Mr Puce, and fired again.

The silence after the second shot was like a black cloud on the darkness. Mr Puce thought out the wickedest word he knew, and said it. Well, he wasn't going to miss again. No, sir! His hand was steady as iron, too. Iron was his second name. And again the gentleman from America found it quite delicious, the feeling that he was not frightened. Attaboy! The drops of sweat from his forehead bothered him, though. Aw, what the hell, that was only excitement.

He raised his arm for the third shot. Jupiter and Jane, but he'd learn that ghost to stop ghosting! He was certainly sorry for that ghost. He wished, though, that he could concentrate more on the actual body of the headless thing. There it was, darn it, at the foot of the bed, staring at him – well, it would have been staring at him if it had a head. Aw, of course it had a head! It was only Quillier with his lousy face in a black wrap. *Sir* Cyril Quillier'd get one piece of lead in him this time, though. His own fault, the bastard.

'Say, listen, Quillier,' said the gentleman from America, 'I want to tell you that unless you quit, you are a corpse. Now I mean it, sure as my name is Howard Cornelius Puce. I have been shooting to miss so far. Yes, sir. But I am now annoyed.'

If only, though, he could concentrate more on the body of the thing. His eyes kept wandering to the hands and arms. Gee, but they sure were long, those arms! As long as the bed, no less. Just long enough for the hands to get at him from the foot of the bed. And that's what they were at, what's more! Coming nearer. What the hell! They were moving, those doggone arms, nearer and nearer . . .

Mr Puce fired again.

That was no miss. He knew that was no miss. Right through the heart, that little boy must have gone. In that darkness he couldn't see more than just the shape of the thing. But it was still now. The arms were still. They weren't moving any more. The gentleman from America chuckled. That one had shown him that it's a wise little ghost that stops ghosting. Yes, sir! It would fall in a moment, dead as Argentine mutton.

Mr Puce then swore. Those arms were moving again. The hands weren't a yard from him now. What the hell! They were for his throat, God-dammit.

'You swine!' sobbed the gentleman from America, and fired again. But he wouldn't wait this time. No, sir! He'd let that ghost have a ton of lead. Mr Puce fired again. Those hands weren't half a yard from his throat now. No good shooting at the hands though. Thing was to get the Thing through the heart. Mr Puce fired the sixth bullet. Right into the thing's chest. The sweat bothered his eyes. 'Aw, hell!' said Mr Puce. He wished the bed was a bit longer. He couldn't get back any more. Those arms ... Holy Moses, long as hell, weren't they! Mr Puce fired the seventh, eighth ... ninth. Right into the thing. The revolver fell from Mr Puce's shaking fingers. Mr Puce heard himself screaming.

IV

Towards noon on a summer's day several years later two men were sitting before an inn some miles from the ancient town of Lincoln. Drawn up in the shade of a towering ash was a large grey touring-car, covered with dust. On the worn table stood two tankards of ale. The travellers rested in silence and content, smoking.

The road by which the inn stood was really no more than a lane, and the peace of the motorists was not disturbed by the traffic of a main road. Indeed, the only human being visible was a distant speck on the dust, coming towards them. He seemed, however, to be making a good pace, for he soon drew near.

'If,' said the elder of the two men, in a low, tired voice, 'if we take the short cut through Carmion Wood, we will be at Malmanor for lunch.'

'Then you'll go short-cutting alone,' said the other firmly. 'I've heard enough tales about Carmion Wood to last me a lifetime without my adding one more to them. And as for spooks, one is enough for this child in one lifetime, thanks very much.'

The two men, for lack of any other distraction, watched the pedestrian draw near. He turned out to be a giant of a man;

and had, apparently, no intention of resting at the inn. The very air of the tall pedestrian was a challenge to the lazy content of the sunlit noon. He was walking at a great pace, his felt hat swinging from his hand. A giant he was: his hair greying, his massive face set with assurance.

'By all that's holy!' gasped the elder of the two observers. A little lean gentleman that was, with a lined face which had been handsome in a striking way but for the haggard marks of the dissipations of a man of the world. He had only one arm, and that added a curiously flippant air of devilry to his little, lean, sardonic person.

'Puce!' yelled the other, a young man with a chubby, good-humoured face. 'Puce, you silly old ass! Come here at once!'

The giant swung round at the good-natured cry, stared at the two smiling men. Then the massive face broke into the old, genial smile by which his friends had always known and loved the gentleman from America, and he came towards them with hand outstretched.

'Well, boys!' laughed Mr Puce. 'This is one big surprise. But it's good to see you again, I'll say that.'

'The years have rolled on, Puce, the years have rolled on,' sighed Quillier in his tired way, but warmly enough he shook the gentleman from America with his one hand.

'They certainly have!' said Mr Puce, mopping his brow and smiling down on the two. 'And by the look of that arm, Quillier, I'd say you're no stranger to war.'

'Sit down, old Puce, and have a drink,' laughed Kerr-Anderson. Always gay, was Kerr-Anderson.

But the gentleman from America seemed, as he stood there, uncertain. He glanced down the way he had come. Quillier, watching him, saw that he was fagged out. Eleven years had made a great difference to Mr Puce. He looked old, worn, a wreck of the hearty giant who was once Howard Cornelius Puce.

'Come, sit down, Puce,' he said kindly, and quite briskly, for him. 'Do you realize, man, that it's eleven years since that idiotic night? What are you doing? Taking a walking-tour?'

Mr Puce sat down on the stained bench beside them. His massive presence, his massive smile, seemed to fill the whole air about the two men.

'Walking-tour? That is so, more or less,' smiled Mr Puce; and, with a flash of his old humour: 'I want to tell you boys that I am the daughter of the King of Egypt, but I am dressed as a man because I am travelling incognita. Eleven years is it, since we met? A whale of a time, eleven years!'

'Why, there's been quite a war since then,' chuckled Kerr-Anderson. 'But still that night seems like last night. I am glad to see you again, old Puce! But, by Heaven, we owe you one for giving us the scare of our lives! Don't we, Quillier?'

'That's right, Puce,' smiled Quillier. 'We owe you one all right. But I am heartily glad that it was only a shock you had, and that you were quite yourself after all. And so here we are gathered together again by blind chance, eleven years older, eleven years wiser. Have a drink, Puce?'

The gentleman from America was looking from one to the other of the two. The smile on the massive face seemed one of utter bewilderment. Quillier was shocked at the ravages of a mere eleven years on the man's face.

'I gave you two a scare!' echoed Mr Puce. 'Aw, put it to music, boys! What the hell! How the blazes did I give you two a scare?'

Kerr-Anderson was quite delighted to explain. The scare of eleven years ago was part of the fun of to-day. Many a time he had told the tale to while away the boredom of Flanders and Mesopotamia, and had often wanted to let old Puce in on it to enjoy the joke on Quillier and himself, but had never had the chance to get hold of him.

They had thought, that night, that Puce was dead. Quillier, naked from the waist up, had rushed down to Kerr-Anderson, waiting in the dark porch, and had told him that Puce had kicked the bucket. Quillier had sworn like nothing on earth as he dashed on his clothes. Awkward, Puce's corpse, for Quillier and Kerr-Anderson. Quillier, thank Heaven, had had the sense not to leave the empty revolver on the bed. They shoved back all the ghost properties into a bag. And as, of course, the house wasn't Kerr-Anderson's aunt's house at all, but Johnny Paramour's, who was away, they couldn't so easily be traced. Still, awkward for them, very. They cleared the country that night, Quillier swearing all the way about the weak hearts of giants. And it wasn't until the Orient Express had pitched them out at Vienna that they saw in the Continental *Daily Mail* that an American of the name of Puce had been found by the caretaker in the bedroom of a house in Grosvenor Square, suffering from shock and nervous breakdown. Poor old Puce! Good old Puce! But he'd had the laugh on them all right . . .

And heartily enough the gentleman from America appeared to enjoy the joke on Quillier and Kerr-Anderson.

'That's good!' he laughed. 'That's very good!'

'Of course,' said Quillier in his tired, deprecating way, 'we took the stake, this boy and I. For if you hadn't collapsed you would certainly have run out of that room like a Mussulman from a ham-sandwich.'

'That's all right,' laughed Mr Puce. 'But what I want to know, Quillier, is how you got me so scared?'

Kerr-Anderson says now that Puce was looking at Quillier quite amiably. Full in the face, and very close to him, but quite amiably. Quillier smiled, in his deprecating way.

'Oh, an old trick, Puce! A black rag over the head, a couple of yards of stuffed cloth for arms——'

'Aw, steady!' said Mr Puce. But quite amiably. 'Say, listen, I shot at you! Nine times. How about that?'

'Dear, oh dear!' laughed Kerr-Anderson. But that was the last time he laughed that day.

'My dear Puce,' said Quillier gently, slightly waving his one arm. 'That is the oldest trick of all. I was in a panic all the time that you would think of it and chuck the gun at my head. Those bullets in your automatic were blanks.'

Kerr-Anderson isn't at all sure what exactly happened then. All he remembers is that Puce's huge face had suddenly gone crimson, which made his hair stand out shockingly white; and that Puce had Quillier's fragile throat between his hands; and that Puce was roaring and spitting into Quillier's blackening face.

'Say, listen, you Quillier! You'd scare me like that, would you! You'd scare me with a chicken's trick like that, would you! And you'd strangle me, eh? You swine, you *Sir* Cyril Quillier, you, right here's where the strangling comes in, and it's me that's going to do it – '

Kerr-Anderson hit out and yelled. Quillier was helpless with his one arm, the giant's grip on his throat. The woman who kept the inn had hysterics. Puce roared blasphemies. Quillier was doubled back over the small table, Puce on top of him, tightening his death-hold. Kerr-Anderson hit, kicked, bit, yelled.

Suddenly there were shouts from all around.

'For God's sake, quick!' sobbed Kerr-Anderson. 'He's almost killed him.'

'Aw, what the hell!' roared Puce.

The men in dark uniforms had all they could do to drag him away from that little, lean, blackened, unconscious thing. Then they manacled Puce. Puce looked sheepish, and grinned at Kerr-Anderson.

Two of the six men in dark uniforms helped to revive Quillier.

'Drinks,' gasped Kerr-Anderson to the woman who kept the inn.

'Say, give me one,' begged the gentleman from America. Huge, helpless, manacled, he stood sheepishly among his uniformed captors. Kerr-Anderson stared at them. Quillier was reviving.

'Gets like that,' said the head-warder indifferently. 'Gave us the slip this morning. Certain death for someone. Homicidal maniac, that's 'im. And he's the devil to hold. Been like that eleven years. Got a shock, I fancy. Keeps on talking about a sister of his called Julia who was murdered and how he'll be revenged for it...'

Kerr-Anderson had turned away. Quillier suddenly sobbed: 'God have mercy on us!' The gentleman from America suddenly roared with laughter.

'Can't be helped,' said the head-warder. 'Sorry you were put to trouble, sir. Good-day, gentlemen. Glad it was no worse.'

Stephen Gregory

The Poet Lewis Bowden Has Died

We ended volume 2 with a new tale by STEPHEN GREGORY, *and we've chosen to conclude volume 4 with his newest story. Gregory has a special knack for ending his stories on a satisfying note – by no means a common talent – which makes this tale perfect to conclude this book with. Gregory is a Valancourt fan favorite, with readers enjoying his cult classics we've republished, like* The Cormorant (1986), The Woodwitch (1988), *and* The Blood of Angels (1994). *In 2019 we collected for the first time a selection of his early short fiction, plus some new stories, under the title* On Dark Wings. *Those who enjoy the following story should definitely not miss that collection. 'The Poet Lewis Bowden Has Died', appearing here for the first time anywhere, is in at least one respect atypical of Gregory's work: it's much less dark than most of his fiction. But we think it's a beautifully written tale with just enough of a ghostly element to belong in this book.*

I WAS FINISHING MY LUNCH in the Flying Fish, wiping the plate with a piece of bread, when I looked up and saw Beasley standing there.

I hadn't seen him for nearly a year. He paused to ask how I was and what I'd had to eat. His wife was impatient to leave. I answered the second question first, I'd had the pigeon casserole, in a red wine gravy with mushrooms and shallots. And then, because he hadn't noticed it parked so close to the table, I pointed at the wheelchair I was sitting in. He frowned and asked me what happened. I could see his wife was fidgeting, so I told him simply I had an accident in a car. My own silly fault, had a few drinks ... they pulled me out, been in this bloody thing ever since.

He edged away from the table, managing to look sorry and judgmental at the same time. If he'd had a moment longer, he would have said it served me right and reminded me of another little incident when I'd had a few drinks and ... but no, he was leaving. I asked him how the school was doing, he made a so-so gesture with his hands and his wife tugged him out of the door.

14th February, 1984. I'd chosen the Flying Fish because it looked over the estuary of the Ouse and had pigeon on the menu. Bumping into Beasley was a coincidence.

A year ago. It was still dark outside, breakfast at 8 o'clock on a miserable February morning. Beasley was coming around the dining room with the mail. He went from table to table, trying to be avuncular because it was Valentine's Day and an opportunity to attempt a joke here and there with the boys.

Worse than miserable. The copper beech was scraping its branches against the windows. Every now and then there was a furious spatter of rain. It had been more difficult than usual to wake the boys in the dormitory, to stir them out of their beds and get them washed and dressed and down to the dining room in time for the headmaster's inspection. But that was my job, seven days a week, term after term, to stir myself from my upstairs room, to splash my face and shave and dress and stumble along to the dorms and muster the boys.

Beasley was trying to be a bit kindlier than usual. I heard him, each time he handed a letter to one of the boys, attempting a humorous remark about Valentine's Day and girlfriends ... but, on such a grimly dark and dismal morning, they were sullen and unresponsive, barely awake.

He tried it with me. He proffered a slim, padded envelope, withdrew it just before I could take it from him, and he affected to sniff it in a clumsy theatrical manner. From one of your lady friends, Mr Boden? Not much of a perfume . . . no, I don't think so . . .

He gave me the envelope and turned away. He adjusted the volume on the big, brown box of a radio in the corner of the dining room, because the rattle of the rain was so loud on the windows. And as we did every day, every morning, we listened to the BBC news. He sat himself at the head of one of the tables, and poured himself tea. I turned to my table of sleepy, befuddled boys.

Most of them had no idea it was Valentine's Day. They weren't listening to the news. A dining room of thirty-five teenage boys, who'd been fast asleep half an hour ago, until Mr Boden had come blundering into the deepest dreams of their faraway homes and bustled them awake and downstairs.

A pale, rather spotty red-headed youth, I couldn't remember his name but he was the only English boy on my table, watched as I opened my envelope. I knew what was inside it, and my fingers trembled with excitement.

The book slipped out. I turned it this way and that, too overwhelmed to look properly and knowing I would have some time, later in the day, to enjoy, to enjoy . . . and I passed it to the boy. He frowned at the front cover, and then turned it over to the photograph on the back. His gingery eyebrows lifted, he squinted closer, and he beamed a quick, boyish beam as he looked from the photo and into my face. Hey sir, is it you? Without your specs? Did you write it? Hey, that's cool, that's really cool . . .

Thank you, thank you, I said and took the book from him. I could have hugged him. Of course I didn't. My eyes tingled, not just for the book but for the warmth of his response. He blushed and turned his attention to tea and toast and marmalade.

The Moon on the Ouse, poems by Lewis Bowden. My youthful reflections on walking the banks of the river on my afternoons and evenings off school, my own real and personal responses to the river in flood and even in spate, the sunsets and moonrises, the flow of the huge salty tides from the English Channel and inland as far as Piddinghoe, and their ebbing to sea again... and somehow, quite unselfconsciously, my yearnings, the anticipation of feelings I'd never yet experienced.

I'd sent them to a publisher in London, they liked them, they would pay me an advance. They suggested the title. They took my photo, asking me to remove my specs. It was my idea to use my middle name, Lewis, and add another W to my surname so that the two Ws would look nice together.

Yearnings? Well, yes. I was Eric Boden and I was 30 years old, an English teacher at The Manor, a boarding school in Sussex. And the living-in housemaster, with a stuffy little room in the roof. Yearnings? Well yes, of course.

Somehow, in a state of bliss, I fluffed my way through the first lessons of the morning. I put the book where I could always see it, where indeed I could hardly take my eyes off it. At break-time, almost sick with nerves, I braced myself to reveal it to the staffroom, as self-effacingly as any newly published poet could possibly manage.

The teachers gathered around and peered at the book. Beasley, who'd told me once that he was writing a novel, came to look. He rearranged his mouth into a quivering smile and examined the front of the book and my photograph, and it was clearly quite painful for him. So painful that he suddenly remembered he had something extremely important to say to his staff ... brandishing a copy of a glossy magazine, he pointed out that someone, a boy of course, had spoiled Lady Diana's smile by blackening one of her teeth. Could we all, please please, be more vigilant in the supervision of our classes in the school library?

A tooth. I had a moment to marvel at how tiny an alteration to her face could make a princess look so ugly, before I was called out of the room to deal with something else. And when I went back, I was just in time to interrupt Beasley reading a poem aloud, in a mock pompous-poetic voice, to his chuckling audience.

Awkward, but no matter. I floated serenely through the day. A day of undiminished gloom and rain, it hardly paused in its icy spattering. The wind which had lashed the copper beech at breakfast was still heaving its branches this way and that, scratching them at the dining room windows, while I was supervising the boys at supper time. A miserable night in February . . . long after all the other teachers had gone home to their families in Newhaven and Seaford and even the suburbs of Brighton.

Gloom and rain? The defacement of Diana, Princess of Wales? Dormitory duty in a boys' boarding school? Nothing could touch me. I was unassailable, the poet Lewis Bowden.

At last, at last. When the lights were all out in the dorms and I'd done my usual security check of the whole house, I was upstairs in my attic room. I switched on my electric fire, and soon the single bar was buzzing orange and red. I liked its dusty, fusty smell. I liked my desk and my scattered books, even the exercise books I should have marked and hadn't. I opened a bottle of good red wine I'd bought and saved specially and poured a big glugging glass. I lay back in my shabby old armchair, stretched my feet to the fire, took a firm hold on my book – which had hardly been out of my sight all day – and raised the glass of wine in my other hand.

Cheers. The rain drummed on the window above my head. The sky was a whirling darkness. Not a star, not a glimmer of moon. After a glass or two of the wine, and then a third, I could understand of course how a staffroom of merely mortal teachers had been unsettled by the book. The dreamily poetic title? My earnestly handsome pose on the back? My nom de plume? If I'd written a novel, something racy or dark or even naughty, we could have laughed it off together, and Beasley might not have been so wounded . . . a thriller, by Eric Boden, wearing glasses. But poetry?

No matter. I read and re-read my poems, loving the ones I'd always liked, liking the ones I wasn't quite sure of. I finished the bottle of wine. And I found another one, not so good, I'd tucked away. The pop of the cork and a slow, heavy, rhythmic glugging.

I must have slept, my head back, my legs outstretched...

Until I jumped awake. A light? Alight? Grabbing the arms of my chair, I struggled to my feet. A tall, yellow flame was flickering on the toe of my right shoe and licking at my trousers. A sudden stink of burning. And there was someone in my room, a noisy shouting blundering someone ... oh my god, what on earth ...?

It was Beasley. He grabbed the bottle of wine, the second bottle I'd nearly finished, he was sloshing it all over my shoe and my trousers and he was blustering ... you bloody fool, you could set the whole place alight and we'd all be burned in our beds ...

He pressed me back into my armchair and appraised me. A steam of wine and molten rubber was rising from my feet and legs. He could see how I was, three-quarters drunk, half asleep. Get to bed for heaven's sake, for everybody's sake ... bloody fool.

Springtime in Paris. Still cold, in the last week in March, but blossoms of magnolia. And sunshine so sharp, there was frost in the air.

School holiday. I took the ferry from Newhaven, slipping out of the Ouse and across the Channel to Dieppe. And a coach to Paris, where I'd booked a room in the very heart of Montmartre.

A poet, in Paris in the springtime. Where else? I had a long weekend to do all the things a young poet would do ... the mornings in a pavement café with coffee and croissants and a newspaper, sitting outside wrapped in a coat and scarf and watching the people, inhaling their cigarettes and perfume, with a pad and a pen on my table to scribble words and phrases and ideas and the very stuff of my future poems and stories and novels.

I wandered the alleyways of the Marché des Puces. I strolled the Rive Gauche, browsing the bouquinistes for musty, yellowing pamphlets of poetry, as odd and as precious as the one in my pocket. And in the evenings, finding the perfect place in this bar or that, in Montmartre, to watch the dusk fall and twilight come creeping, and settle into a night of slow, unhurried drinking ... Pernod and a few splashes of ice-cold water, the shock of the aniseed and then a leisurely savouring of its utter Frenchness.

And the theatre, in Montparnasse ... I booked a seat in Le Théâtre de la Gaieté, high in the gods, to see a music-hall singer called Claudette de la Touche. I had no idea who she was or how good or how awful she might be, but I sat and drank three or four glasses of Pernod in a bar, Le Petit Sommelier, before strolling along ...

I was dazed. Not drunk, but dazed enough to be dazzled by it all. High in the gods, so cramped that my knees were crunched against the seat in front of mine and I had to duck to the left and right of a pillar to see the stage ... in the gods? I was in heaven. An exquisite theatre, a jewel of fin de siècle Paris ... so fine and delicate and so intimate ... I sat in a swoon and the songs of Claudette de la Touche lifted me higher and higher, until I was swept into the starlit sky ...

Claudette? Her voice was thrilling. I couldn't understand a word, but I knew she was singing about love. What else would a woman want to sing about, in such a place, in Paris, in the springtime? Her smile ... although I was so far away from her, a diffident, shyly self-effacing young man bending this way to see her from the cheapest seat in the house, she shone her smile at me. And she was lovely.

A stage-door johnny. The phrase came to me. Well, why not? When the show ended, with a succession of encores and my Claudette overwhelmed with the flowers which were tossed onto the stage and the bouquets pressed to her, I tumbled down the stairs and out into the cold night air. Cold, yes ... it hit me like a slap on the forehead. I took a few long deep breaths, tugged my coat around me and the scarf around my neck, and turned the corner to find the stage-door.

The back door of the theatre. In a side-street of Montparnasse. Just me, for a few minutes, although further down the street, in the deeper darkness, I could see the lumpen shape of a car, waiting, the engine running silently and sending a haze of exhaust smoke into the air, blurring its shadowy outline.

She emerged, in a waft of perfume, swaddled in a big fur coat. I leaned forward with my programme, a picture of her divinely smiling face. Without looking at me, in fact glancing sidelong into the street where her car was purring towards her, she scrawled her autograph. And then, as the car paused beside her ... la grande Citroën, of course ... and as she reached to open the door, she lifted her face towards me.

She smiled. She smiled into my eyes, as though for a moment she recognized me, as though we'd met before, somewhere, at some time. And then she ducked into the car and disappeared and slid away.

I drifted through the sweetly seductive streets of Montparnasse, into the giddy streets of Montmartre, and yes, what better than to lubricate my intoxication with another little Pernod or two? Outside, at my pavement table at Le Petit Sommelier, around the corner from the Théâtre de la Gaieté ... snugly enfolded in my coat and scarf on a frosty night in March, under the blossom of a purple magnolia. With my autographed programme.

The following night, I did the same. A few drinks beneath the blossom. I didn't go into the theatre, but I was waiting at the stage-door when the show was over. She appeared, in a fume of Chanel or Givenchy or something like that, wrapped in her furs, and just before her car came whispering towards her, I gave her a rose.

She took it, Claudette de la Touche, and again she gifted me her smile . . . somehow knowing me, as if we'd been friends or even lovers, in a different place, at a different time. And then she was gone.

And my last night in Paris? I had something special for her. I'd been pondering it all day, over my morning coffees and in my gentle strolls by the Seine. But when at last she came out of the stage door, the moment I'd been imagining and embellishing in my mind since the previous evening, I could sense something was wrong.

There was a shadow around her. A darkness. Perhaps she was tired. It was the last night of her run at the theatre, and maybe she was disappointed, that it hadn't gone as well as she'd hoped. She hurried out of the door, staggered and almost fell as she caught her heel on the step, and she brushed past me without even seeing I was there. The car came. It slithered out of the dark side-street like some kind of beast, its eyes swivelling left and right.

As Claudette bent to get inside, and I knew in my poetic heart that I would never see her again, I pushed forward with my book.

She flashed a look at me. She had no choice but to take the book because I was angling it into her hands. She slammed the door shut, and I was aware of two things happening, both of them bitterly painful.

First of all, her face. She smiled, but it was a practised smile of years of show-business, a look of weary disdain. Yes, she knew who I was, after nearly recognizing me the previous two nights. I was a stage-door johnny. She'd met me before, a hundred times. The other thing, she'd nipped the two middle fingertips of my left hand in the door, and I had to step smartly along the pavement with the sudden movement of the car before I could pull them out. The car swept away and was swallowed into the traffic.

I slunk into Le Petit Sommelier and sulked. My fingers

were hurting. What else to do, but assuage my feelings and my fingers with a glass of Pernod, and then another? And I was cold. I'd established myself outside on my usual table and was too wounded to bother moving inside. I huddled deeper into my coat, let the alcohol flood into my arms and my chest, and I thought of the poets who'd come before me, to this table at this bar, to escape the chill of their garrets and warm themselves with the cloudy yellow anis.

And absinthe... la fée verte... the drink of the decadents, of Verlaine and Rimbaud and Baudelaire. I caught the waiter's eye and he manoeuvred himself among the tables to see what I wanted. Absinthe? He rolled his eyes, exasperated by just another tipsy tourist, put my bill onto the table and turned away.

A blurry few minutes later and I was heading down a flight of pitchy dark stairs and into Le Tournesol, a cellar bar with just the perfect corner for me to slide into. And the waiter, a big blurry shape smelling of patchouli, who wasn't as sniffy as the one upstairs in the limelight of a Parisian street... he brought me what I'd asked for.

I watched in wonder. A glass of brilliantly green liquid, a touch of theatre with a silver spoon expertly balanced on the rim... a cube of white sugar... a silvery flask which dripped water onto the sugar and slowly dissolved it into the glass. Droplet after magical droplet, the neon green liquid was clouded and ready to drink.

And so I drank. Slowly, savouring every sip which rolled around my mouth and then filled my throat and my chest with a miraculous fire. The bitterness of wormwood... the heat and the sensation of a decadent pleasure. I was gradually ... no, I was suddenly supernaturally aware of my surroundings, of every cobweb and speck of dust of the candlelit subterranean room, the very pores of the man who loomed towards me and made sure that the magic was working... his silvery spoon and the sugar and the icy-cold water, performing its miracle on the distillation he'd deigned to deliver me.

He delivered another. I saw every detail of his immaculately filed nails and the skin of his skilful fingers and the oily black hairs on the back of his hands, although the man himself was only a shadow. And then? And then I was a beating heart ... I was a deep, heavy beating of blood in my heart, and in my head, and in my fingers ... throbbing so loudly I thought everyone in the room must have heard it ...

The face of Claudette de la Touche swam in front of me. I had the programme on the table, the smile of a goddess and the scrawl of her autograph. A goddess ... I'd seen her car come wallowing out of the side-street, a clumsy beast with swivelling eyes ... la grande Citroën, la DS ... la déesse, a swollen overblown monstrosity ... and then wallowing into the traffic with my goddess inside it, as though she'd been swallowed by a hippopotamus ...

I drained my second glass. My head was pulsing. My fingers were pounding. I waved at the waiter, like a drowning man he might think about saving, and heard a snorting of laughter from him and some people at the tables nearby. Somewhere in the room a woman was laughing at me. Was it Claudette? And yet I'd given her the best and most precious thing I'd ever made ... I peered closer at her photo and yes she was laughing, I could see it on her lips, the scorn for me, the disdain, and see it in her eyes.

On an impulse, as my whole body swelled with the ridiculous nonsense of what I was doing in such a place, and moved to tears of self-indulgent, self-inflicted unhappiness, I rummaged in my pocket for a pen. I bent over my programme and I scratched as hard as I could. I blackened a tooth, and I leaned back and marvelled. How a few strokes of a pen could make a goddess so ugly!

A minute later? A large and patchouli-pungent person was manhandling me from my table and towards the foot of those stairs. I'd left money. And the programme. Someone had seen what I'd done to it and was shouting angrily after me.

My body was hurting, somewhere in a faraway extremity, and my heart was aching. And yet I was perversely, painfully happy.

Not so the following morning. I was sorry for myself and sorry for what I'd done. Coffee and more coffee on my favourite terrasse.

An artist settled himself at my table and started to sketch me, with charcoal on a big pad of paper. He was handsome, young, unshaven, the stereotype of a Parisian pavement artist. I told him to stop, or rather, not to start, but he was charming and he was used to getting his way with tourists. When I mumbled my schoolboy French at him and tried to establish how much I might pay for my portrait, he shrugged and waved his hands in a long-practised quintessence of Frenchness, and plucked a figure out of thin air. I let him get on with it. And at the end, after I'd salved my hangover with a couple of coffees and swallowed a croissant, he asked me for twice the amount he'd suggested. I paid him. He left, charmingly.

I appraised his work, in smudgy charcoal. Yes, he was an artist. He'd got me perfectly, my wounded demeanour, the pain in my eyes. The poet Lewis Bowden ... a worldweary man of the world, who'd been in love with a beautiful woman and given her the best of himself, who'd been cruelly spurned.

No really, I managed to laugh at myself. I showed it to the waiter and attempted a joke in my floundering French, as I paid and left. It was my last day in Paris, I was catching my bus to Dieppe. On the way past the Théâtre de la Gaieté I stopped to see if I could get another programme, wishing I hadn't so childishly spoilt the one I'd had signed by Claudette de la Touche. Her photographs were still on display, but the box-office was closed.

Sorry? Yes. In love? A little bit. Heartbroken? I'd had my fingertips crushed in the door of her car.

And so, Mr Boden, back to school for the beginning of the summer term.

The boys called me sir, of course. Among themselves they referred to me as Eric. On the first day, at the staff meeting, there was chit-chat about where we'd all been during the Easter break. And when it was my turn, Beasley managed a sideways remark ... how romantic, and had I fallen in love? I joined in the laughter, and stopped myself from saying, well yes actually, I had. I bent my head and blew on my blackened fingernails.

He took me aside afterwards. I'm afraid we're going to lose you, Eric. He'd never called me by my first name before. Even with the influx of foreign students, the numbers were falling. From September he himself would cover my classes and take over the supervision of the boys. He pulled a face and tried a joke about, oh dear, having to set his alarm a bit earlier to get the boys up in the morning ... and should he read them a story at bedtime? But seriously, I wouldn't be needed. And he winced, reminding me of the little fire I'd had when I was celebrating the publication of my book, as though he needed another reason to let me go. We could all have been burned in our beds ... nothing to joke about.

No matter. For the next two months, I applied myself diligently to being an English teacher and a housemaster. When I'd first come to the school there'd been three dormitories of normal, naughty boys tussling and scragging, and my job was to get them washed and changed and into bed with lights-out at ten, and then patrolling for another quarter of an hour if they were still fooling around.

Not anymore. They were teenagers from Iran and Egypt and Lebanon. Some of them had beards. They showered and then covered themselves with talc, and then they lay on their beds with their headphones in their ears, listening to the music of their faraway lands. Tussling and scragging? No, they lay in the dorm like patients on life-support, eyes closed, twitching their fingers to the beat of their tinny, percussive songs. I switched off the lights, and five minutes later I was up in my room, swirling water into the first of my two or three glasses of Pernod. And it was summer, no need for the buzzing electric fire to be toasting my toes . . .

A schoolteacher, Eric Boden. In the staff room there was an occasional, deliberate slip of the tongue, and someone would call me Lewis. Whenever it happened, I would glance at Beasley and get a shiver of pleasure at the way he flinched. I meant to ask him one day if he was still writing his novel and trying it with a publisher. In fairness, when my book was actually published and I gave him a signed copy, he had the grace to show it to his pupils and put it into the school library. He slipped it into the poetry section, between Betjeman and Byron.

My blackened fingernails grew out. The term slipped by . . . sports day, exams, cricket, the end-of-year garden fête. I went through the motions, in a Sussex summertime haze.

One evening, after turning the lights out and doing my final lock-up of the house, I drifted into the library to sit and think about my time at the school. I was leafing the pages of an old *National Geographic*, and there was a *Paris Match*. To my surprise she was in there, Claudette de la Touche, at some kind of showbiz bash . . . I hadn't realized she was in the league of *Paris Match* celebrity. I was so taken aback to see her smiling at me, that for a while I just stared and blinked, without trying to read the accompanying text.

Then I read it, and I read it again. She had died. In a fire. At her house in France.

I sat for a long time in the school library. It was a night in June, and a big yellow moon had risen behind the copper beech on the lawn outside. I read the article two or three more times. I remembered how she had shone her smile at me, when I was

perched in the gods and falling, almost falling in love with her
... and at a silly, hapless stage-door johnny.

The moon. When at last I closed the magazine, I looked for my book. I wondered if she'd ever done more than glance at it, whether she'd opened it and wondered what the poems were about. *Moon on the Ouse*, by Lewis Bowden. Someone had crossed out the name, scrawled Eric across the cover, and added specs to the photograph on the back.

Not sure whether I should laugh or cry, I took it up to my room. There, I swigged a glass of Pernod, and another. I conjured her smile. I'd seen it flicker and fade into disdain, and now it was lost forever. I'd been in love, just a tiny bit, enough to have felt its joy and its sorrow. I swirled my glass and raised it to her. I unrolled the charcoal portrait of myself, done in Montmartre, and saw that it had captured my mood that morning ... hunched in my coat, blurry and smudged and bruised.

Later that night I awoke, my mouth dry, my head whirling with music and laughter, and a throbbing pain in my fingers as though they were nipped in the door of that great, whispering car.

The end of term. What to do? So, to France.

July in Charente. I'd driven down there, with not much more in my car than a few clothes and a clutter of books I'd accumulated in my room at The Manor. My plans were pleasantly vague. I might pootle around for a month, staying in a village here or a small town there, and I could always go back to Sussex if the idyll of France in the summertime started to pall. I had a brisk and bossy aunt in Brighton who would put me up, not an especially exciting option but a room and a bed.

Intrigued by the name, I stopped in a village called La Touche. The river ran through it and under an ancient stone bridge. The countryside was in full, dense, green leaf, vivid and fresh before the drowsiness of August would turn the leaves darker and drooping. In a bric-à-brac shop in the village square, among piles of books and old newspapers, I found a theatre programme ... Le Théâtre de la Gaieté, with my Claudette on the front cover. And then I saw there was a display on the wall, partly hidden by the notices that people had stuck into the corners of the frame, adverts for builders and handymen and kennels and catteries ... a display of her cuttings and glamour photos.

The old man in the shop told me that Claudette had lived here. She was a local, much-loved celebrity. She'd taken her stage-name from the village where she'd been brought up. And as she'd become more successful in the bright lights of Paris, she'd come back and bought the manoir, a grand house just a mile away, and returned whenever she wasn't gracing the stage in Montmartre or Montparnasse.

I bought the programme. I told the old man that I'd seen Claudette, on stage in Paris. He directed me, shruggingly, if I might be interested to see the remains of the manoir, by the river, where she'd lived and died. And he added, as I was leaving the shop ... le pigeonnier est à vendre ... so bewildering, like a clue from a cryptic crossword puzzle, that I didn't have the gumption to ask him to repeat it.

I found out what he meant when I stopped and got out of the car to appraise the manoir. Its burnt-out remains. A broken skeleton. A gable end and a tall chimney remained standing, enough to show that it had been a fine, big house. But the inside of it had collapsed into an enormous pile of charred timbers ... the bones of the house, exhausted by fire and then crushed by the weight of thousands of tiles.

There was another car, with English number plates, parked by a curious building a hundred yards away from the ruins: a dumpy, circular stone tower, like a pepper pot. It had a slate roof, a tiny window below the line of the roof, another tiny window lower down. Otherwise it was no more than a dungeon, oddly stout and robust ... a grain store, or maybe a place for hanging venison or wild boar? A flight of roughly hewn stone steps went up to a doorway no more than five feet high, from which a very dusty and scowling man emerged. He glanced at me, nearly overbalanced because he was carrying a cardboard box full of tools, and he wobbled down the stairs and across to his car.

A woman came out behind him, as dusty and as unhappy as him. A long story, short? Yes they were English, and in the spring they'd bought their dream project in France ... a pigeonnier, part of the manoir, and they were converting it into their second home in France. They'd had a fosse septique put in and so there was water, the wiring was done and there were lights. There was a wood-burning stove. I peered inside and saw he'd put down a timber floor and built a kind of loft upstairs with a ladder to it, which was going to be a bedroom.

The man told me all this, half exasperated to have me nosing around, half relieved to have a break from emptying their stuff from the tower and into the car. His wife didn't speak. Her eyes were reddened with dust, and also by tears. She blew her nose very loudly and glared at her husband to stop talking and come and help. Very upset, they both were. She went back inside, snuffling. He told me they'd been in the pigeonnier, enjoying their very first night there, when the fire started. Horrific, such a sudden and engulfing blaze that no one could get near. They'd heard screams from within the flames. Horrific, they would never forget it. By the time les pompiers had arrived, the inside of the house had collapsed, swallowed into a crushing inescapable inferno.

Yes, they'd heard screams. She was still in there. How could they stay any longer, in their idyllic French retreat? Horrible, they could still smell it, he said, the smouldering timbers.

I could smell it. On a lovely afternoon in July, I could smell the burning. It rose from the ruins in a faint haze of smoke. Screams? No, no screams.

Le pigeonnier est à vendre. For sale? I mooched back to

my car, and I stood and watched the river slipping smoothly by. The lovely Charente, so shallow and clear, flickering with trout, reflecting the oak and ash and the willow in the fullness of their summer foliage on the further bank. A perfectly blue, over-arching sky, brimming with cumulus.

And a miserably squabbling couple. They couldn't wait to get out, swearing and struggling from the tower to the car with their cardboard boxes. When I saw the wife come out, crack her forehead on the lintel of the door and spill a clattering boxful of pots and pans all over the grass and then burst into spluttering tears, I went over to help.

On an impulse, I suggested they leave the pots and pans. Leave them, I said. I could use them. Leave me the pots and pans, and the key ... a great clunky iron key, as old as the tower.

He found a bottle of wine among the jumbled supplies, she dabbed her sorely reddened nose and found three glasses. We all took big deep breaths and we talked. We exchanged details and I gave them a cheque, a nominal amount for using the pigeonnier for the rest of the summer. They could go home and clear their heads, and I'd camp out while they put it on the market and waited for another day-dreaming English couple to make an offer ...

They left, a bit happier, or less unhappy. I explored my pigeonnier.

The dove-cote or pigeon-house of the manoir, since the 17th century, from the days when a good number of pigeon-holes was a sign of prosperity. More than just a status symbol, there would always be pigeons to be eaten, and the rich mulch of their droppings to be shovelled from the floor of the building and spread onto the kitchen garden.

Like a dungeon inside, not much light but a cobwebby blur in the two little windows. A dark, circular tower, the thick stone walls with their dozens of pigeon-holes. I clambered up the ladder to my loft, where somehow they'd managed to haul a bed ... overhead, ancient timbers, riddled with woodworm ... daylight through the chinks in the slate roof and from a kind of slatted chimney at the very top, where the birds used to come and go.

But it was summer in Charente. I would be outside in the sunshine, under a huge blue sky.

A balmy summer. I loafed on the riverbank, in shorts and sandals and one or other of my schoolteacher's shirts. Sometimes I wandered to the ruins and stared into them. A heap of wreckage. Depending on the angle of the sunlight, I could make out the twisted remains of things which had not been entirely consumed by the fire ... the hinges of a door or shutters, the ironwork of a stove, the cradle and dogs of a grand fireplace ... and in a part of the shattered building which might have been a barn or a workshop or a stable, the buckled frame of a cart or a carriage. Scattered nearby, there were spars of wood which had only been scorched, as though they were morsels too small to be devoured by the flames and had been spat aside by the blast of heat. Firewood for me, I thought, in my pigeonnier, if I stayed long enough to need it.

A cat came out of the ruins. He strolled towards me, yawning, and rubbed himself against my legs. He would be my cat, he was saying in the electric vibration of his sleek, black body. He would visit me in my tower and deign to stay, in return for food and affection. He had lived in the manoir and been the companion of a beautiful lady ... but now she had gone, and the manoir as well. So he would be my cat. I picked him up. He smelled of smoke.

And the owl came. Not the first night I climbed up to the loft and lay staring at the splintered moonlight, but long into the third or fourth, the white owl came. La chouette, as they knew her in French ... she startled me awake with her scream, and when she settled into the slatted chimney which the pigeons had used long ago, she roosted there, snuffling and wheezing. She retched up a pellet, the compacted remains of some unfortunate shrew or vole she'd eaten. And then she slept. I could hear the scraping of her claws on the timber as she fidgeted and shuffled and snored. She came every night, to digest her dinner and sleep.

Long summer days and nights, not at all lonely with my cat and my owl.

A stroll into the village, and I met my French neighbours at the market in the village square, selling their home-grown vegetables and fruit, their pâté and cheeses, and there was fresh fish from La Rochelle. I introduced myself as Lewis Bowden, a writer, and they asked how I was settling into the pigeonnier. They'd seen the previous occupants leave abruptly and unhappily. They made shrugging references to the manoir and its ugly ruins, suggesting that one day the mairie would organize its clearance... but in the meantime it was too soon, in respect for their darling Claudette, to disturb the silence with noisy machinery.

It hung in the air, the silence, and the feeling that she was still in there, somewhere, if not in body but in soul, and should be left in peace.

Me, I was a curio... a writer, and I'd met Claudette? My summer blurred into an idyll of French country life. A haze of wine at lunchtime and a hazy afternoon, and then a long, longed-for sunset. I sat outside my pigeonnier with the first of several glasses of Pernod. And then a bottle of the local merlot, as dark and fruity and as full of deep, rich song as the blackbird, le merle, after which it was named. The blackbird sang me through the dusk and the twilight, until a moon rose over the river.

No, not a moon. The moon, my moon. My moon on the Ouse had become my moon on the Charente. I would spend an hour or three outside, with my wine and my smokey cat, until the moon set behind the trees, and it was time for bed. Up the ladder and into my loft, with the cat springing beside me and snuggling on the bed. And my owl. A scream in the night, and she was there, snoring me gently asleep.

But sometimes, waking with my fingers hurting and my head full of voices and laughter, I would go outside. And then I was ridiculous, sleep-walking in a fume of wine and anis, a teacher sacked from a failing school in Sussex, a poet in a pigeonnier...

Drunk. A pompous-poetic voice was reading aloud, and people were laughing. A beautiful woman, swaddled in fur and a waft of perfume, was laughing. I would shake my head and try to spit, although my mouth was so dry. And I might walk, barefoot, through the long grass to the burnt-out ruins of the manoir.

Burning, I could smell burning. Was it the cat, pungent of smoke, which had followed me outside and was rubbing his long black body against my legs? Or was there still a silvery-blue haze of smoke from the remains of the house? And what was that sound? A movement in the rubble. A shifting of timbers. It was the cat, he had scented a mouse and slithered in stealthy pursuit. A scream? It was the owl. I looked up and saw her, a silhouette against the sky, where she had perched on the top of the remaining chimney. I saw her float down, silent, and drop into the deepest core of the ruins.

The cat, or the owl, or both... they made a secret whispering in the darkness.

And so the summer grew tired. Tired of itself. It had been so sappy and green, but in the air there was a weight of weariness. Enough of being breezy and blowsy and a great blustering warmth in the deep green trees. Make way for the autumn, which would try so hard, fragrant and brilliant in yellows and golds and reds, to be lovely and to be loved...

But even the autumn, in all her loveliness, could never postpone the reality of what would come next.

Thursday, 22nd December. The shortest day. How could I have known it would be my last day in the pigeonnier?

I was cold. I crouched in front of the fire. My face was reddened but my back was like ice, and I wondered why I was still there. It had been dark until mid-morning, and then, after a few hours of silvery-grey sunlight, it had fallen dark again at four o'clock in the afternoon. Now, at nine o'clock in the evening, it was the dead of night.

The autumn? It had blazed briefly and made a surreptitious exit, like an end-of-the-pier magician whose act fell flat. In November, the river itself seemed to shrink and stale, oozing bubbles of methane. The woodland was stripped of leaves. The trees were skeletons, their bones hung with parasitic clumps of mistletoe. The pigeonnier soaked up the damp, the walls bloomed a black, foul-smelling mould.

I'd posted another cheque to my erstwhile landlords, who didn't seem bothered one way or the other. Winter came overnight and I'd been lighting the fire in the stove. Every morning and into the dimly shortening afternoons, I scavenged the ruins of the manoir for wood. All the spars which the fire hadn't wanted, which it had tossed aside in an explosion of heat and collapsed the building and crushed everything inside it, I collected by the armful and brought into the pigeonnier. Sometimes, in search of more fuel, I pushed deeper into the rubble of the house and its stables, closer to the core of the fire ... no more wood, only a tangle of iron it had torched and twisted.

I snuggled the smokey black cat on my lap. And the owl had come ... I'd heard her screeching outside, as though to presage her arrival, and she'd wafted into the chimney above my head, to retch up the indigestible remains of her dinner. I sat even closer to the stove. It was toasting my feet and my legs, without throwing any heat into the tower.

The damp, the mould, the woodworm ... I didn't care, I had all the company and comfort I needed, the cat and the owl and a glass or two or three of Pernod and a bottle of wine. I would need more wood, somehow, from somewhere.

I fell asleep in front of the fire, with the cat on my lap, my legs outstretched.

And when I awoke, as a splinter of wood fell out of the stove and shattered into pieces on the floor, I jumped to my feet. For a second, in a confusion of dream and memory, I heard a voice, a man's voice in fear and panic and felt a splattering of wine... because my shoes were burning, there was a puther of smoke and a tall yellow flame was flickering on my shoes and scorching my legs... for a moment I was in my stuffy upstairs room in school and the fire was buzzing and a man was shouting and splashing wine and...

And then I yelled and I was awake, in the pigeonnier. The cat sprang away. I snatched up the nearest thing I could find to swipe and swat the flames, and they were gone. Only a stink of rubber, from my shoes. I slumped back into my chair. The fire was going out. There was a mess of embers on the floor. And in my hand, the theatre programme I'd used to put out the fire ... the lovely smile of Claudette de la Touche was singed and blackened.

Two ways to keep warm and somehow survive the night without shivering to death... I groped by the side of my armchair for the bottle and poured the last few drops into my glass. A mean slosh of water, enough to cloud the anis into a yellowy swirl without wastefully weakening it. And tip it wonderfully into my throat. A few staggering moments later, I'd swathed the scarf around my neck and wriggled into my coat and I was outside with a torch... somehow, somewhere, no matter where, I had to find more wood.

The midwinter night hit me right between the eyes. I followed the wavering light of my torch, it seemed to lead me onwards and onwards, sparkling on the first fingers of frost which lay on the grass. I paused to piss, a marvellous heady head of steam, the only warmth and energy in a world of deadliness, and I was off again in pursuit of the torchlight. It took me to the ruins of the manoir, but it was feeble in the wreckage, there was nothing but dust and darkness which swallowed the beam and snuffed it. And there was nothing which would burn in my stove. It had already burned. It was exhausted, nothing but charcoal and a tortured skeleton of iron. But what was it, the mess of metal? I aimed the torchbeam, and I saw it was a car.

Crushed into nothing. A frame, a chassis, the blackened wheels, almost flattened by the weight of all the timbers and roof tiles which collapsed on top of it.

I turned and pointed my quivering light back towards the pigeonnier. What did they say in France? Reculer pour mieux sauter? Go back, revive the remains of the fire with a bit of kindling or an old magazine or even break up and burn a bit of the furniture which my kindly predecessors had left behind, and I would recover myself and return...

Inside again, I felt for the bottle. It was empty. I felt into the box I'd brought back from the shop in the village. Empty? Inconceivable, that the three or four bottles I'd tucked away were already gone. But they were gone, or rather not gone but rattling empty under my armchair when I pushed it aside and rummaged there...

Nothing. And nothing to burn. A pigeonnier, a symbol of wealth, where dozens of plump, warm, well-fed birds had snugly roosted ... it was a mouldy damp tower with a poet shivering inside it.

Drunk enough to do grand poetic things, indeed I did two things. An old magazine? I took up the theatre programme which was already so scorched and disfigured and swished it towards the fire, which was simmering to ashes and yet hungry for fuel. I placed it ceremoniously into the stove. Where it curled and crisped and burst into flames.

The other thing, more important. I knew it was somewhere. I went banging and stumbling around the pigeonnier, which didn't take long in such a relic which should have been knocked down and had its stones more usefully reclaimed a long time ago ... and I found it.

La fée verte. The green fairy.

In the last light of the burning programme, her face flickering into the flames, I poured the neon green liquid into my glass. A teaspoon and a lump of white sugar, and I arranged it onto the glass. I dripped a little water onto the sugar, so that it dissolved into the dazzling clarity of greenness and made a beckoning, bewitching cloud.

I drank it down. I stared into the fire and it stared back at me. And I did it again, the otherworldly ritual, a bit of alchemy, a miasma of magic. It was beautiful, the way her picture curled and blackened and folded into flame, the brief and beautiful heat it gave, and the heat which filled my body. The heat, the electric greenness of it, it flared into my fingertips and hurt in a sweet pounding of pain and filled my head with a powerful pounding of blood ...

And so I took the torch outside again. Wrapping the scarf around my throat, too enfeebled to button my coat but letting it flap around me, I followed the torch. Into the darkness, my mind whirling ... wormwood woodworm ... moon on the ouse moon in the ooze ... the heat the hurt ... la fée verte ... la déesse ... Betjeman Bowden Byron ... I stumbled into the rubble of the manoir, where the chimney loomed above me, where there'd been a hallway panelled with oak and a stately staircase ... and into the barn or the stable ...

The torch picked out the skeleton of a car, crushed almost flat, entombed. I clawed my way towards it, crouching and bending, until I fell on my knees and scrabbled deeper and deeper into the wreckage ...

And then I was writhing on my belly. Strangely calm and warm, the heat in my head and in my throat and ... although my fingers were numb, the fingers of my left hand, and they dropped the torch once, and then a second time, and again, and I felt for its yellowing beam in piles of ash and rust and exhausted embers. I crawled head-first into the remains of the car.

La grande Citroën. I was inside the belly of it, I'd seen it come wallowing from the shadows of the side-street, its headlamps swivelling like beastly eyes, I'd seen and smelled its whispering fumey breath...

I was inside it, my coat and scarf entangled around me. I tried to turn, I couldn't. I pushed myself backwards, I couldn't. My coat, my scarf... I was bundled in a sooty, smokey space which pressed onto me and around me.

A scream? It was the owl, watching from the top of the remaining chimney. I heard screams and laughter... a fall of rubble, a slither of dust and a shifting of the timbers which had fallen across the wreckage of the car... it was the cat, somewhere in the ruins and following me...

My fingers were useless. I dropped the torch, fumbled for it in the carcase of the car, a carcase which had been devoured by the fire, nothing had survived in there, in the devouring heat.

A gleam in the torchlight, like a pearl in the powder of ash. I strained to reach it, to sift it between my numbly frozen fingers. And then I brought it closer to my face, where the fog of my breath and the whirl of dust confounded my eyes...

A tooth. It was all that remained of her. I heard myself calling her name... Claudette? Are you here? Is this where they never found you? In the car? Ive found you, I've found you...

And then I lay silent. The owl screamed. I thought it was the owl. I heard screams, again and again and again, in a terrible dying sadness. And a slithering of debris, louder and more impatiently groaning, as though it had waited and waited long enough and had had enough and was tired of waiting. A cracking of spars. Somewhere above me, where the timbers had been broken by the collapsing of the roof and had settled on the car, the rubble groaned. There was a cracking and cracking, like breaking bones. And the whole weight of burnt-out building dropped another inch, no more, and settled.

An inch or two. I heard it groan and creak and settle. Bending the frame of the car flatter still. Enough to pinch me and hold me where I was.

A pain like fire, as though I'd been pierced in the small of my back by a burning spear. I cried out, horribly high-pitched, and the pain flared and melted into a sweet benumbing heat.

Forwards or backwards, I couldn't move. I was crushed, with Claudette, with her tooth in my hand. I knew, in the heat which flowed and ebbed in my body like the tide of a great river, that I would never get out.

I felt the bones of my broken body relax like the bones of the building which had crushed me. No more pain. Nothing to be done except wait for the end, with the little light of my torch, into the long hours of the longest night. I flickered the beam around me. Like a child, I shone it across my face and under my chin. I was foolishly smiling as I mouthed the words of my own obituary ... the poet Lewis Bowden has died, his own silly fault.

Valentine's Day, 1984. Very good, the pigeon casserole, and a lovely view across the Ouse. I took another piece of bread and wiped up the gravy. My aunt would be coming soon, brisk and bossy, to help me out and take me home. While I waited, I took the book from the pocket of my coat and put it onto the table.

My favourite copy. A curio, the one I would always keep. The name crossed out on the cover, and Eric scrawled across it. On the back, my face with specs.

My aunt came in and called across the room, Eric are you finished? And again, because I was moved to a confusion of laughter and tears and hadn't answered ... Eric Boden, are you finished?